Unfaithfully Yours

# Unfaithfully Yours

Nigel Williams

corsair

Constable & Robinson Ltd.
55–56 Russell Square
London WC1B 4HP
www.constablerobinson.com

First published in the UK by Corsair,
an imprint of Constable & Robinson Ltd., 2013

A copy of the British Library Cataloguing in
Publication Data is available from the British Library

ISBN: 978-1-47210-674-2 (hardback)
ISBN: 978-1-47210-683-4 (ebook)

Printed and bound by CPI Group (UK) Ltd, Croydon, CR0 4YY

1 3 5 7 9 10 8 6 4 2

'More than kisses, letters mingle souls.'
John Donne

# Cast of Principal Characters

## *In order of appearance*

*Elizabeth Price*, a classics teacher
*Orlando (Roland) Gibbons*, a private detective
*Gerald Price*, a successful barrister, married to
    Elizabeth Price
*Mike Larner*, a retired BBC producer, late of the
    Natural History Unit
*Mary Dimmock*, wife to Sam Dimmock, a dentist
*John Goldsmith*, a Putney doctor in general practice
*Sam Dimmock*, a Putney dentist
*Barbara Goldsmith*, a novelist, married to John Goldsmith
*Pamela Larner*, career mother, married to Mike Larner,
    now deceased

The novel is set in SW15. Now.

*Dear Mary –*

*I thought I would put together all the letters that passed between what I still cannot help calling the Puerto Banús Eight. Nine, I suppose, if you included me, but I was never – thank God – conscripted into one of those villa holidays.*

*I come over as an absolute jerk. I think that is what I was in those days. Maybe that is still a good way of describing me, but at least now I am an absolute jerk who is loved by you.*

*Don't ask me how I got hold of them. That's my job. I am rather proud of being a snooper – and getting better and better at it with every new marital breakdown in Putney. I am no longer ashamed of who I am – and have even been known to own up to the fact that I went to a minor public school.*

*These aren't all the letters, of course, and, as well as letters, there were emails and phone calls; but I think the letters say more about us all than any of the more casual traffic. Your prose style tells the world more about you than almost anything else, which is perhaps why now I take more trouble with it.*

*I have typed them up – so that you don't get John*

*Goldsmith's unusually neat doctor's hand, Barbara G's wild scrawl, Mike Larner's prim italic, Sam's bold cursive or your wonderful way of managing to make the alphabet look as if it was eating itself. The butch, broad strokes of Gerald Price's Parker pen are also absent – as are the hideous, spider-like marks made by my (now abandoned) Mitsubishi Uniball. The only handwritten letter I have left as it was is the last and, I think, rather touching, message from Elizabeth Price to me.*

*Her handwriting was not as I had imagined it. It was crazy. There were wildly irregular spaces between words, sentences and even, sometimes, different ingredients of the same character. Significant?*

*Here they are anyway – Elizabeth and Gerald Price, Sam and Mary Dimmock (that's you!), Mike and poor Pamela Larner and the Perfect Couple Who Weren't – John and Barbara Goldsmith. They come over as clear as day, don't they?*

*That is the beauty of letters. There is nowhere to hide. So here you are. I thought it might amuse you. I've touched them up a little and added a few chapter headings, but – I promise – I have not seriously interfered with what any of us wrote to each other. This is Putney, red in tooth and claw. My version of the Great Putney Novel, the one I often talked about writing back in the day. All You Ever Wanted to Know About Sixtysomethings – a group I have only recently joined.*

*Enjoy!*

*XXXX Orlando*

# PART ONE

# Chapter One

## *Mrs Price Hires a Private Dick*

From:
Elizabeth Price
PO Box 132
Putney
12 June

To:
Roland O. Gibbons
Gibbons Detective Agency
12 The Alley
Putney, SW15

Dear Mr Gibbons,
I am writing to you because I think my husband may be having sex. I am not sure with whom he is having it but it is certainly not with me.

He may, for all I know, be involved with more than one person. I use the word 'person' advisedly. He may be doing the deed of darkness with females, males, or some combination of the two, since, as far as I can gather, at his public school, a boarding establishment, homosexuality was more or less compulsory for the younger boys. I am fairly certain he is not a paedophile, however, which is some comfort. We have two children and, as far as I know, he has never interfered with either of them. Indeed, it has been something of a struggle to get him to even acknowledge their existence.

I have studied various kinds of detective agency but none of them seemed entirely convincing. Indeed, from the general tone of their advertisements, I gained the impression that many of them would have joined, enthusiastically, in whatever it is my husband is doing.

I am not, at this stage of the proceedings anyway, interested in photographic recordings of him committing adultery. Nor am I sure, at the moment, what I will do with the information you obtain or, indeed, what it is I expect you to uncover. It may be that he is not having sex with anyone at all. Though, from my observation of him over more than twenty years, I think that highly unlikely. He once told me that he would 'shag the Archbishop of Canterbury if that was the only thing on offer'. A joke – of course - but people reveal themselves through their jokes. Don't you think?

We have – as people do over the years – grown apart and, to be honest with you, he has become, in many respects, a complete mystery to me. I want, in other words, to find out more about him without having to go to the trouble of asking him. It may be simply that he has discovered a new hobby and is not keen to tell me about it. He may have bought a boat. No fewer than three men married to friends of mine have done precisely that – without telling their wives.

I want information about him, Mr Gibbons, and I want it gathered with complete and utter discretion. I suspect you are well placed to supply that commodity. If only because – during the quite extensive period of time in which I have lain in wait outside your offices – it has become clear that you are about the only person who ever visits them.

There may well come a time, Mr Gibbons, when I will require professional surveillance of his activities even when he is on our premises. We have a five- bedroom house and it is not always possible to keep track of him inside the property; but, for the moment, I am only interested in finding out what he does when I am not there. I see no reason why you and I should ever have to meet.

For reasons of security I do not wish you to reply to the address at which – for the moment – I am forced to reside with him.

Perhaps you would write to me care of the Post Office and let me know your rates and the kind of details you might need to help you begin the complex and probably unrewarding task of tracking the man to whom I am, unfortunately, married.

I look forward to hearing from you,
Yours
Elizabeth Price

PS I think he may be contemplating the prospect of doing away with me. I have seen him giving me some very suspect glances when we are watching television and he thinks I have not got my eye on him. For some reason this often seems to happen when we are tuned to Channel Four. I am pretty sure, however, that he has not got the kind of nerve it would require to stab, gas or strangle me.

From:
Roland O. Gibbons
Gibbons Detective Agency
12 The Alley
Putney, SW15
14 June

To:
Elizabeth Price
PO Box 132
Putney

Dear Mrs Price,
Thank you very much for your letter.

I was *really* glad to get it. I know I should pretend to be 'cool' and look as if I can only just manage to fit you in – but – yowzas! A job! This was my reaction. The recession has affected our business very badly and small private firms such as mine are seriously at risk from the major conglomerates.

Well done with the 'research' too. I will admit to feeling slightly 'weird' that someone has been doing a 'snoop job' on me (shouldn't it be the other way round????) but, in fact, Mrs Price, I completely understand you wanting to make sure that we would be a 'good fit'. I do not know if you have been following me home or monitoring my telephone calls and emails but, if you have, I hope you didn't find any real dirt on yours truly!

Your letter does not suggest what it is that has made you feel Mr Price is having an affair, although you seem to imply that, whatever he is up to, it is pretty serious.

Are there stains on his clothing? Has he been making or receiving phone calls that he has attempted to hide from you? Has he been visiting inappropriate websites? I do appreciate your need for privacy but, obviously, in order to make an assessment, a 'face-to-face' meeting would be helpful. Perhaps you would call by the office. You seem to have had no difficulty finding it and I am pretty much free most of the time at the moment.

I'm not a hermit! I do occasionally get out for a light snack at the La Mancha Tapas Bar in Putney High Street. I usually bring a selection of sandwiches (cheese, ham or coarse pâté and pickle) to work or – on special occasions – order a delivery from the Royal China in Chelverton Road. Their Steamed Eel in Black Bean Sauce has brought me more moments of real ecstasy than – for example – my first wife. Although that would not have been difficult!

If you would prefer to telephone – and I often feel that, if a physical meeting might cause embarrassment, a chat over the 'blower' can be more helpful than words on a page – I enclose a leaflet, which, as well as giving our email and telephone details contains our mission statement and a few selected testimonials from satisfied clients.

I remain, yours respectfully,
Roland O. Gibbons (MA [Reading], PIAA registered)

From:
Elizabeth Price
PO Box 132
Putney
17 June

To:
Roland O. Gibbons
Gibbons Detective Agency
12 The Alley
Putney, SW15

Dear Mr Gibbons,

I fear it will not be possible for us to meet face to face. I am not horribly disfigured and am not more noticeably hideous than other late-middle-aged women of my acquaintance. I am, however, trying to keep our relationship as secret as I suspect my husband has been keeping his extra-marital activities. Although you may think you are adept at snooping, Mr Gibbons, you have no idea of the talents of the women of Putney in this area. Very little escapes their notice, and, were you and I to meet, even at a prearranged location many miles from this area, it would not take them long to rumble us.

I do not anticipate you and I ever having to go through a face-to-face encounter. I would prefer to restrict our contact to the form in which it is presently enshrined. I have used email, but it is, on the whole, a barrier to successful communication. People begin sentences in the middle, abandon paragraphs before they have got to the point and are – with some reason – usually so frightened their words will reach people for whom they are not intended that they do not bother to make the smallest attempt at honesty.

I am afraid I did not find the leaflet you enclosed very

informative. The quotations from clients were positively off-putting. Who is 'Mrs L.B.' of Raynes Park and why did she think you were 'utterly smooth and professional'? Why on earth does 'Mr C. Lewis' of Southfields believe that 'your enquiries saved his marriage and restored his faith in humanity'? Are these people real? And, even if they are, is their opinion of any value?

You say your rates are 'between £125 and £150 a day depending on the type of surveillance required'. I am not quite sure what this means. Do you concentrate harder if you are being paid more? I am sure I do. I am sure that keeping my husband under observation is worth at least £150 *per diem*. Although large, he is physically agile and naturally suspicious. He is a lawyer. Need I say more?

Perhaps – if you are willing to undertake this job – you could write back to me and give me some details about yourself and your working methods. I always think it is possible to deduce all one needs to know about a possible employee from studying their prose style and, indeed, their handwriting – should you feel moved to scribble your reply.

I look forward to hearing from you.

Yours,
Elizabeth Price

PS Inverted commas should only really be put at the beginning and end of directly reported speech.

From:
Roland O. Gibbons
Gibbons Detective Agency
12 The Alley
Putney, SW15
30 June

To:
Elizabeth Price
PO Box 132
Putney

Dear Mrs Price,

I am sorry to be late replying to your letter. I was called away to Norwich on a difficult case involving a missing animal.

If you do not wish to meet – let's not meet! I want what you want, Mrs Price! I am not one of those private investigators who argues with the chap (or lady!) who is paying his bills! I am happy to accept your terms. Indeed, in the interests of 'transparency' you will have noticed that I am writing this reply with a black Uniball 'Eye' pen, made by the Mitsubishi Pencil Company. You are welcome to make what deductions you may from my handwriting!

A graphologist, who did some work for yours truly, once told me that my signature was 'a cry for help'. My wife said she started to lose faith in me when she received my first love letter to her in what she called my 'pathetic, spidery writing'.

Well, Mrs Price, you are in charge, and if the style and formation of my letters lay me open to you, I am happy for it to be that way! You is de Boss Lady!

Your typed letter tells me diddly-squat about you, ma'am! It was written, I would guess, using the Microsoft Word Program and printed with an HP LaserJet 2015 that is nearing the end of its cartridge life, which might suggest that you are a person who writes for a living. Your quite stern attitude to the old 'references' and my habit of being a bit too free with the 'inverted commas' tells me you may be a teacher of some kind (English possibly?) but otherwise, Mrs Price, I am quite happy for you to remain a mystery.

I would warn you, however, that the more I find out about your husband the more I am likely to find out about you. What is it the Spanish say? 'The husband wears the wife on his linen; the wife wears the husband on her face.'

What can I say about myself?

I am fifty-four years old and have a degree in English from Reading University. I was married for twenty years and am now divorced. I was brought up in a working-class household in Putney and was the first person from my family ever to go to university. Hence my 'penchant' perhaps for 'inverted commas'. I have been a private investigator for over thirty years and I take my calling very seriously indeed. I may not seem an appetizing person, Mrs Price – though I hope your sighting of me did not make you feel I was the shabby 'man in a mac' of detective stories – but in my quiet way I am a moralist.

I am very happy to start at the rate of £150 per day, which I usually reckon at eight hours. If I have to observe him after the hour of eleven p.m. there is a surcharge. I will obviously need a current photograph of your husband and some idea of where and when he is to be found. You mentioned that he is a lawyer so I presume he visits an office on a daily basis. Adultery is, in my experience, often committed with work colleagues – sometimes, I am sorry to say, even in the workplace itself. Perhaps he goes on 'away days' – a modern management notion that has done wonders for marital infidelity.

Does he, for example, have hobbies? You mentioned a boat. I have done several cases in and around Portsmouth where the bunks of seagoing yachts were not always being used for the purposes for which they were intended. Is he a keen sportsman? Leisure centres are a hotbed for this kind of thing. Is he, perhaps, a member of a local dramatic society? You mentioned your fears that he might be a homosexual and, of course, it is in these sorts of places that our 'gay brothers' are often to be found! I am also, at some stage, going to need to know your home address – if only so that I can make sure I go nowhere near it! Believe you me, our motto here at the Gibbons Agency is total and complete discretion at all times.

I say 'our'. It's just me here. I often joke that I am so discreet I usually do not have a clue what I am doing and why I am doing it!

Seriously, though, I take your confidentiality seriously and your address will not be divulged to anyone. I will make sure all my letters are directed to the 'PO Box number' you have given me.

Yours,
Roland O. Gibbons

From:
Elizabeth Price
PO Box 132
Putney
3 July

To:
Roland O. Gibbons
Gibbons Detective Agency
12 The Alley
Putney, SW15

Dear Mr Gibbons,

I am impressed! You got me in one! I have taught classics at a girls' public school in Putney for twenty-five years! I am generally reckoned to be pretty strict but – of course – I have a heart of gold! Don't we all?

Classics, actually – not English. And, yes, I am working on a long book about Propertius, though I am not sure it will ever see the light of day.

I am a terrible snob, I'm afraid. I think people should have heard of Beethoven even if they haven't listened to him. I think there are rules of grammar that should be obeyed, if only because they help to clarify our thoughts. An inverted comma, like a full stop or a semi-colon, is there for a precise reason. Sloppy language leads to sloppy thinking. Well – it *is* sloppy thinking and that is all there is to it. I only found out recently, through my daughter, that Big Brother was not – to most people – a character in a novel by George Orwell but the name of an unusually witless television programme.

I will say, however, that, while I might be rather tough on your homework were you to have the misfortune to be a pupil of mine, I knew from the moment I caught sight of you in the little alley off Putney High Street that you were the man for me. Do not, please, misinterpret that remark. I have no interest in forming another sexual relationship – not that 'sexual relationship' (I am using quotation marks here, Mr Gibbons, because I am quoting myself) is in any way a description of my marriage.

You do not want a private detective to look distinctive, do you? I do not mean this to be offensive, Mr Gibbons, but it took me some moments, on my first inspection of you, to realize that there was a person there at all. You blended into Putney High Street with a skill I don't think I have seen anyone else achieve. You hinted in your last letter that you have to struggle against putting on weight but, like many plump men, you are surprisingly light on your feet. There was a rather unpleasant-looking dog in the doorway to the stairs leading up to your office and I admired the way you flicked it out of your way with the toe of your rather extravagantly pointed shoe.

Most importantly, Mr Gibbons, you exude cunning. Even from behind you seem almost dangerously intelligent. That is the thing that counts – not inverted commas – as I often tell my girls. You have the kind of pale, watchful blue eyes that make me glad you are working for me and not my husband!

*À nos moutons*!

I am enclosing a picture of my husband and £750 in cash, which should take care of five days of close observation of him. His name is Gerald O'Shaughnessy Price, although there is nothing obviously Irish about him. I think he just added his middle name to spite me when, in the late seventies during a brief period of feminist activism, I announced my intention of using my maiden name, which is, unfortunately,

Smellie. We live in Heathland Avenue, Putney, a small road lined with large houses very close to Putney Heath off the top of Putney Hill. There is little through traffic, a lot of grass and a great many trees. You could easily fool yourself into believing you were in the country, so it is a place where a private detective might prove to be conspicuous. We are, unfortunately, also very close to the Telegraph pub, where my husband is quite often to be seen drinking pints of Guinness and slapping strangers on the back.

It might be a good place to observe him at weekends. He is usually in there from about one p.m. to three p.m. on Saturdays and from seven p.m. to ten p.m. on Sunday nights. He works as a barrister, specializing in medical negligence. His chambers are called Highleybury Parkside and they have a website bearing that name, which carries photos and contact details for all their employees. Take a careful look at Sandra. She has blonde hair and a big nose but that would not necessarily stop him.

He travels to work every day by bicycle, and as he wears a bright yellow jacket, a bright green helmet, luminous socks and there are two large red flags attached to the front and rear of the vehicle, I imagine he will be hard to miss. Next week he is going into chambers on Monday, Wednesday and Friday. He is in Kingston Crown Court the week after that. He leaves Heathland Avenue, on chambers days, at approximately nine a.m. It is quite possible there is an organized gang of adulterous cyclists, somewhere along his route, who use this absurd method of transport as a way of shaking off their legitimate spouses.

It is interesting that you mentioned the possibility of a local dramatic society. He is, as it happens, a member of the Putney Thespians, a group who meet regularly at a church hall in the Lower Richmond Road. He is currently playing

Hamlet in a production of the Shakespeare play which bears that name. That might be a possible place to start. Whenever he returns from rehearsals he has a furtive look about him.

I hope this is satisfactory. Send a written report of progress to the above address when you think you have used up five full snooping days!

Yours,
Elizabeth Price


From:
Roland O. Gibbons
Gibbons Detective Agency
12 The Alley
Putney, SW15
4 July

To:
Elizabeth Price
PO Box 132
Putney

Dear Mrs Price,
When I came in this morning, your hand-delivered letter was waiting for me.

I am starting to understand why you prefer letters to emails. I can't imagine daydreaming about the person behind, say, Horace@googlemail.com, but the hand that typed a paragraph on a screen, sent that paragraph to the printer, wrapped it in an envelope herself and then posted it through my humble letterbox – along with £750 in crisp red fifty-pound notes! – that conjures up a woman, who is, well, interesting. It is the unknown in other people that attracts us. You'll turn me into a writer yet, Mrs Price, and, so far, in this letter anyway, I haven't used a single inverted comma.

The photograph of Gerald is very disturbing indeed. He is – and I hope you will not mind my saying this – a sinister-looking man. His face is typical of the kind of adulterer with whom I have had dealings over the years. His lips, I note, are thick and sensual and, although the hat he is wearing makes it difficult to be certain about this, he seems to bear a strong resemblance to a gorilla.

The eyes struck me very forcefully. They are set very closely into his – large – nose. They suggest to me that he may very well have something even worse on his mind than sexual relations with people to whom he is not married. Is he violent, Mrs Price? I would guess so from his expression. Do you have pets? Has he been cruel to them? He looks like the sort of a man who might well kick a dog. You mentioned that he might, at one point, have planned to kill you. From the look of him I would have said he was well up for strangling.

His hands are large and he has wide shoulders, as well as a thick neck.

There is something fairly suspicious about the way he is looking at the two small boys next to him, although this may have something to do with the fact that they seem to be hitting each other with what look like broadswords. I assume they are plastic. Perhaps they are your children. Or grandchildren! If they are, the way he is looking at them is not natural. What I can see in his face may be dislike rather than sexual desire – in my experience, the two are often very close – but if they are your children, Mrs Price, and your letter made mention of a daughter, I would ask you to try to make sure that he is not alone with them too often.

I will start work tomorrow and report at your earliest convenience.

Yours,
Roland O. Gibbons

PS While I fully understand your reluctance to use telephone or email as a form of communication, I am assuming your husband has no such scruples. It may, therefore, at some point in the future be worth considering my monitoring his mobile and landline phones and, of course, his computer.

PPS Sorry about the inverted commas! You can take the boy 'out of the housing estate' but you can't 'take the housing estate out of the boy'.

PPPS I do not think of myself as a 'snooper' but as someone who is valiant for the truth!

From:
Roland O. Gibbons
Gibbons Detective Agency
12 The Alley
Putney, SW15
12 July

To:
Elizabeth Price
PO Box 132
Putney

Dear Mrs Price,

No! I have not melted in the heat. I have been hard at work on Mr Gerald O'Shaughnessy Price.

On Monday, at 0850, I put on a pair of baggy shorts and a T-shirt and got out my old 'Holdsworth' drop-head racer from the shed at the back of my block of flats. I am using inverted commas because it is a brand name. I have not ridden it for some years and am a little shaky.

I was headed up Putney Hill towards the Green Man when I saw a figure that was, unmistakably, your husband. He has aged considerably since the photograph you sent me (do you have a more recent one, perhaps?) but it was definitely the same man. He was coming down the bus lane at a speed of at least forty miles an hour. The wind whipped through his surprisingly luxuriant hair as he pulled out to overtake a bus, raising the third finger of his right hand and pointing it at the driver, shouting, as he passed him, 'Out of the way, you cunt!'

He then rode through the red traffic lights at the junction of the hill and the Lower Richmond Road. He kept the middle finger of his right hand pointed up at the sky during this manoeuvre and, as he wove out into the middle of the road to make an illegal right turn into Disraeli Road, which is, as I am sure you know, a one-way street, I think I heard him shout, 'Die, motherfuckers!'

He did not, I have to say, look like a man with adultery on his mind. Suicide seemed a bit more like it.

I am, as you were pleased to remind me, Mrs Price, more than a little overweight, but I do take pride in my physical fitness and I did not find it difficult to keep him in my sights. I followed him, illegally, up Disraeli Road, through to Putney Bridge Road and down towards the Wandsworth one-way system. As we reached the park that lies between the main road and the river he slowed and I thought, for a moment, that he might be easing the pace in order to enjoy the beautiful morning. The sun was sparkling on the river and the trees on the far side of the park were crowned with summer light.

In fact, just ahead of us, a young female cyclist was hoisting her buttocks high off her saddle and your husband was thrusting himself forward in a manner that, if left unrestrained, would undoubtedly have led to his sniffing or, possibly, penetrating her behind with his nose. As we drew up to a set of lights he slowed to pull up next to her and, as I watched, from a safe distance, he struck up a conversation. At first I thought he might know her and, indeed, that she might be the woman with whom he was having a relationship; but it very quickly became clear that the easiness of his manner was just that.

He has charm, Mrs Price, I will admit. Within a few seconds she was laughing at something he had said and, when they pulled away, they rode together for a few hundred yards until the young woman turned right, down towards Tooting, just before Wandsworth Bridge. He waved a cheery goodbye to her. For a moment I was beginning to think the better of him and then, as I came behind him at the next set of lights, I heard him say to another fellow cyclist, a young man in his twenties, 'Lovely arse on that!'

Not the sort of thing one would usually say to a stranger but, again, it was done with a certain charm. It did not seem as offensive as it ought to have done. His teeth, I noted, were brilliantly white and his eyes – very pale blue – sparkled with the kind of intense life that is very difficult to resist. Oh, Gerald! I thought, as I pedalled on, thirty or forty yards to his athletic rear. 'You devil! You're up to something! I wonder what it is!'

The rest of his journey to work was, I am afraid (or pleased) to report, without incident. I followed him all the way to his chambers and paid particular attention to his demeanour as he entered the building. I will obviously look into his office life further. As I think I said, work is an erogenous zone. But men of Gerald's age and type, when conducting an affair, do not usually risk being seen by their 'fancy bits', wearing bicycle helmets, Lycra and a hairstyle so blown about by the wind it resembles a haystack in a hurricane. He did not look like a man with filth on his mind. I cycled home – a journey for which I have not charged you, Mrs Price – convinced that he is 'playing away' 'close to home'.

On Thursday night I went along to the church hall in the Upper Richmond Road where the Putney Thespians meet.

It is not an inspiring location. There is a draughty, gloomy entrance hall and, beyond, an even more draughty and gloomy high-ceilinged room in which there are some chairs, a large table and a poster saying, 'ARE YOU A CUSTARD CHRISTIAN? DO YOU GET UPSET OVER TRIFLES?' There were only about five or six people in the room and they were sitting, all well apart from each other, with the air of those who have been waiting for a train that they are starting to suspect will never arrive.

A woman in her late fifties was the only one to rise. She had what I think is called strawberry blonde hair, which looked – I am afraid – as if it were not her natural colour. She had, also, a strawberry blonde complexion and, as she was wearing a pink cardigan, pink slacks and what looked like a pair of pink slippers, my first impression was that she was, for some psychological reason perhaps, too heavily involved with the colour pink.

She had, however, two of the largest breasts I have ever seen on an Englishwoman. In fact, on first sight of her upper half I was convinced there might well be more than two of them. Her lower half, too, spread outward from her waist in a manner that reminded me of the upholstery of an old but very comfortable sofa. As she came towards me, smiling brightly, she wobbled all over in a way that was not, although at first it threatened to be so, unpleasant.

'Hello!' she said, with some eagerness. 'I'm Ophelia! Are you Rosencrantz or Guildenstern?'

'I'm afraid,' I said, 'I'm even more unimportant than those two characters. I'm not even a member of the club. I just saw the sign outside and wondered whether you might need a hand backstage.'

'Oh, gosh, how marvellous!' said the pink woman. 'How absolutely marvellous! We need all the help we can get backstage! Perhaps you could play Rosencrantz or Guildenstern as well! Or both of them! We could...sort of...merge their two characters, couldn't we? They are pretty much the same, don't you think? And we just haven't got enough bods, have we, Rachel?'

A small, grey woman with a squint looked at her with real dislike.

'There are some who maintain,' she said, 'that we haven't got a Hamlet!'

The pink woman became even pinker. 'That's a horrible thing to say, Janet,' she said. 'I think Gerald is going to be one of the great Hamlets of all time!'

The grey-looking woman took out a packet of cigarettes and, without making a move towards the door, got one out and lit it. I thought, these days, that that was a pretty brave thing to do, but she must have been sure of her ground, as none of the other members of the cast made any move to stop her.

'If we can talk him out of the German accent,' she went on, inhaling deeply, 'he might be adequate. With a few more years of rehearsal!'

As she was saying this, your husband came through the doors of the hall. He looked, I have to admit, very like Hamlet. He was dressed entirely in black – black jeans, a black polo-neck sweater and a black jacket. He also had the look – common, I have found, in people who play this part – of a man who was about to contradict the next thing that was said to him. He is, I suppose, Mrs Price, a handsome man. His jaw is too large but built on very secure lines. His nose – as I think I said – is a possibly over-ambitious structure but those pale blue eyes have a kind of life that is clearly hard to resist.

Janet, the grey woman, became suddenly faintly girlish. Whatever she might say about him behind his back, she looked glad to have him in the room. And my pink friend was trembling like a blancmange that has been set down too violently upon a table.

'"Soft you now!"' he said, holding out his right hand in what looked a little like a Hitler salute. '"The fair Ophelia!"'

I began to suspect he was already 'in character' since – as the grey woman had suggested earlier – there was definitely a Germanic edge to his accent. Perhaps there is a 'Nazi theme' to the production. The effect on the pink woman was striking.

She went towards him and, taking his hand, led him towards the centre of the room. I could not quite hear everything she said but I caught the words '"How does your honour for this many a day?"' To which he replied, 'Fucking brilliant, darling!'

It was not, however, what they said, but what they didn't say. Suddenly that shabby church hall was reeking of sex. I had the impression that, at any moment, Mr Price was going to throw her on to the floor, pull down her pink trousers and have her right there in front of the core members of the Putney Thespians.

I am writing this in my living room, Mrs Price, and the man next door seems to be trying to run over his dog with his lawnmower. I will try to give you a more detailed report tomorrow. Suffice it to say that, from what I have seen of these two over a period of only two days, I am convinced that something is 'in the wind' between them. I will need further proof, quite obviously, and this will involve detailed surveillance of 'Mary Dimmock', which may involve extra expense. Do, please, let me know your thoughts. If you could bear to telephone or email me that would certainly speed things up!

Yours truly,
Roland O. Gibbons

From:
Elizabeth Price
PO Box 132
Putney
14 July

To:
Roland O. Gibbons
Gibbons Detective Agency

Dear Mr Gibbons,
Just received your letter. No, I will not phone or email you. This woman Dimmock was known to me although I have – thank Christ – managed to avoid her for the last fifteen years. There was a nasty moment in 2003 when I sighted her while crossing Hotham Road and had to duck down behind a parked car until I was sure she had passed. Keep your distance and on no account let either her or my husband suspect that you are what you are.

I want to know everything that happens between them. If you have to use a telephoto lens – use it. Tape record whatever seems necessary. You have my permission to hide under whatever bed they may be using to do what they do – if you think that is advisable.

Yours,
Elizabeth Price

PS When the time comes I will act appropriately. I am relying on you to keep our correspondence completely secret. In fact, I would recommend you to burn all my letters as soon as you receive this. I have to go away for a few weeks. I am enclosing £850 in cash. Do not stint in your endeavours while I am away.

# Chapter Two

*Mr Price writes a letter of condolence.*
*Mike Larner tries to avoid him*

From the desk of
Gerald Price QC
112 Heathland Avenue
Putney, SW15 3LE
20 July

To:
Michael Larner
24 Lawson Crescent
Putney

Dear Mike,
I felt I had to write to say how sorry I was about Pamela.
I know it happened a long time ago. I think I only heard
she had passed away a few years after she actually got the
ultimate P45; and I always felt bad I didn't write to you with
a bit of the old 'she was an unrecognized genius' sort of
thing. We had all lost touch, had we not? It's taken me yonks
to get your address.

I was reminded of her because I ran into old Norman

Staines in the Northumberland Club and we got talking about people stiffing – as you do – and your missus was mentioned.

'Was it cancer that got Pamela Larner?' I said to him. 'Or was it her heart? She was always a tense sort of person!'

He dragged his bulbous nose out of his pint and said, rather mysteriously, 'I heard it was suspicious circumstances. Although I couldn't quite say where I heard that.' You could have knocked me down with the proverbial feather, Mike. Suspicious circumstances!

'What kind of suspicious circumstances?' say I.

'I'm not exactly sure,' says Norman, 'but there was something dodgy about it.'

It seems only yesterday that we were all standing around the playground at St Jude's Primary and watching Conrad and Jasper and Barnaby and Molly (or was it Milly?) and dear little Elaine (did she become a nun, I wonder?) skip around in their green uniforms. Do you remember Conrad absolutely fucking up as the Roman soldier in the nativity play? And 'Find a Bin'?

> Find a Bin
> Find a Bin
> Find a Bin and PUT IT IN!

Jesus, we're all getting so old. Where did the years go, Michael?

Suspicious circumstances! Pull the other one. It's usually cancer, isn't it? Was it cancer? Almost everyone I know seems to have cancer. Toby Loosestrife has a brain tumour and is clearly on the way out. I saw him in the Green Man at the top of Putney Hill the other day, wearing a woollen cap, presumably to hide the scars on his bonce, and staring into his beer as if it was about to suggest an answer to the question 'What Was It All For?'

God knows, mate. You go to school. You manage to slither through to university. You are a lawyer. You have 2.4 children. You die. That's about it. Oh, in my case, it's more like 1.75 children since no one in their right mind would dare to suggest that Conrad is a fully developed human being.

Mavis Whatever Her Name Was had a stroke apparently and Peter Vansittart is in a coma – only this time it's official! Don't mean to sound callous. I sometimes feel making a joke is the only way to get through it all.

Don't get me wrong. I'm not about to try to raise a few cheap laughs about the demise of your wife. Although – as you will remember from the old days – Gerald is a man not averse to the cheap laugh. Do you remember the time when I locked 'St' Johnny Goldsmith in the lavatory at Courseulles-sur-Mer? Served the pompous fucker right – and I did let him out eventually.

Seriously, Mike, Pamela was a really special person. She was one in a million. She was always so well turned out, and the work she put into those children was phenomenal. Norman seemed to think they had all got into Oxford, which is amazing. Molly was always bright, wasn't she? And Barnaby and Leo, I seem to remember, could read and write Latin from the age of three! Maybe Barnaby bullied Conrad a bit, but bullying is about the only way to get through to Conrad.

God knows what happened to Jas and Josh Goldsmith. Extended prison terms for both of them, I imagine. Dr John Goldsmith may be a paragon of virtue but his and Barbara's kids should, in my humble, have been strangled at birth.

But Pamela! My God! Pamela! I remember her in the kitchen with Elizabeth knocking up banquet after banquet while we men lounged around and played tennis. She was a very beautiful woman, Miguel – at least, she was fifteen years ago. We're all getting senile, Mike, and it won't be long before we, in our turn, are being shipped down to Putney Vale Crematorium in a rented saloon.

We are still jogging on. Elizabeth is still tormenting the daughters of estate agents at Dame Veronica's, and I am still doing the old medical negligence. Every time a heart surgeon's scalpel goes wide of the mark or an anaesthetist tries to take forty winks in the middle of a bladder operation, it's 'Send for Gerald'. I have just finished a very lucrative eight weeks demolishing some hopeless loser who seemed to think he knew as much about the large bowel as I did. Professor of fucking Surgery! I don't think so!

The wife has been a bit depressed of late. Maybe it's being married to me; but I suspect it might be something to do with the Conrad situation. I do wish he would get a job. Or at least look as if he's interested in finding one. She won't read him the Riot Act and I am forbidden to force his head into the toilet bowl in order to emphasize any points I want to make to the little bastard. Elizabeth spends hour after hour locked up in her study. I suspect she may be writing a novel. Do we really want any more novels? Aren't they all written by lesbians for lesbians? I did read a rather good one recently about an SAS man taking apart the fellaheen. He reminded me of me.

Anyway, my little troubles are, obviously, nothing compared to yours. Unless, of course, you were glad to see the back of her! You always had a pretty combative relationship, I seem to remember. There was a real bust-up one night when the six of us were staying in that villa in Corsica – though I think it might have been to do with tensions between Mrs Dimmock and Mrs Larner. Scratch away, girls!

It is possible you and Pam got divorced years ago. But even if you weren't speaking when she hit the buffers, I'm really sorry, mate. Really sorry. She was one of my all-time favourites. If you want the God's honest truth – I always fancied her rotten. Which is a compliment to you, Mikhail. I'll never forget her in that Portuguese place, hoovering the stairs in her nightie. Way to go, Pammie!

All my best, mate,
Gerald Price


From the bed of
Mike Larner
24 Lawson Crescent
Putney
26 July (probably)

To the desk and indeed the front hall of
Gerald Price OBE by now, why not?
112 Heathland Avenue
Putney-on-Sea

Dear Gerry,
Nice to hear from you. Well – 'nice' is not quite the word but I was glad you wrote to me. It's been years, hasn't it? Fifteen? At least that and maybe more.

We're still here, though. Well, I am anyway. A letter of condolence – even from you and nearly ten years late – is always appreciated. You took the trouble to write it – I'm assuming you did give it *some* thought – and, perhaps even more importantly, when you had written it you bothered to dig out an envelope and the appropriate stamp. I write far more letters in my head than on paper and even the ones on paper do not always make it to the pillar-box at the end of Lawson Crescent.

Pamela died over ten years ago. There were no notices in the papers. She just died and that was it. I can't remember whom I told. All I can say is that it is not a night I will forget in a hurry. I don't want to go into detail. Suffice it to say that she should not have died in the way that she did. Almost anything would have been preferable.

I don't see many people now. I took early retirement from the BBC. Which is actually virtually indistinguishable from working for it. I don't think I miss it. They don't seem as committed to serious wildlife programmes as they once were. David Attenborough – The Man Everybody Likes Apart From Me – has somehow smarmed his way into total control of all animals everywhere.

He has always had a prejudice against fish – as far as I can see. 'Oooh, isn't that Arctic fox cute as it burrows away in the snow?' There is no longer the space for the poor old mackerel, the fascinating and intense story of, say, how sprats mate, or the willingness to sit down and take a good long look at the life cycle of the perch. Small fish, for some reason, are beneath contempt for the present-day gurus of natural history films. Back in the eighties I was allowed five hours of airtime to do a really in-depth study of gudgeon. The programmes won awards because they were a serious study of the lifestyle of a particular fish. We went into the subject in fantastic detail. Nobody questioned the fact that it took me four years to make the show or questioned my expenses, which were considerable.

Thanks for asking about the children – although I am afraid none of them got into Oxford. Milly spent three unrewarding years at Exeter and is now working part-time in local radio. She lives in Leeds – with a tall, thin, self-righteous boy whom everyone, apart from me, calls Spon. Barnaby and Leo never really showed any aptitude for Latin. I can't think where you got that idea.

At least you didn't suggest we meet up for a drink. I went through a phase of doing that. Drinking alcohol with people I don't really like. And then I realized it was completely pointless.

I don't see anyone these days – and certainly not people from Putney. Even though I still live here it is remarkably easy to avoid them. Maybe they're at home, hiding behind drawn curtains, avoiding me. I'm sitting up here in my bedroom, looking out at the rain-swept garden, filled with an awful empty rage. The summer seems to have given up trying, doesn't it? In the street, a woman in a grey coat has just come out of the house opposite. Her husband died of a stroke three years ago. She fiddles with her handbag. I know she's checking if she still has a key. I know her son lives in Norwich and she hardly ever sees him. I know she's lonely. I know I'm lonely. But there's no point in talking to her. It would only emphasize our complete isolation – from the world and from each other.

The children never call. They have their own lives. Leo married a truly ghastly woman from a place called Budleigh Salterton, in, I think, Devon. I only went there once, for the wedding. I paid for it – but that was about the extent of my involvement. Jacinta (where do they get these names? Who are they trying to impress?) wore a beautiful white dress. She was the bride's mother. Her daughter, who is called Jazz or Jizz or something like that, wore a slightly less glamorous white dress. The best man made a speech in which the word 'cock' was mentioned twelve times. He closed by saying, 'Leo is a queer!' which drew gales of laughter and a huge round of applause.

It was as well Barnaby wasn't there. I don't think I can face bringing you up to date with what's happened to Barnaby. It's not a pretty story. Pamela used to say it was all our fault for giving him that fucking stupid name but I don't think being called Dave or Alan would have stopped him doing what he did.

Am I angry about Pamela's death? I suppose I'm angry about a lot of things. I'm as angry about what happened to Pamela as I am about the decline in the standard of wildlife programmes on the BBC. But, as you have probably gathered, I am really pretty angry about that. Did you see that sickening elephant programme the other day? Insulting, self-congratulatory rubbish. 'Oooh, look – they've got big ears and they like each other!'

But nobody cares what I think about wildlife programmes. Nobody cares that my wife died in such peculiar circumstances. The rain has started again. It's beating against the shrouded windows of the house three doors down on the other side. Gordon Bliss lived there for nearly forty years. He was a civil servant and now he's dead. Who cares?

I've had a few whiskies. Thanks for writing anyway. I think I'm grateful. Though I'm not sure. We both know what we think of each other, don't we, Gerry? I don't think either of us has any illusions since that last sponsored cycle ride, but at least you bothered to pick up the pen and write. Not that it will bring back Pamela. I suppose, if I'm honest, your letter had a bad effect on me because it reminded me of what Pamela and I went through and of that awful night in November when she died . . . Whoever said the suburbs were peaceful?

Best anyway,
Mike Larner

From the desk of
Gerald Price QC
112 Heathland Avenue
Putney, SW15 3LE
5 August

To:
Michael Larner
24 Lawson Crescent
Putney

Dear Mike,

Bloody hell, mate, you sound in a bad way! I tried to find
your number but no one seemed to have it and when I tried
Directory Enquiries, which, like everything else, has gone
completely down the tubes and is full of smooth-talking people
with regional accents offering to connect you for ten quid a
minute from a BT line, they said you were 'ex-directory'.

Oho! Very important and mysterious. Have you been
shagging someone you shouldn't? Or do you just owe a fuck
of a lot of money like the rest of us?

Sorry to hear about the Beeb. I have great respect for
wildlife programmes. I always thought you had an absolutely
jammy job, Mike. They are the only things I watch, apart from
the footie. And the rugby, of course. And, oh, well, yes, the
tennis and the winter Olympics and hockey – or girliehock,
as we like to call it – and it is true that I always find time to
sneak a look at anything to do with sailing or athletics or
boxing, wrestling, cricket, fives and good old squash!

I did actually see the elephant programme you mentioned
and found it pretty riveting. I know what you mean about it
being a bit too cute and giving them names and that woman
practically blubbing in the commentary when one of them

fell down that hole and couldn't get out. But, that being said, I did find I was really rooting for Tonga the Bull, pride of the herd, and when he did that neat bit of tusk work on his rival Bimbo Baggins, or whatever his name was, I was there for him, perhaps because I identified with his need to keep all the other fucking elephants in line. Literally. I thought old Tonga definitely deserved his go on Zimbo or Zimbu or whatever she was called – the Marilyn Monroe of the herd. She may have looked like a wrinkled London bus to us humans but she clearly meant a lot to the male trunkmeisters. And when she moved her five-foot-wide arse and let Tonga know she was ready to accommodate his three-foot long schlonger you could really feel the heat of it. Even in Heathland Avenue! Not a venue in which the resident human female does a lot of arse-spreading I can tell you, mate.

You really do not want to hear about Elizabeth and me. Not the whole story. We kind of get along okay, I suppose, but certain things have happened...Me and...well...me and her and Julia and that business with Conrad and the cider. Jesus!

I must have missed the gudgeon programmes. When did you say they were on? I caught something about stickleback a few years ago – or was that made by some foreign geezer? Apparently the male stickleback looks after the children full time. What a fucking tosser!

What did happen to Pamela? I've been ringing round trying to find out if anyone has any info but absolutely no luck. Maybe you're still in touch with the dreaded Dr John 'Hands Off My Halo' Goldsmith. I seem to remember you two got on okay. I assume he still lives in Putney but I seem to have managed to keep out of his way for twenty years. To my surprise, I find I still have the bastard's number but I draw the line at picking up the phone and calling him.

What about these 'suspicious circumstances', then? It obviously wasn't the big C. I got the impression from your letter that it all just came in one wallop. Heart attack? Was she run over by a lorry? Was it bacterial meningitis? A mate of mine had that. We were on the tennis court at eleven. At around lunchtime he had a headache and by the time *Newsnight* came on he was in the old sliding drawer at the hospital morgue.

Don't want to sound ghoulish but I really would like to know. I mean, if it was so ghastly you really cannot bear to talk about it please forget I ever asked. Maybe you reversed over her while she was standing in the drive of your house. I damn near did that with Conrad when he was about five. I can still see him looking up at me in his Osh Kosh dungarees, as I hurtled towards him in the Volvo. The expression on his face was so piteous I was minded to keep my foot on the accelerator and spare the little bastard the misery so clearly in store for him over the next twenty-odd years.

Do try and let me know how old Pam got her dismissal notice. I don't know why but I sort of feel the details would help me come to terms with it. I don't need twelve pages on how she bled out during major surgery at Kingston Hospital. Just a word or two, if that's all you can manage. 'Brain haemorrhage'. 'Traffic accident'. That's all you have to write. And if you're fed up with this correspondence and find writing letters as tedious and unusual as I do – call me or drop me an email.

All best
Gerry

PS You don't mention them in your letter so I suppose you've lost touch with John and Barbara Goldsmith. John G swore he would knock me down if he ever set eyes on me again. If I ever do run into him, I hope to give him the chance to try. Let him make one move and I'll alter his face so considerably that no woman in Putney will ever again describe him as a DILF – Doctor I would Like to Fuck.

From the overgrown back garden at
24 Lawson fucking Crescent
Putney Les Deux Arseholes
10 August

To the no-doubt immaculate luxury mansion of
Sir Gerald the Invincible OM, VC, etc.
112 Heathland Avenue
SW396 Very Superior Postcode

Christ, Gerry!
You are unbelievable. You are fucking unbelievable. I don't know why you are the way you are. I seem to remember meeting your mother once, back in the days when we all used to socialize together, and thinking she was quite a pleasant woman. You, however, are and have always been a complete and utter cunt.

I tried, when you wrote to me, to reply pleasantly. I thought maybe I could handle communication with you by letter – at least in writing a letter you have time to stop and think about what you're going to say – but here I am, in spite of all my good intentions, scribbling away, unpacking my heart like a very drab to let you know what I really think of you.

I don't know how you have managed to get away with it for so long. Some people seem, actually, to like you. But I know you're a cunt. I think you know it too. I think deep down you're aware of what a cunt you are; perhaps that is your strength. Perhaps, like Stalin and Hitler, you know how to walk the narrow line that divides truth from falsehood, insult from compliment, mateyness from hostility. You give people just enough hope there might be a decent person lurking under that façade of crudity, racism, selfishness and deliberately contrived ignorance to entice them into treating you as a human being. I think it's time someone pointed out a few simple facts to you. Such as – you are a cunt.

'That's Gerry!' is what people in Putney used to say about you in the old days. 'He does that! Yeah. He sticks champagne bottles into the groins of his friends' wives because...well...he does that!' I always remember you saying at one of those first ghastly dinner parties you gave, 'Oh, Mike Larner is built like a bottle of Beaujolais!'

I was supposed to take it in good part and laugh. Very funny. Mike Larner was not one of the boys. He wasn't John Goldsmith, the most handsome GP in south-west London. He wasn't even, really, in a league with chunky bluff northerner Sam Dimmock, dentist with the biggest beard in SW15. He was just the vaguely effeminate guy with the sloping shoulders who did a programme about gudgeon that nobody ever watched! And old Gerry Price was...you know...a bit tactless but that was good old Gerry. Who never really thinks about what he says, just comes out with it!

But, of course, your offensiveness is not simply ignorance. You are a highly intelligent individual. Everything you do is done for a reason. Everything you do is done for the greater good of Gerry Price. Letters of condolence that are not, really, letters of condolence, or insults disguised as compliments or any of the other tricks you have up your lawyer's sleeve are all there to progress the only cause in which you really have a firm belief – you.

You're cautious too, aren't you? Do you remember when I reversed into that car in Montserrat Road and I was about to drive away? You said, 'No – leave a note under their windscreen. Put a false address and disguise your handwriting! You don't want some busybody reporting you to the cops!'

I sometimes wondered, in the days when we all went on holidays together, whether you might be shagging Pamela. You are, really, just like a great big red penis, aren't you? And although women – especially pseudo-feminists like Pamela – like to pretend they're not interested in great big red penises, in fact they probably think about little else – especially when locked up in a Mediterranean villa for two weeks.

I don't think so, though. I think Mary Dimmock was the most smitten. I can remember her on the beach at Quinta da Praia, watching you smother yourself in sunscreen. I think Pamela and Barbara Goldsmith and, even, perhaps, your long-suffering wife had had enough of the ape-man routine by day three of each holiday.

Pamela and I didn't always have an easy time of it, but we loved each other. We talked, Gerry. We talked about life and art and politics and design and, yes, fish. Pamela supported me throughout the making of my gudgeon films and, when I was in real despair about getting the kind of screen time I thought the fish deserved, she was there for me. We were friends, Gerry – something I'm not sure you and Elizabeth ever were. I miss her more than I can say.

Don't bother writing to me again. I won't reply. Don't bother to try to find out my number either. I'm getting rid of my phone – partly to avoid the possibility of people like you calling me.

Mike

From the desk of
Gerald Price QC
112 Heathland Avenue
Putney, SW15 3LE
12 August

To
Michael Larner
24 Lawson Crescent
Putney

Whoa there, tiger!
I did try door-stepping you, old boy, because I thought you
sounded in a bad way. From the look of your front garden
you're seriously in need of a bit of the old psychotherapy. I
don't think I've ever seen a privet hedge in quite such distress.

All the curtains seemed to be closed too. I hope you haven't
gone and topped yourself, *mon brave*. And if you have, can
I not be the one who breaks in through the downstairs
window and finds you rotting away in front of Sky Atlantic?

Look, I'm sorry if I behaved like an oaf. I am an oaf, *cher
Michel*. A full-time oaf. It's how I am. It's what I do. I can't
help it. I really would like to know how dear old Pamela
died. I feel quite upset about it.

Were the police involved on the 'awful night in November'?
And was old Norman just talking balls about 'suspicious
circumstances'? If there had been a murder inquiry or
anything I suppose it would have been in the papers, but she
just seems to have popped off without anyone really knowing
quite how. Or, indeed, when! Was it November 2002? Or
November 2003? I keep trying to think where I was ten years
ago but all I can recall about that period of my life is that
Conrad was an adolescent, which is why I have probably so

40

effectively suppressed all memories of the period. I know we have had our differences but, for the record, I would like to state that Beaujolais is a highly entertaining and fruity wine that comes in rather beautifully shaped bottles.

Really all my best,
Gerry

PS This summer has – if I'm honest – been a pretty intense one for Gerald Price QC. I am not all penis, old thing – although I will grant you that Percy does tend to run my life. I can't go into the full emotional dossier now but it has to do with a production of *Hamlet* in which I am due to 'open' – as we say – in September and a pretty heavy bit of cruising at the Waitrose cheese counter in Putney Shopping Centre. If you want to see sex in the raw try to get along to St Jude's Church Hall in September where you will see yours truly in the old black tights. Jude Law, be warned! I bet my cock's even more impressive in close-fitting doublet than yours!

PPS Talking of being a nut bag (no offence, Mike), I've been having the feeling, just lately, that someone is following me. Is this something to do with being a sixtysomething? Or do you think some woman is trying to get her hands on my love stick?

PPPS If Pam's death was murder – do you have any idea who might have done it?

# Chapter Three

*Mary Dimmock writes to the local paper for sex advice. Dr John Goldsmith is surprised*

From A Worried Woman of Putney:
I do not wish to give my real name or address but am prepared to supply if necessary. This is a *genuine* enquiry!
15 August

To:
Dr Wise, c/o His Column in the *Putney Guardian*, which I read with great pleasure

Dear 'Dr Wise',
Though I am sure that is not your real name. I know it says in the paper that you are a genuine doctor but I do not believe anything I read in the papers.

Why then, you may ask, am I writing in to your column?

Because, whoever you are – even if you are actually three different reporters working for the *Putney Guardian* – the answers you give to people's problems really sound genuine and sincere and thoughtful and kind. It is so important to be kind, isn't it? The answer you gave to the woman who was having a discharge from her vagina was so sweet and tasteful. What you wrote to the man whose wife was having an affair with his father and two of his brothers was moving and gentle and intelligent and full of sound, practical advice.

I have many, many problems, Dr Wise. I am a person with an artistic temperament, trapped in a marriage to a man who does not really understand my needs and aspirations. I do not know whether you have read *Madame Bovary* by Gustave Flaubert. It is a wonderful, wonderful novel and when I read it I cried aloud to the empty room in which I was sitting at the time '*Madame Bovary – c'est moi!*' It is – though I am sure you know this, Dr Wise – a French book.

I am married to a dentist. This is the first of my problems. And, while I am interested in painting and music and ballet and theatre and the novels of Ian McEwan (I hope I am spelling that correctly), he is really only ever excited by teeth. In the early years of our marriage, when we made love he would quite often break off to examine a suspect molar or a dodgy bicuspid. When he says – as he still does after many years of marriage – that I have a lovely mouth, it is not because he wants to kiss it. From the way he looks at me I can tell he cannot wait to force it open, lay pieces of cotton wool along my gums and get to work with his miniature pitchfork and odiously intrusive silvered-mirror-on-a-stick!

He never folds me in his arms, Doctor, and whispers the words all women long to hear from a man. He has never been anything less than respectful but we have not had sexual intercourse since 12 August 1981. I am not even sure that that is the right way to describe what happened on that particular occasion – although it is etched in my mind with the vividness of a Daumier *engravure* (if that is the right word).

Gradually, Doctor, as he has lost interest in me, I have found myself drawn to other men. Although my husband is a well-built and handsome individual, with a particularly striking beard, I have found my eyes wandering. Many years ago while on a mixed villa holiday in Portugal – I have long since lost contact with the other couples involved – I found myself excited by the sight of one of our party. He was a distinguished lawyer, thrusting and powerful in conversation, but he was also a superb physical specimen. In the early morning, after a swim in the villa pool, he would do gymnastics on the lawn of the property and I was quite often weak at the knees at the sight of him balancing on one hand and moving his well-formed legs in a slow scissor motion. His buttocks were particularly beautifully shaped and in the wet swimming trunks he often seemed to be wearing, even at lunch, he was a powerful spectacle for a woman in her thirties.

Quite by chance I ran into him again, quite recently, as he joined a drama club to which I belong and we both gained prominent roles in a forthcoming production of a Shakespeare play. I talked with him about the old days and, though we were friendly and even slightly flirtatious, I did not feel the passion that had once so disturbed me.

Then some weeks ago I found myself by the cheese counter at Waitrose in Putney Shopping Centre. I was moving my trolley forward when I caught sight of a man's behind raised in my direction as he stooped to pick up a tranche (is that the right word?) of Jarlsberg.

The sight of his bottom must have triggered some deep feelings that I had been struggling to suppress for years. In rehearsal for our play there had been many slightly dangerous moments – especially when he laid his head in my lap in the scene in which Ophelia is taken to the theatre. But this was different. It was intense. Suddenly the memories of those villas we had shared in northern Corsica, southern Portugal and western France came back to me with the force and vigour of one of this man's swallow dives hitting the surface of a shared holiday swimming pool all those years ago!

Pretending an interest in Norwegian, Swiss and other hard, nutty cheeses, I leaned forward and found myself once more looking into his long, muscular face. He has a wide mouth and I have heard people say he reminds them of one of the larger and more menacing sharks. His hair, still abundant I noticed, continued to start up from his forehead in a bold, masculine manner and, in spite of the many years that had passed since we last met, he could easily have been mistaken for a man of forty-five.

We talked, for the first time, with real intimacy. He told me about his family. I had always found his wife a somewhat snobbish woman who often paraded her learning at the breakfast table and corrected my attempts to speak any language apart from English (although even that sometimes came under her scrutiny). I gained the impression he was unhappy. He has a son who became dangerously addicted to cider at university and a daughter who works for an organization dedicated to preserving Rwandan gorillas.

'Perhaps,' he said, throwing his head back with a booming laugh, 'they remind her of her old man!'

He inflated his chest and beat upon it, violently, with his fists, uttering a throaty cry as he did so. The effect was overpoweringly erotic. After we had talked for several minutes he gave me his mobile number and suggested we meet one evening for a drink.

'I won't tell the wife if you won't tell the old man!' he said, with another of his deep, attractive laughs, and, with these words, strode off in the direction of the fish counter.

As he left me, Doctor, a sudden and disturbing image came to me. I am almost embarrassed to write it down but I feel you need to know all the facts of the case. It was no more than a fleeting vision but it has stayed with me and I cannot get it out of my mind. *I was being penetrated by him in the open air.* It was – I am fairly sure – mountainous terrain and there was a crowd of peasants or tribesmen, or people of that sort, watching me and applauding as I allowed him access to my body.

I find myself constantly thinking of this man and, although I have always been something of a feminist, I find my dreams of him often involve his taking me by force – very much as Ledaia (is that her correct name?) was taken by Zeus, who had disguised himself as an animal of some kind in order to take advantage of her. I do not know whether to ring his mobile. I feel that if I do it may lead to events I will be unable to control. But I am very tempted to call him. What should I do?

Yours truly,
Worried W, Putney

From Dr Wise
*Putney Guardian*
9 Industrial Way
Salford
Greater Manchester NTR 345Z
18 August

## A DOCTOR WRITES

Dr Wise is a working medical practitioner with a wide experience of medical and emotional problems. He will answer your questions – which should be sent by post to DR WISE'S BUREAU at the *Guardian* – in complete confidence but regrets he cannot enter into any private correspondence.

## LETTER OF THE WEEK

*Should I or shouldn't I?*

Dear Dr Wise,
I have recently become attracted to a married man with whom I have been re-acquainted after losing touch for many years. I am very worried about where this may lead. I am married to a man who is completely absorbed by his work and with whom I have not had sexual relations for some time. The married man has asked me to call him in a way that suggests he would like to take the relationship further. What should I do?

Yours truly,
Worried Woman of Putney

Dear Worried Woman,

It is clear from your letter that you are suffering from something that the French call *un coup de foudre*. There is no recognized medical term for this condition – in which long-repressed feelings come to the surface in a way that makes them very difficult to control.

The married man you describe is clearly making advances to you without in any way offering you the chance of a serious relationship. You need to raise this – and the whole issue of your marriage – with your husband before you fall into the trap of seeking solace with someone who does not sound as if he is deeply committed to you or, indeed, anyone else.

That being said, it is, of course, everyone's right to have a satisfying sexual relationship and the problems you have described in your letter are serious ones. It may help you to seek the advice of a therapist – either with or without your husband – but I would advise you not to do anything you may regret later.

Best wishes
Dr Wise

From:
Mary Dimmock
24 Beeston Crescent
Putney
22 August

To:
Dr Wise
c/o *Putney Guardian*
9 Industrial Way
Salford
Greater Manchester NTR 345Z

Dear Dr Wise,

I suspect I am not supposed to write to you again and I cannot expect you to write to me. I am sure it is against your professional code of ethics to write to a person's home address, and although my husband would never do anything like open my mail, I suppose it is possible he might do so inadvertently.

I feel I have to write, though. I have to pour out my heart to someone and you are so calm and reasonable and gentle. I can tell this from your column and the sensitive way you edited my rambling thoughts for public consumption! Writing tells you so much about a person, doesn't it?

I write myself and can spend hours describing things, like the way an ant moves. I also write poetry.

It seems strange that you are based in Greater Manchester and not in Putney, where I – as you will see from the address – live! Although I suppose that means there is less chance of me bumping into you on the high street!

I have, I am afraid, already disregarded your advice and now feel I am paying the price for it. Forgive me, Doctor.

I have not only telephoned the married man in question. I have also made love with him five times. All these sex acts took place in the open air. One of them happened in a tent in Richmond Park. Gerald brought it along for that specific purpose. As we were doing it a large dog tried to get under the canvas to join us. I am afraid this only made my sensations more intense!

At first this was because we had nowhere else to go. My husband's surgery is in our home so he hardly ever leaves the premises and my lover is – in spite of his great physical strength – very afraid of his wife. He says she is capable of murder and sometimes seems to suggest she has actually committed it!

But now it has become something of a compulsion for both of us. I am in the middle of a maelstrom. If that is the correct expression. Last week we did it in the bushes on the towpath not more than two hundred yards from Putney Bridge. I think – though I cannot be sure – that other people were also doing it in the near vicinity although it was not late. The sex is very passionate and enjoyable and I nearly always have an orgasm, although none of them seem to have quite matched up to the one where the dog tried to get into the tent.

It is, however, Doctor, a purely animal affair. We meet, go for a brief stroll and then, before we have really had any conversation at all, I am grabbing his penis, which is enormous, and thrusting it into me, quite often within earshot of late-night pedestrians and, on one occasion, an entire rowing team in the middle of a training session.

If we do talk it is about the old days when – as I think I said – I and my dentist husband often went on villa holidays with him, his wife and two other couples. But I find these conversations even more disturbing than the casual violence of our physical relationship. I do not feel I can go into it here, Doctor, but it seems that one of the members of our villa parties back in the 1980s may have died in suspicious circumstances!

Please help me, Dr Wise. I do not want to be having sex with this man. And yet I do. I am! I am behaving like a slut!

Yours in despair,
Mary Weston

PS My married name is Dimmock. I do not feel I have the right to use it, given the way I am behaving with this man.

PPS We have now had intercourse twenty-eight and a half times. The half was in Richmond Park's Isabella Plantation. He took his penis out in the rhododendron bushes and I made him put it away but he ran after me with his trousers at half-mast with his cock waving around in the dusk like a conductor's baton. Eventually he fell over and we both laughed about it, but there is nothing to laugh about, is there, really? We could both be arrested for indecency. They are very strict about that in Richmond Park. You are not even allowed to let your dog have a poo – although I do not have a dog – without the Royal Parks Constabulary coming down on you like a ton of bricks. I have one daughter to whom my husband and I are totally devoted. What would she think if it got into the papers?

PPS We often do it 'doggy style'.

From:
Dr John Goldsmith MRCGP, DRCOG
101 Fellen Road
Putney
26 August

To:
Mary Dimmock
24 Beeston Crescent
Putney

My dear Mary,
I have been agonizing about whether to reply to your letter. I
suppose the mature thing to do would be to do nothing. It is
often, I find, the best thing to do. But I am afraid I just had
not got the heart to do that. I am somehow programmed not
to be able to sit back and watch people suffer. I wish it were
otherwise. I don't claim any credit for it. It is just the way I
am. Unhappy people make me unhappy and so, for purely
selfish reasons, I always seem to find myself trying to solve
their problems. Which gets me into terrible trouble.

A quiet word with you on your own?

Not really. The telephone, like email, is a distressingly
public medium. I suppose I could have organized a trip to the
dentist. Are you still Sam's nurse? I do not think, however, we
would have been able to snatch a few words on our own. And,
in any case, I am afraid I don't think I would ever have the
nerve to show old Sam the inside of my mouth. When we were
at Puerto Banús in the weird place that looked like a castle
in a horror film, I found I had to keep my lips closed even
when eating meals. Not an easy thing to do when chomping
spaghetti. Your old man, Mary, was always a hell of a dentist.

So – a letter. If you decide to answer, it might be best to

address your thoughts to me at the paper. Yes – this is not Dr Wise talking to you but John Goldsmith whom you knew all those years ago on the villa holidays. I've been doing the job for about a year – as a cushion against impending retirement.

My God, Mary, you and Sam always seemed such a perfect couple. And you were both absolutely devoted to Elaine. She was a delightful little girl. I can still see her, with her long, red hair and snub nose, walking through the villa in a pinafore dress and a total dream. I seem to remember once she walked into the kitchen door – I think it was on that first holiday we all took in Brittany – and said, when I had picked her up off the floor, that she had been 'worrying about Rapunzel and whether her hair would be all right and not hurt from all those people climbing up it'.

Did she become a writer, perhaps?

I am so sorry to hear the physical side of your marriage is not good. I hope that, at least, you are still friends. I do remember Sam being a very amusing bloke. Some of his anecdotes – especially that one about the chap with the cleft palate – were hilarious.

Gerry Price. Well – as you probably noticed all those years ago – I cannot stand the fellow. I think he is arrogant, totally selfish and not nearly as good at tennis as he thinks he is. He is also completely callous and uncaring as far as women are concerned. Some of the remarks I heard him make about his own wife – to my mind a very sweet and compassionate person – made me want to punch him on his substantial nose.

Sex is obviously something that has been a problem in your marriage and you are seeking it elsewhere. That's fine. But – and I am speaking as a friend rather than a doctor – please, please, please not with Gerry Price. Actually I think

I am speaking as a doctor as well as a friend. I imagine the man is seething with sexually transmitted diseases of one sort or another!

I hope you won't think I am being impertinent in saying this. My own relationship is not exactly in great shape. What relationship is after forty years of marriage? Barbara's demands in the sex department are often really hard to satisfy. It's difficult to know how to put this but she has a pretty well laid-out formula for the way in which we're supposed to make love. Well – after years of marriage I suppose that's inevitable. And I don't blame her in any way for demanding it be strictly adhered to. I won't say any more about it except that it involves a particular piece of music and an item of footwear that is not usually worn indoors! *Sauve qui peut*, old bean! Don't wish to embarrass you with such revelations but, as I have had such access to the intimate details of your marriage, I feel I should, in fairness, be as open as you were with me. I can appreciate you probably feel rather vulnerable after pouring out your heart to someone you thought was a complete stranger! And I would like you to know that you are not alone.

Do feel free to write again. I would like to help. My boys Jas and Josh have left university, got married and even come up with a few grandchildren for the old man. The effect on Barbara is not always good. The other grandparents seem to bring out the inner Nazi in her. I am accused of being 'remote'. My God! If someone wasn't remote something even worse than murder would have occurred in the Putney area last Christmas. My life these days is divided between work in the surgery and trying to make sure my two dearly beloved louts are not nagged narrow by their wives. Not to mention avoiding their in-laws. Which is, as it happens, not an easy thing to do.

All best and I mean that about writing again,
John Goldsmith

PS I think I may have heard somewhere that poor Pamela Larner died. Although I can't recall who told me or when it happened. Is this true? Did you hear anything? I always thought, back in the old days, that Mike Larner was quite definitely one of those husbands who might one day lose it totally and run at her with a meat cleaver. Was it her you had in mind? And what were the suspicious circumstances? Or has someone else from the old villa circle finally got what is coming to us all? I'm afraid I'm dying to know more details. I hope it wasn't Mike Larner. I was always rather fond of him. I've never seen a man get so worked up about fish! I always thought he was gay. But, then, I think every bloke I meet is gay. I went to an English public school, for God's sake!

From:
Mary Dimmock
24 Beeston Crescent
Putney
28 August

To:
Dr John Goldsmith MRCGP, DRCOG
101 Fellen Road
Putney

Dear, dear John,
You haven't changed! Same sweet old thing you were back
in Uzie-les-Trois-Chapelles (if that was its name.) Always
ready to listen to people's problems. I can still see you at
the table at Puerto Banús, watching us all get drunk with
that sad, noble face of yours that always reminded me – I
hope you will not be offended by this – of a horse. I love
horses. I always felt that wonderfully noble forehead of
yours should have a white stripe down the middle of it,
like Gentleman Billy who won the Derby in, I think, 1995.
Your eyes were the beautiful pale blue I always associate
with the jockey who rode Laughing Lady, who broke her
leg at Sandown Park in 2003 and your determined chin
was always the kind of chin I felt a prizewinning stallion
might have.

And those wonderful, youthful blond curls! You looked
like that marble statue of a Greek god in the British
Museum.

You are, of course, quite right about Gerry. I should have
had no more to do with him. I will stop seeing him. I will. I
promise. It's a fling, that's all. I am drawn to him in a way
I simply cannot control. Last week I put my hand down his

trousers while we were having lunch in the La Mancha tapas bar on Putney High Street and the manager—

There I go again! I really must spare you these details!

Actually, I don't want to talk about Gerry. Or, at least, not about my doings with him – although they seem to have slackened off a bit, perhaps because of the weather. It's been raining non-stop, hasn't it?

Gerry told me about Pamela Larner's death. He was very strange when he talked about her. He just said 'Pamela died, apparently'! Then he added, 'The *on dit* seems to be she died in "suspicious circumstances". Whatever that means.'

'I suppose,' I said, 'it means she was murdered.'

He looked really thunderous at this. 'Why on earth should you think she was murdered?'

' I – I don't know ...' I stammered. I was a bit frightened suddenly.

'Any man with red blood in his veins would want to top her,' he said, with a really weird expression. 'She was a class-A bitch!'

Then he got control of himself. He told me he had been doing a bit of sleuthing to try to find out how Pamela did actually die and what the 'suspicious circumstances' might be. He has been in contact with Mike Larner for precisely that reason. Which I thought strange. He never liked Mike, did he? I seem to remember him making some rather horrible jokes about him in Corsica.

At first, he said, he hadn't had much luck finding out anything. It seems Mike Larner has become a bit of a hermit since Pamela died. He wouldn't say anything about it to Gerry and would only communicate by letter! Gerry kept going round there as Mike pulled all his phones out of the wall a few months ago during some wildlife programme to which he took exception. My *liaison problematique*, if that is the correct phrase to describe G, finally had to sort of lie in wait for him as the poor chap was going out to get the milk.

Mike told him, when they finally met, that poor Pamela took sleeping pills. Quite a lot of them! Awful! And, for some reason I can't quite fathom, Mike seems to think it might not have been suicide but something meant to look like suicide, i.e. murder. It seems she was smothered with a cushion as well! Or possibly even strangled!

Gerry said Mike was making all sorts of wild accusations and, when they met in Mike's front garden, he started saying that it was all the fault of people like Gerry. Accused him of having an affair with her! They had a screaming row in the middle of the street, apparently, which was embarrassing as people were watching. Mike has also got some kind of obsession with David Attenborough, it seems. He thinks he's in league with the devil. Which does suggest that poor Mike may have gone a bit potty. Everyone loves David Attenborough, don't they?

But Gerry is very strange when he talks about Pamela. Something about his manner worries me. Do you think he did have an affair with her? I don't want to think about Pamela, really. She wasn't a very nice woman, was she? She once told me I had a big bottom. It was nearly thirty years ago but you don't forget things like that, do you? Gerry seems to like my bottom a lot. A few days ago on Putney Heath he—

Sorry, darling John. I will heed your advice. I know it is the right thing to do. What should I do about this Pamela business?

Love,
Mary 'Scarlet Woman' Weston that was.

PS A funny little man who walked into one of our drama-club rehearsals a few weeks ago – and joined the Thesps as prompt boy and general dogsbody – has just enrolled as one of Sam's patients, claiming to have gingivitis. He is called Gibbons, and if he has gingivitis I am a Dutch sea captain. From the kind of questions he asks me – which are nearly all about G – I have got it into my head that he is an undercover policeman investigating Pamela's murder. If it was a murder.

PPS Do come to *Hamlet*. It is in the St Jude's Church Hall on 24 October. G is fearfully good as the Great Dane and my Ophelia is getting some pretty good reviews from other cast members. Who says Ophelia wasn't a fifty-eight-year-old woman with a big bum? We have a very long rehearsal period, as we are all too old to remember our lines!

PPPS I hope you and Barbara are all right. I was always terrified of her, actually. She is fearfully intelligent, isn't she? And has actually published books as opposed to writing them – which is about all I seem to manage to do!

From:
Dr John Goldsmith MRCGP, DRCOG
101 Fellen Road
Putney
1 September

To:
Mary Dimmock
24 Beeston Crescent
Putney

Dear Mary,

It was nice to get your letter. I shall certainly try and get to *Hamlet* and will bring Barbara – if she is back from teaching women how to write feminist history by then. I think she is actually just telling them how to be cruel to men – something about which she knows a very great deal. What is feminist history anyway? Is it history written by feminists or history written about feminists? In which case it has a rather limited field in which to operate. Boudicca, Elizabeth I and Florence Nightingale and you've about done it, haven't you?

I do not mean to sound even more grumpy than I actually am. I spent this morning with three cases of depression, five malingerers and a bloke who had bleeding from the anus. As I got the old rubber glove on and shoved my finger up his bottom he said, in a deep voice, 'I can cope with this, Doctor – but can you?' Which was actually the high spot of my day.

I went into medicine to try to help people. If I had known I would spend my time arguing about drug budgets with thirtysomethings who seem to have gone into the field for the opportunities it affords to acquire expertise in management, I would have stopped before I started. Bit late now. I was trying to palpate some bloke's abdomen the other day and found he was sending a text as I did so! What a job!

It sounds as if you're cooling a little towards Gerald. I'm very happy to hear that, Mary. He really is a very destructive person who is only interested in himself. I can remember playing tennis with him once in Puerto Banús and forgetting, for some reason, to concede him a set. I had only just realized it was 6–4, 6–3, 6–2, 6–4 when his racket came hurtling over the net at me, followed, rapidly, by Gerald himself. He actually tried to bite me, puncturing the skin as he did so. He tried to laugh it off afterwards as part of his famous 'Wild Beast' impression – the one he used to practise on Pam Larner at the Larners' parties, remember? – but he meant it all right.

And he was sweet on Pamela. No question. She tried it on with all the men, didn't she, Mary? But with Gerry she didn't need to try. There were times in that place in Corsica when I really thought they might actually be doing the deed of darkness on the property. It was always rather hard to tell who was where in the afternoon. I remember a lot of stuff about going off to look for mushrooms. I do not think it was mushrooms they were looking for. I felt really sorry for poor old Mike Larner.

I would imagine Pam could be very demanding. She always reminded me of one of those puppets we had as children. Either that or a rather sickeningly cheeky elf from some sentimental Christmas film. She had a button nose, button eyes and tiny little pointy breasts that she always thrust into your face when setting you right about Greenham Common – or whatever it was that was exercising the ladies back then. And the way she always carried on about going to Oxford when everyone knew she was at something like the polytechnic, as it was called in those days. Or maybe even a secretarial college. She seemed to resent the fact that poor old Mike had actually been to Balliol or something, even though he had ended up in some backwater of the Beeb being tortured by one of its many faceless managers. Head of Small Mammals or Controller of Regional Squid or whoever they were.

My God! I can just see her leaning too hard on Gerald and him losing his rag and getting those huge meaty hands of his round her neck and squeezing away for England. I think you should ask him some subtly probing questions about Mrs Larner and his relationship with her. Or maybe you shouldn't. Let's not even think about what happened to poor Pam. It doesn't sound as if there's much we can do about it – there wasn't even a police case all those years ago. I expect the poor woman really did top herself.

There are plenty of reasons to top yourself in Putney. Looking out of your front door for starters. Trying to park in Sainsbury's. Looking into any individual face on the high street. Trying to avoid the eyes of the Africans who want to wash your car in Putney Shopping Centre car park. Watching people eat in Wagamama. I could go on but I won't.

Do let's meet up one of these days. From the sound of it, involving either of our spouses sounds a bad idea. Do try to talk it through with Sam. I always thought he was such a nice bloke. I'm sure if you're good friends you'll find a way back to each other. Gerry Price is a very dangerous individual. I find it quite easy to believe he murdered Pam Larner – and got away with it too!

All my love, Mary,
John Goldsmith

From:
Mary Dimmock
24 Beeston Crescent
Putney
3 September

To:
Dr John Goldsmith MRCGP, DRCOG
101 Fellen Road
Putney

Dear John,

I think it is all over with both the men in my life. The Gerald story is so truly awful I don't think I can bear to tell it just yet. But there are other things. Things I can hardly bear to talk about. I am in fear of my life, John, and do wish I had listened to your sound advice earlier.

I think I may have mentioned that, just recently, I had the feeling I was being followed by a mysterious entity. I couldn't exactly pin it down. It was just that – when walking home from rehearsals, for example – I often felt there was a mysterious figure somewhere in the shadows. And then, last night, I decided to take a route back along the towpath. It was late, about eleven o'clock, as we had been doing the scene in which I go mad and throw flowers at people while laughing in a high-pitched voice. Some of the cast are very enthusiastic about the way I do this but the others feel it is a little 'over the top' and Nasty Jean recently told Amanda Fluestatter (who told me) that I could not act my way out of a paper bag.

In my mad scene I do actually put a paper bag over my head, as it happens, and I think I act my way out of it rather powerfully. It is a modern-dress *Hamlet* set in a church hall in Putney where an amateur drama group are doing a production. I think it is a brilliant *mise-en-scenario* – if that is the right phrase.

Anyway, you will see all this on the night, John.

I was walking past some bushes, and remembering some of the exciting minutes that Gerald and I had spent inside them, when I thought I heard a rustling sound in the darkness over by the wire fence that separates the towpath from the playing fields on the other side. I called out but no one answered. I assumed it was an animal of some kind. Then, just as I was coming up to the Sea Scouts boathouse, I heard footsteps behind me. I thought at first they must be those of a jogger – they were coming towards me at quite a speed – and then something very heavy hit me on the side of the head and I fell forward on to the damp earth.

Whoever it was ran back the way they had come. They did not attempt to rob me or to interfere with me sexually, just hit me on the head and ran off. Who would do a thing like that? It seems so pointless. Why club a fifty-eight-year-old dental nurse over the head? As I listened to the footsteps pattering off through the summer night I could have sworn they were those of a woman!

I have been wondering if it was Amanda Fluestatter. She has had her eye on the part of Ophelia for some time, although the idea of someone of sixty-seven playing the part is patently ridiculous!

As if this was not bad enough, it may be, too, that my marriage is in even worse trouble than I had thought.

I opened a drawer in Sam's office the other day and found several books containing pictures of naked men. They were doing gymnastics so at first I thought it was all about Sam's fascination with sport. One of them showed some men playing football without any clothes on. He is keen on watching the game and it may well be that naked football is a thing, these days – really, when one looks at Channel 4 one sees things like men's penises and women's breasts and hears people using four-letter words almost every night. I really am sure the day is not far off when that man Peter Snow will grin out at one from the screen and say, 'Here's the fucking news!'

I leafed through the pile of books and found they were all of naked men. They were not all playing football. Some were lounging around in the open air in what looked like a meadow. One was standing on a diving board displaying himself. In one volume, entitled *Ganymede* and published, I think, in Germany, the men, all naked, seemed to be working on agricultural machinery and in one, in which they seemed to be taking off and putting on what looked like leather shorts, they were shown spanking each other with hairbrushes.

There were also a number of quite large black-and-white photographic prints, which, at first, I thought had been taken by Sam. Photography is something of a hobby of his. He has also always been keen on sailing and, though I tried hard to stop him buying a boat, he has, finally, got a part share in one with a man called Root, who was, he tells me, in the Royal Navy a long time ago. I hate it. Really, they are very expensive and all you do is cruise around places like Portsmouth, which I don't like.

This was more like a nineteenth-century sailing ship. It was a picture of a man climbing a mast and he seemed, as far as I could tell, to be quite a long way from the deck. He was wearing something that looked a little like a Santa Claus hat and, on close inspection, proved to be precisely that. Although the picture was in black-and-white they had coloured the hat bright red. The man was about thirty, I suppose, and he was absolutely naked. What was most noticeable about him, however, was that he was sporting something I have not seen on Sam for nearly thirty years – an enormous erection.

I know we are writing to each other, now, as friends and I am not talking to you in your professional capacity but the question that comes to my mind is: 'Is my husband a homosexual and, if he is, what should I do about it, Doctor?'

Your friend
Mary Dimmock

# Chapter Four

*Mr Gibbons dishes dirt to PO Box 132*

From:
Roland O. Gibbons
Gibbons Detective Agency
12 The Alley
Putney, SW15
4 September

To:
Elizabeth Price
PO Box 132
Putney

Dear Mrs Price,
It is now about several weeks since I started surveillance on your husband and, as you said you were planning to be away for a few weeks, I have not 'bothered you with detail' in respect of his extra-marital sexual activities. I am not sure whether you are 'still with us', by which I do not mean that I am wondering whether you are dead but whether you are still in Putney. Mind you, the two things are not dissimilar!

Your husband, Mrs Price, has done things with the woman known to you as Mary Dimmock that have even shocked me. I have twenty years' experience as a private investigator but I have never seen adultery as flagrant as this.

I am sending you only a few selected images. The others are, frankly, far too shocking to be entrusted to the 'post'. Even the ones I am sending – particularly the wide-angle shot of them underneath the table in the garden of the 'Coach and Horses' (it was taken after hours) – may well disgust and anger you.

I have been watching Mr Price very closely. It is not a pleasant task.

I often find that really intense surveillance can often be achieved by making a relationship with the subject. To that end I not only have continued my involvement with the Putney Thespians but have also made several trips to Mrs Dimmock's husband's dental surgery – which is a hotbed of vice and sexual intrigue of the kind that I understand were common in and around the Emperor Caligula's summer retreats. When in rehearsal your husband and Mrs Dimmock are fairly discreet. They do address each other as 'darling' but then so do most of the other Putney Thespians, who are clearly under the illusion that this is how professional actors carry on at work.

When he is having his teeth fixed, however, their behaviour is little short of certifiable. It may be that their *'liaison dangereuse'* is one of those that thrive on danger. I have often encountered this kind of thing. A couple I watched for most of the autumn of 2005 seemed to get most pleasure out of having sex on public transport (particularly tube trains) and it is clear that the close proximity of Mr Dimmock 'adds spice' to the proceedings.

I realized this when, overhearing them at the end of a

rehearsal of Mrs Dimmock's mad scene in which, for some reason, the director had decided that Mr Price should enter, halfway through, wearing swimming trunks and carrying a dustpan and brush. The idea – as far as I can make out – is that everyone in Denmark, or the royal palace anyway, is either mad or pretending to be mad, which is why Polonius spends most of his performance wearing a nappy. Anyway, as the 'lovebirds' were discussing their performances, I heard Mrs Dimmock say to your husband, 'You should come and get Sam to look at your gums!'

'Oh, really?' said Mr Price. 'My gums!'

'Yes!' she replied. 'And I can...give your molars a good going over!'

She said this in an openly suggestive manner and Mr Price laughed, long and loud, as he does whenever she says anything that could be construed as having a sexual implication. I have noticed, by the way, that their 'love chat' – much of which I have on tape – often uses dental metaphors. This exchange occurred at 15.49 on 20 July, and a full transcript is available, should you wish to see it.

'Come on Thursday at two thirty!' she said. 'I will book you in!'

The Dimmocks' house is a large and gloomy affair in one of the quiet streets that lie between Putney Heath and the Upper Richmond Road. I arrived deliberately early for a 15.00 appointment. There were no shops nearby and no people visible on the wide pavements. The only thing that distinguished their house from those near it was a mast in the front garden, which, to my surprise, was decorated with a flag that (although furled on the windless afternoon that I visited) was almost certainly a skull and crossbones.

The front door was open. There were several rhododendron bushes in the front garden, and the hallway and the front reception – which doubled as a waiting area – were both dark and cool after the brilliant sunshine outside.

I did not announce myself but slipped into the waiting room without anyone realizing I was present. I am, as I think you observed in one of your letters, Mrs Price, a man who 'blends in' to almost any background. Your husband was 'in the chair' when I arrived and, from my seat by the window, I could not only see his feet and legs but hear his 'small-talk' with the invisible Mr Dimmock. To my surprise, they seemed to know each other quite well. Mr Dimmock – who has a pronounced West Country accent – talked a great deal of his boat, which is apparently called the *Jolly Roger* and is moored at Portsmouth. He interspersed a fairly detailed account of what he called 'caulking its bottom' with loud and often aggressive commands to his patient. 'We got the keel up on the ramp and we – OPEN WIDER WIDER WIDER – managed to seal the resin on the back timbers but – DO NOT MOVE YOUR TONGUE, GERALD – I always think that commercial resins in this country are not a patch on those from the Dutch marine suppliers, like Burgwaal de Kock. I AM GOING TO SQUIRT WATER ON YOUR GUMS NOW.'

Then he fired off several direct questions to his patient, even though Mr Price was obviously unable to speak. This did not stop him trying, of course, although he sounded as if his mouth was propped open with the dental equivalent of an RSJ.

At 14.25 precisely Mr Dimmock broke off and said to his wife, 'Is it time for Yo-ho-ho?'

I thought at first he was referring to refreshment but Mrs Dimmock answered, 'It is, darling! They are showing extracts from the Guernsey Regatta with some of those sloops you liked!' It was, clearly, a TV channel devoted exclusively to sailing.

Mr Dimmock said he would not be gone long, and as he rushed off to get a look at those sloops, I had my first glimpse of Mary Dimmock's much-cuckolded husband. He was much bigger than I had expected and his beard was enormous – far bigger than almost any I have ever seen. It was reddish in colour. He was also, again to my surprise, irretrievably bald.

Immediately he had gone, Mrs Dimmock and your husband began to make love. At first I thought he was giving her oral pleasure and then I realized that the noise he was making was muffled by whatever Mr Dimmock had put into his mouth. Cotton wool? A steel clamp? Both, possibly. Whatever it was, their needs were obviously so urgent that neither thought to remove the device. Perhaps it enhanced his pleasure.

It was certainly the most interesting ten minutes I have ever spent in a dentist's waiting room. It was hard to work out what they were doing and I am afraid I did not manage to get any photographs but I do have a fairly good-quality sound recording, which is among the attached documents. I have also transcribed Mrs Dimmock's comments, most of which are, as you will see, commands along the lines of 'Harder! Faster! Deeper!' and 'Fuck me, Gerald!' – which she says several times. From the movements of Mr Price's feet, I think full intercourse was almost definitely achieved.

When they had finished – and I timed the act at four and a half minutes (which is, as I know from past observations, roughly what it usually takes) – Mrs Dimmock started to move about the surgery once again. I caught fleeting glimpses of her as she crossed and re-crossed my line of vision. She was – on first viewing anyway – naked from the waist up.

'God,' I heard her say, 'I love it when you put your hands round my throat!'

71

It was still hard to make out Mr Price's response (I have not bothered to try to transcribe his replies) but he said something that sounded like 'Gy guh gucking goo!'

To which Mrs Dimmock replied, 'Did Pamela Larner like that?' He did not answer this comment but she went on to say – and I have this comment on tape too so I did not mishear the remark, 'Did you strangle her?' He did not answer this. She went on, 'I bet you wanted to kill her, didn't you? I must say I wanted to kill her. Odious woman. With her pointy breasts and her three children who could all read at three months and were all going to Oxford. I would have wanted to kill her. You can tell me. I shan't mind. Good riddance, I say.'

There was a pause and then she added, 'She said I had a big bottom.'

His only answer – which was cut off by the return of Mr Dimmock – was, 'Gat's ger woh hun I e'er hagg i' a genckiss care!' A remark I still do not completely understand.

When I was sure the 'coast was clear', I went out again and re-entered the premises, after first pressing the bell.

I think we now have definitive proof of his adultery and, should you wish to use this material in a legal context, divorce or custody settlement or simply to confront him with it before trying to 'make a go' of your marriage, I am at your disposal. I will say, however, that 'making a go' of any relationship with the fiend to whom you are so unfortunately yoked will be a difficult task.

If you wish me to investigate the circumstances surrounding the death of this mysterious woman 'Pamela Larner', if it should turn out to be murder and if your husband had anything to do with it, he should obviously be punished. I think Mr Price is owed at least fifteen to twenty years in a maximum-security prison. Though he might do rather well in that kind of place!

I do, however, appreciate that you may not wish to learn anything more unpleasant about Mr Price and, if you feel I have 'done my job' I enclose my bill for your kind attention. As you will notice, your cash advance did not quite cover all the time I have spent on this case. I hope you will feel I have been 'fair'. I have not charged you for my dental expenses for the exploration of a (fictional) gum disorder or for my time in rehearsals of *Hamlet* – although were I to allow myself the luxury of billing for this difficult task, it is not easy to think of an amount of money that would fully compensate! It bids fair to be one of the worst productions of the play ever seen anywhere in the world!

Best wishes
Roland O. Gibbons

PS I have now been asked to play the part of Horatio in *Hamlet*. I get the impression that if a Labrador wandered in off the street they would offer it a part. Mind you, I think a Labrador would make a better job of Laertes than the bloke who is now playing the part. He is called Norman Staines and he cannot seem to remember his lines. He keeps moaning about having to 'go to the hospital' but I cannot see anything wrong with him. He seems to be a buddy of Mr Price's – since your husband is unusually pleasant and almost protective towards him. I have accepted the part but do not feel I am right for it. I personally fancied the Norwegian ambassador role, which is less demanding but has been cut – along with many other things, including the 'To be or not to be' speech!

From:
Elizabeth Price
PO Box 132
Putney
6 September

To:
Roland O. Gibbons
Gibbons Detective Agency
12 The Alley
Putney, SW15

Dear Mr Gibbons,
My word, you have been busy!

I have only just returned to Putney, and thank you for your last letter. I say 'letter' – it was quite a parcel! I have now viewed your footage, some of which has been filmed really superbly and, for me, recalled some of the most pungent moments in documentary *noir*. The sequence in which *la* Dimmock masturbates my husband in the children's play area next to the Barnes tennis courts was powerful, vivid and full of an unexplained menace that was all the more potent for never being sufficiently explained. Who was the man in the white coat in the distance? Was that a dwarf on a bicycle disappearing, at speed, in the direction of the Lower Richmond Road? Why did Gerald shout, 'Banzai!' at the critical moment? Was she rubbing his semen into her hair and, if so, why?

Do I sound as if I am above all this, Mr Gibbons? I hope so.

I am, as you have probably already gathered, no mere jealous housewife, and your researches have not been commissioned simply in order to enable me to get rid of my husband quickly and easily. I don't think, actually, that anyone can quickly or easily get rid of someone they have once loved. Believe you me, Mr Gibbons, I once did love Gerald a lot, unbelievable as that may seem.

I want more fuel for my hatred of him. I want to know everything about what he gets up to with that unspeakable woman. I've started something I suppose I'll have to finish. Perhaps I should talk more frankly about Mary Dimmock. And, indeed, Pamela Larner. Pamela Larner – it is easy for me to say this to you because I know we will never meet – was a self-centred, self-opinionated, profoundly silly, vulgar woman of a kind that was all too common in the St Jude's Putney Parents and Teachers Association twenty years ago.

For some reason still not clear to me, I found myself on holiday with her on several occasions. Her odious, talentless children went to the same primary school as my dear Conrad and my desperate Julia. Mary Dimmock and her ridiculous husband were also, usually, of the party when six of us St Jude's parents went off to southern Europe, in search of sunshine, all those years ago. God knows why. I think Conrad liked their Elaine. It was pretty clear to me, too, that *la* Larner had designs on my husband.

You probably do not understand, Mr Gibbons, what it is like to love someone and to be betrayed by them constantly, as I have been betrayed by my husband for at least thirty years. You have probably never felt the self-hatred, the fury and inexpressible loneliness that goes with loving someone who does not love you back.

Sniff around the Putney Thespians. Sniff around Mike Larner – if you can bear it. Bring me film and recordings and prose descriptions that make me cry. Get to know this ludicrous Dimmock woman. I certainly never want to see her again, but I like hearing about her, in just the way you scratch at a scab or open a newspaper in which you have been criticized. By all means go to the dentist – and allow me to pay! Ingratiate yourself with Mary's equally loathsome husband. I will fund root-canal surgery if that is what is required.

I enclose cash to the value of the amount you requested.

Yours truly,
Elizabeth Price

PS I didn't want to write 'yours truly' but the word-processing program made me do it. Even in letter-writing, surely one area where one might have thought that free will was still an option, we are being constrained!

PPS Use as many 'inverted commas' as you like. Feel free to violate the rules of the thing what is called grammar; and be careless with the semi-colon. Question marks???? Why not???? Exclamation marks are good!!!! Perhaps the tone of my letter surprises you. I am certainly not the rational schoolmistress who wrote to you first, am I? But, then, I have just sat through a three-hour video of my husband performing sex acts with a dental nurse in her late fifties.

From:
Roland O. Gibbons
Gibbons Detective Agency
12 The Alley
Putney, SW15
8 September

To:
Elizabeth Price
PO Box 132
Putney

Dear Mrs Price,

Try not to worry about all this. I will take care of everything and, perhaps, in a few weeks we will have enough information to gain you a very satisfactory divorce settlement. It is a beautiful day and London is wonderfully empty. I do hope you are managing to enjoy it.

I am, as you asked, getting more information about Mrs Dimmock; but, in some ways I feel that Mrs Dimmock is a victim. She has often – as I think you will see from the transcripts – expressed a desire to stop the affair. I feel sure that as soon as you have separated yourself from Mr Price all will become clearer. If, however, you do decided to confront him with the information, recordings and video footage I have supplied to you, I would be glad if you would not mention, at this stage anyway, that they came from me.

I have, I will admit, become a little obsessed with a case that does not – at the moment – seem to have anything to do with the reason you hired me! I am talking about the mysterious death of the woman called Pamela Larner. She was, I have now learned, a hairdresser, a physiotherapist, a Pilates instructor and a Jungian analyst! I cannot, by the way, quite work out whether she did these things all at the same time or whether they form a kind of career path. If they do I am at a loss to work out in which order they came, but everyone seems to agree that she was abnormally unpromising at nearly all of them. Although even Mary Dimmock seems to think she had some talent for hairdressing.

Was she murdered? And, if she was, who murdered her? Was it your husband? I have not been hired to find out whether it was him although it may well be that if I come across proof that he did slaughter her in cold blood it may provide additional grounds for your divorce. I could, if you wanted, 'throw in' an element of murder investigation to add to my final bill, although I am not qualified to do this kind of work and any results I produce would not have any legal force and should not, probably, be even mentioned to the police.

What does it matter? She has been dead for ten years.

Let me know how you wish to proceed.

I remain yours faithfully,
Roland O. Gibbons.

PS I do not think, as far as I can tell, that Pamela Larner actually qualified as a Jungian analyst. This may or may not be relevant to the circumstances surrounding her death.

From:
Elizabeth Price
PO Box 132
Putney
10 September

To:
Roland O. Gibbons
Gibbons Detective Agency
12 The Alley
Putney, SW15

Dear Mr Gibbons,

Keep digging away at Mrs Dimmock. She is a fat and artful woman who is about as far away from being a victim as am I from being a downhill racer or a concert pianist.

Yes, my husband is quite capable of murder, and if you find that he has done such a thing I will expect you to furnish me with evidence, in as much detail as possible, but I am not, repeat not, interested in why or how or even when Pamela Larner died. It is very sad that she did so but it is not something I wish to think about. You do the job for which I hired you and I will do mine. Which is, as someone in Dante observes, to get on with the business of suffering. Jealousy, whether current or retrospective, is a horrible feeling, but disapproving of it, even in oneself, does not make it go away.

Yours
Elizabeth Price

PS Ha! Beat you, Microsoft Word Tyrant!

PPS I would be glad if you did not mention Pamela Larner again. I really do not wish to think about her.

# PART TWO

# Chapter Five

## *In which two Putney men discover things they never knew about each other*

The *Putney Free Sheet*

Affiliated to the *Wandsworth, Balham, Clapham, Croydon, Reigate, Banstead, Coulsdon, Raynes Park, Tooting, Earlsfield and Southfields Free Sheet*

PERSONAL ADVERTISEMENTS

For terms and conditions, please see page 13.
Payment terms, see page 23.

9 September

MEN SEEKING MEN

Box 1001A

Professional, early-middle-aged man seeks masterful type for sex, fun and discreet relationship. I am boyish and artistic with a strong interest in wildlife. South-west

London preferred. I enjoy outdoor activities of all kinds and long to find someone to keep me in order. Serious enquiries only. Recent and authentic photograph helpful. Reply to 'Young 'Un' at above box number.

From :
'Bo'sun'
Name and address can be supplied

To:
'Young 'Un'
c/o Box 1001A

Dear 'Young 'Un',
I have never written a letter like this before. It has taken a great deal of time to pluck up the courage to do so. About forty years at least.

I first of all realized I had homosexual feelings when I was at school in the West Country many years ago. I was at a prep school not far from Taunton. Do you know Taunton? Not far is not far enough as far as Taunton is concerned.

There was a boy there called Garland. He was small, plump and, at first sight anyway, not an attractive sexual proposition. He had a house near the school and I would often go there for tea on weekdays. After tea we would always be sent upstairs by his mother. He was an only child and he had a large bedroom, crammed with all sorts of mechanical toys, in which I was not really interested.

Neither – as it turned out – was Garland.

After some brief, desultory conversation Garland would say, 'Would you like to wrestle?' and I, who have always been very fond of contact sport, would strip off to the waist and leap upon him with a war cry that I had devised for use in playground games with the other boys of my year. After some grappling on his bed (Garland would also strip, often to his pants) the two of us would lie side by side, staring up at his ceiling, and the memory of this comradely moment is what stays with me to this day. We had no genital contact of any kind but those encounters were positively drenched in sex.

Garland is now a happily married man with five children, or so he claimed in his last letter to me, but those encounters remain some of the most vivid of my early years.

I married quite young, soon after I had left university, and although the physical side of my marriage has never been spectacular, we did manage to conceive a child, to whom we are both devoted.

I knew that I was drawn to men in naval uniform but, at first, was not at all conscious that there was a sexual dimension to my feelings. I have always been interested in boats, and I am now the proud owner of my first sloop, but, from an early age, the crew of any ship has been of as much interest as the vessel. When crossing to Cherbourg on the ferry, as a young boy, I found myself drawn to the sailors as they coiled ropes or walked purposefully along the upper decks. I think – if I thought anything of it – it was simply that I liked the look of mariners and imagined that I, too, one day, might find myself tossed about on salt water, feeling the wind in my face as a wild nor'easter drove down the Channel.

I was always particularly drawn to the younger *matelots* and when, later, at my public school I joined the Sea Scouts I soon found one of my greatest pleasures was to drill a group of lads in the basic skills of seafaring. I once took a few junior boys on a trip round the Isle of Wight and, though nothing improper took place, I did find myself attracted to a young rating called Edgar, who allowed me to guide him through the basic principles of knot-tying and shared with me his own unquenchable passion for the briny.

I was in my early twenties when I began to be plagued by a recurrent dream. In the dream I was the commander of a naval vessel in the Second World War. I was, for reasons that are still not clear to me, German although I am fairly sure I was not in Nazi uniform. We were chasing an English frigate through coastal waters off a landscape that looked a little like the Dorset coast and, after we'd fired a few shots across her bows, the vessel surrendered.

When we boarded her we found, to our surprise, that it was crewed by a group of young men some of whom were wearing gym shorts, and some of whom were completely naked. As the captain, I ordered them all to parade on deck and rebuked them strongly for being improperly dressed. I announced that I myself would administer six strokes of the cane to the naked buttocks of each one of them. A junior officer handed me a weapon and I ordered the captured sailors to bend over one of the ship's guns, which, curiously, seemed to be of eighteenth-century design. I was approaching the first backside when I realized (in the dream) that I was sexually excited. I was just about to give the English seaman
his first whack when I noticed that his belt had made a red mark around the line of his waist. I remember thinking how white his flesh was when I ejaculated, violently. I awoke with a feeling of profound joy.

It was after this that I became involved with the Putney Sea Scouts.

I am proud to say that I have never made a physical approach to any of the lads in our outfit, although I did get dangerously close to a German recruit called Gunther, but, during my time in the Service, I became increasingly aware that I wanted to do a lot more to the lads under my care than equip them with basic navigation. I was known as a strict but fair captain and I will admit that, when my wife is out of the house, I quite often behave inappropriately with myself. And that, quite often, the physiques of my imaginary partners bear a strong resemblance to the naval cadets for whom I have been responsible. I have now resigned from the Sea Scouts and devoted myself to my newly acquired sloop the *Jolly Roger*. I share it with a man called Bert for whom I have no sexual feelings. He is seventy-four.

I am looking for an obedient lad who will join in sexual fun and games with me. I am very happily married and do not wish to interfere with the stability of my home life. I work from home and my wife is an extremely supportive partner, who has little interest in sex herself. I would very much like to undertake discreet experiments with a submissive, youthful soul who, like me, has a genuine enthusiasm for things maritime.

Do write to the above box number: you sound as if you might be the perfect partner for me. You describe yourself as early-middle-aged, and a boyish nature is more important to me than someone who has been on the planet for many fewer years than the fifty-nine and a half I have spent burying my true sexual nature. I would like to meet – if you think I might be your type.

In anticipation,
'Bo'sun'

PS I am heavily bearded but my preference is, obviously, for clean-shaven men.

From:
'Young 'Un'
c/o Box 1001A
The *Putney Free Sheet*
12 September

To:
'Bo'sun'
c/o Box 1001A
The *Putney Free Sheet*

Dear 'Bo'sun',
I was very excited by your letter. It stirred things in me that
I have tried to hide for many years. Indeed, until I placed
that advertisement I had never really thought that I was
that kind of person. Like you, I have lived an outwardly
conventional life as a married man. I have, indeed, fathered
three children, who are all extraordinarily talented and
intelligent.

To the world I am a successful and well-known filmmaker,
but inside I am a very different person. I was the youngest
of eight and until I was twelve my mother was unable to
remember my name. Even then she quite often got it wrong
– most often confusing me with the older sister nearest to me
in age, Dorothea.

About my earliest memory is of me screaming, 'I am not
Dorothea!' greatly to everyone's amusement.

I was treated, from a very early age, as the lowest form
of life. For some years, indeed, this was what my family all
called me. 'Where is the lowest form of life?' my father, an
eminent scientist, would say, and one or other of my brothers
or sisters would answer, 'Oh – he's in the garden!' or 'I think
he's in the cupboard under the stairs!' a place where I spent

much of my childhood. I was always the one asked to run errands or help my mother clean the floor.

It was only when I was sent away to boarding school that I began to suspect my upbringing had influenced my sexual preferences in a way that, at first, I found difficult to accept. Although my boarding school was in North London we had very little contact with the outside world. Our headmaster, a man with an OBE and very little else to recommend him, used to call School House together and warn them, graphically, of the danger we faced from prostitutes.

'Prostitutes,' he would say, 'operate freely in this part of London! And they are rife with disease!'

Our school was in Hampstead.

His most fearsome warnings, however, were of the dangers of homosexuality. 'If you give your body to a homosexual,' he would say, 'you will give away the most precious thing you have!' He never said what that thing was – although the boy next to me whispered, 'Your bum!' and sniggered. All I remember thinking was that giving your body to a homosexual sounded very interesting indeed. It certainly sounded more interesting than hanging around the games field in a pair of ill-fitting shorts or trying to learn Latin verbs with Mr Davenant, who smelt of aftershave and once tried to put his hand on my knee.

'I need to warn you of Smith-Parker!' the headmaster once said to us at morning assembly. 'He is a homosexual!' Smith-Parker, a squat, spotty boy of about sixteen, sat there looking vaguely smug as the headmaster said this. I remember thinking that Smith-Parker might be a useful person to get to know; but – and this is important – my interest in other men was purely theoretical.

Until I was about thirty-five I thought that having sex with men would be a bold and radical thing to do – a bit like joining the Communist Party or growing one's hair below one's collar. But I didn't think it was something I would actually end up doing.

And then I had the opportunity to observe the mating behaviour of the Amazonian river dolphin – a species that, like many middle-class humans in the south-west London area, indulges in group sex. As you may know, dolphins have a high sex drive and can mate up to twenty times a day – although the act only usually takes about twenty seconds. They also have astonishingly lithe, prehensile penises and they are prone to insert them into anything that looks convenient. Including, on occasions, the blowholes of their male companions. I had occasion to see some footage of two male dolphins indulging in this activity and found it powerfully erotic.

I was particularly struck by the expression on the face of the male submitting to nasal sex. Dolphins, as the Hoeffer-Lübeck study in the 1960s definitively proved, do have a wide range of facial expressions. According to Hoeffer-Lübeck, and, subsequently, Joachim de Ribeiro, although his results have been questioned, they have been sighted 'grinning', 'sneering', 'smiling openly' and 'looking triumphant'.

The passive male in this footage seemed in a state of ecstasy I have seldom seen in any species. His tail made the rapid threshing movements associated, in the Hoeffer-Lübeck study, with the 'profound satisfaction and self-worth' usually found only in relation to fish capture or shoal domination of 'an extreme kind'. I did not need any scientist to tell me that. This was one very happy dolphin. He was gratifying a powerful male, nicknamed, for the purposes of the study, 'Big Boy'.

This was a Damascene moment for me. I was, at the time, trapped in a deeply unsatisfactory marriage to a woman who was not my intellectual equal. She and I had been initially attracted because I conformed to the 'obedient' stereotype of the kind of man who looked as if he might indulge her need for control. She would bark commands at me, very much in the style my own family had used to do, often shouting in what seemed the grip of ungovernable rage as she said, 'Take out the bins!' or 'Hoover the stairs!' Woe betide me if I failed to 'wax the kitchen floor' or 'fold the dishcloths neatly neatly neatly'! She very often repeated key adverbs several times as if afraid that I was too stupid to understand their import.

I could see that my children disapproved of my passivity in the face of her behaviour but I was powerless to alter the balance of our relationship. I should stress that I gained no satisfaction whatsoever from being asked to empty the washing-up machine or take out the recycling bags.

Had she asked me to Hoover the stairs naked, I might have been more interested!

I loved this woman, in a twisted kind of way, but she never really satisfied me sexually. Female domination is a subtle and all-enveloping thing. Male domination of another male is, somehow, clean and simple and straightforward. As soon as I saw this dolphin, nicknamed in the study 'Nancy Boy', I knew that his role was the one I craved. I set out on a long – and intensely private – study of homosexuality in the animal world.

I found I felt a great affinity with the five-spined stickle-back. The males among these tiny but courageous fish are responsible for the upbringing of the young, very much in the way in which I was always the one designated to do the school run or to pick up my progeny from lacrosse, karate or choir practice. I was intrigued to note, too, the happy way in which a group of male stickleback would rub themselves off against one particular fish, usually the one primarily involved in child care. And one particular fish, designated, in the study I made, Passive Stickleback A205 – yes, he was named after the South Circular Road! – fascinated me. From very early on I noted that he exhibited behaviour always associated in the stickleback family with deep and lasting satisfaction. Stickleback do not, of course, have facial expressions in the accepted sense of the term but, 'Bo'sun', you know when they're happy!

I became very interested in penguins. Long before the celebrated 'gay penguins' of Toronto Zoo, I tracked down a pair of male Emperor Penguins in Regent's Park who were not merely exhibiting the kind of beak behaviour associated with courtship but proceeding to the nearest thing to full intercourse that is possible for these flightless birds. The penguin has no sexual organs as such but each animal is equipped with a cloaca in which waste products, eggs and fertilizing agents are all stored. Usually the female, after a bit of rear-entry pecking – will lie full length to receive the male, and these two penguins, unnoticed by keepers or any of the public, were doing exactly the same thing. 'Sailor Boy', as I nicknamed him, would lie out with his flippers extended while 'Butch Cassidy', again my own name, waddled up to him and shot his load.

They always, I noticed, chose to do it behind a particularly large rock, which is probably why this couple of lovers were – and, as far as I know, still are – unnoticed by those members of the public, keepers, naturalists and other busybodies who make it their business to spy on the private life of other species.

What I did notice, however, in the three or four months in which I observed this obviously happy couple was the way in which they exhibited all the mating behaviour of penguins – enlarging, trumpeting, walking together – but always in a place in which they thought themselves unobserved. Which, of course, they were – apart from by me! And, when 'Butch Cassidy' had finished I was particularly struck by the behaviour of 'Sailor Boy', who performed an ecstatic action almost never observed in Emperor Penguins in captivity – the 'Victory Roll' in which the penguin jumps up, falls flat on its face and then rotates on its stomach while beating its flippers up and down at high speed.

Passive male animals had a much better time of it than their more 'masculine' brothers. 'Butch Cassidy' never exhibited this ecstatic behaviour. In fact, after intercourse, he often seemed rather depressed and would wander off to a corner of the penguin terraces and stare at the ground for hours. As I went deeper and deeper into my researches, I found that almost all of the passive males I studied lived longer, more contented lives than any other sexual type in the studied group. One African elephant, who had allowed himself to be penetrated by no fewer than nine other bulls in the course of an afternoon, showed positive signs not only of self-worth and freedom from tickworm, *bula bula* fly and trunk psoriasis but also of improved survival skills, the finding of waterholes, general navigation and so on.

And then, about eighteen months ago, like you, I had a dream.

I had never been interested in anything nautical but in the dream I found myself to be a cabin boy on some kind of pirate ship. My task was to serve food to a group of pirates, all of whom, interestingly enough, in the light of your letter, were heavily bearded. One of them, a villainous-looking fellow with very hairy arms and a large ring through his nose, told me that I had 'prepared the sprouts all wrong' and that I would have to go to his cabin for some 'private time'. All the other pirates laughed coarsely when he said this. I laughed in what I hoped was an innocent fashion but, in fact, of course had a very good idea what 'Cap'n Bob' had in mind.

For he was – I realized, in the way one realizes things in dreams – the captain of the ship. It was only when we got to his cabin, which was decorated in pastel colours and, to my surprise, contained a large double bed equipped with a fluffy white duvet and an assortment of freshly laundered pillows, that he told me he was 'only behaving like that in front of the other boys because of peer pressure' and that, deep down, he was a sincere and kindly individual who only wanted to make me happy. I told him I did not know what would make me happy. He said he thought he knew. I replied, 'How could you possibly know?' Although I knew – as one does in dreams – that he did know and that he was about to show me.

At this point in the dream he started to undo his belt and lower his pirate breeches and I had an orgasm.

I think that was the moment when I realized I might not be a fully heterosexual man and it was not long after that I placed the advert in the *Putney Free Sheet* to which you replied. I must say that, from the tone of your letter, we may very well be suited and I would very much like to meet as soon as possible. I am based in Putney but could easily come up to the West End if necessary. Anything east of Fleet Street is, however, taboo as far as I am concerned.

Perhaps, 'Bo'sun', you will allow me to sign myself, 'Cabin Boy'.

From:
'Bo'sun'
c/o Box 1001A
The *Putney Free Sheet*
14 September

To:
'Young 'Un'
c/o Box 1001A
The *Putney Free Sheet*

Dear Cabin Boy,

What a wonderful letter!

I read it with a mounting sense of excitement! I really felt that we were two people who might have 'larks' together! Even if we do not rise to the heights achieved by 'Butch' and 'Nancy Boy' (or was that the dolphin?), I am sure we can share some good masculine time together and achieve some of the things of which we have both, so long, only dreamed.

I suggest we meet in a pub called the Spotted Cow on Putney High Street. Next Tuesday? 2000 hrs? They used to have a good quiz but I do not imagine that you and I will be answering too many obscure questions about Tamla Motown!

We have things to do, Cabin Boy! Let's get aloft. You will easily recognize me as I have a large beard!

Your new friend
'Bo'sun'

From:
'Young 'Un'
c/o Box 1001A
The *Putney Free Sheet*
18 September

To:
'Bo'sun'
c/o Box 1001A
The *Putney Free Sheet*

Dear 'Bo'sun',
I really look forward to our meeting. I feel sure I will know you instantly.

    Your obedient
    'Cabin Boy'

From:
'Young 'Un'
c/o Box 1001A
The *Putney Free Sheet*
22 September, around 11 p.m.

To:
'Bo'sun'
c/o Box 1001A
The *Putney Free Sheet*

Dear 'Bo'sun',
We must have missed each other! These arrangements are so hard to make.

There were no fewer than six men with beards in the Spotted Cow this evening. One of them was obviously not you since he was sporting a goatee and a small moustache. I did think, however, that he was looking at me in a suggestive manner. Indeed, all the bearded men who were out tonight seemed to be taking a definite sexual interest in me – though that could simply have been to do with the fact that I was in a state of considerable anticipation as a result of the letters we exchanged.

Were you the one with the army fatigues and the George V 'tache and beard – a style I have always found attractive? Or were you the very tall, thin man with the side-whiskers and pepper-and-salt square cut?

If you were either of these do please get in touch. It wasn't possible for me to make contact as I met a very old friend, whom I have not seen for years, in the pub and was unable to avoid conversation with him. He is a thoroughly nice person and I spent several holidays with him many years ago but whatever else Sam Dimmock may be he is certainly not 'Bo'sun'. There is nothing gay about Sam. He is, actually, happily married, as you say you are, and his relationship has always seemed to me an exemplary one. His wife is perfectly nice, even if she has delusions of being artistic.

Sam, as it happens, does have a beard as well – and a large one. It is one of the kind that sprouts out in every conceivable direction and I think it may well be one of the most hideous things I have ever seen in my life! Although, apart from that, he is rather a good-looking chap. Funnily enough, I had always thought he was from the north of England – although, in talking with him tonight, it emerged that he was brought up in the same part of the world as you, i.e. the West Country. That must be about the only thing he has in common with you, apart from the beard.

I had been meaning to get in touch with Old Sam – as everyone used to call him – in connection with a rather irritating dental problem, as he is, though a little on the dull side, an absolutely brilliant dentist, but I could never quite face it. I have also lost his address! Anyway, we got talking about our kids. I don't know why, by the way, I pretended any of mine had gone to Oxford – it was a delusion of my late wife's, which she always made me keep up with our so-called local friends – as in fact they are all something of a disaster.

One of them did something so frightful I cannot even bear to mention it. It was in Thailand – but that does not make it any better.

So it was not the night for me to explore a hidden part of my sexuality. I have told no one else I know about these feelings. They are totally private. I often identify, violently, with 'Sailor Boy', the penguin I told you about – yes, 'Nancy Boy' was the dolphin – in his urge to hide behind a rock when consummating his love for 'Butch'. Isn't all human sexuality meant to be private? Why should we let everyone know what we are feeling and thinking? Why do 'gay' people all have to line up together as if they were part of the same fucking football team? My sexual feelings are nothing to do with anyone else at all . . . apart, of course, from . . . you 'Bo'sun'!

Let me know which of the bearded men you were. I long to meet you and be your faithful, submissive and ecstatically happy

'Cabin Boy'

From:
Samuel Dimmock
Dimmock Dentistry
'Because Teeth Matter'
24 Beeston Crescent
Putney
24 September

To:
Mike Larner
24 Lawson Crescent
Putney

Dear Mike,

I hope you will forgive this letter. I had a devil of a job tracking down your home address. You are not in the phone book and, as I do not see any of the people we used to know from St Jude's, I had no means of tracing you via Johnny Goldsmith or the horrifically conceited and odious Gerald Price.

In the end, to my surprise, Elaine had a contact number for Conrad. The poor little bugger is still living at home and trying to write his novel about the Spanish Civil War. He, for some reason, is in touch with Molly (or is it Milly?), who seems to have had a bit of a hard time herself recently, and she gave me, at long last, your details. It seems she got pregnant by some bastard in local radio, had an abortion and has decided she is a lesbian. Although I suppose you know all this. I do remember you having a wonderful and glamorous job at the Beeb and all of us teasing you about whether you knew David Attenborough. Isn't he just great? Did you see him with those wolverines the other day?

Is it true you have ripped your phone out of the wall? And made a vow not to see anyone for five years? That was what

Molly (or should that be Milly?) told Elaine. I could not believe it, Mike. You were always the life and soul of the party in the old days. You seemed pretty chipper the other night

I suppose Milly, or Molly, is following in your footsteps. She was always a tough, no-nonsense little girl. I do remember her thumping Elaine once in Mont-Verlaine-les-Deux-Arbres, or whatever that ghastly place in Brittany was called. Whatever happened to Barnaby? He was such a talkative, lively little chap with a finger in every pie. I remember one night in Spain he got hold of Gerald Price's underpants and cut them into thin strips. I could see Mr Price was dying to thump him – or at least scream at him the way he screamed at poor Conrad – but he was too frightened of Mrs P to do anything about it. My God, there was a scary woman, eh? I bet her Latin class have all had nervous breakdowns.

It was so nice to meet you by chance in the Spotted Cow the other day. It is not a pub I usually visit, the quiz night notwithstanding, and it was great to get a chance to catch up. We never really talked on those villa holidays, did we? I am quite a shy person and was usually pretty preoccupied with Elaine. As were you with your brood. Anyway – I was just the boring old dentist with a beard and you were the glamorous director with many hilarious stories of films you had made and famous personalities with whom you had had lunch.

I was so sorry to hear about Pamela. She was an incredibly lively person – always up and doing, often, I seem to remember, at five or six in the morning. I can still remember her calling out to you and giving you your marching orders for the day. I don't think I have ever seen a man scrub a patio floor quite so hard! I wasn't quite clear, from what you said, about how she died, but I did gather there was something not quite right about it.

Mary and I rub along OK. I have got to go and see her in *Hamlet* in a few weeks' time, which I am dreading. She says Gerald Price, who is also in it, is absolutely dreadful. One of the things I enjoyed most about our chat was the chance to have a good old bitch about the Butch Barrister, as we used to call him. But she has made a new friend there called Gibbons, who's become a patient of mine. He is in and out of our surgery all the time. A bit of a dental hypochondriac, I suspect. I rather like him and am hoping he will take her off to the theatre to see those plays to which she is always dragging me.

I would rather be out on the open sea myself. If you ever fancied a trip in my boat I would love to take you out in her. I can easily show you the ropes and though I am a bit of a Fascist when on board I will try to be gentle with you – for the first few hours anyway! If you don't like using the phone just drop me a line to the above address ...

All the best
Sam Dimmock

From:
Mike Larner
24 Lawson Crescent
Putney
28 September

To:
Samuel Dimmock
Dimmock Dentistry
'Because Teeth Matter'
24 Beeston Crescent
Putney

Dear Sam,

Very kind of you to write. I don't have enough human contact these days. I suppose I have got very wrapped up in myself and my own problems. Pamela always said I was self-obsessed. Although I must say I never spent a quarter of the time she spent looking in the mirror, examining my own weight or going over my relationship with my mother with the kind of care and attention shown by medieval commentators to the Bible. To her, 'self-obsessed' simply meant 'not interested enough in her'.

It is very kind of you to ask me out on your boat. I never thought of you as a sailing man. Finding out that you are has started to alter my perception of you. We have stereotypes of people, don't we? And they often do not correspond to what the person is really like at all. Maybe by writing to each other we can get to know each other a little better.

I am not really a man for the ocean wave. Except, of course, in my fantasy life! I must admit that I quite like the idea of discipline and – make of this what you will – I never have problems obeying orders if those orders are given by another chap! But I wouldn't like to think of you being disappointed in me as a possible crew member. I would hate to let you down.

I once had dinner with John Goldsmith, years ago, on a yacht that belonged to a friend of his, and, though we only spent an hour or two on the thing, and St Katharine Dock was always in full view during dinner, by the end of the evening I felt as if I had just done twenty years in the Château d'If.

Letters are about all I can cope with at the moment. Face-to-face contact with anyone brings me out in a cold sweat. But that was not the case with you! It was incredibly pleasant to meet up and chat with you after all these years. Actually, I sometimes think Pam had a point and that, for much of the time, I never really noticed other people at all! Something to do with working at the BBC for thirty years. A place, which, as George Orwell said, combines the worst elements of a lunatic asylum and a girls' boarding school. It was really interesting to hear you talk about teeth in such depth. I promise to brush more regularly, Sam, and will take your tip about flossing very seriously indeed. I do have bleeding gums and never really knew what caused it until you filled me in the other night.

No – it was a good chat. I suspect in the old days we were all so busy droning on about our lives that we never really listened to either you or John Goldsmith. What a nice guy he was, wasn't he? I'm sad to have lost touch with him.

But his wife was absolutely not a nice guy, was she? Barbara Goldsmith! My God! I thought I saw her going into the Putney Odeon about eight years ago and, although I had tickets for *Bridget Jones: the Edge of Reason*, I ran and hid in what was then, I think, still the Café Rouge on Putney Bridge Road.

Perhaps I can open my heart to you, Sam. I'm not sure it's a good idea, but I feel I want to. You mustn't take anything I say the wrong way but I will admit to you that, in many ways, I am not the man I thought I was and I am beginning to feel that you may be basically a different person from the Sam Dimmock we all knew in the old days. You may have interests that go well beyond dentistry. If you take my meaning.

I hated my wife, Sam. I really did hate her. That is an awful thing to say but it's true. I never felt I was who I was when I was with her. If you know what I mean. And I am beginning to suspect you do.

Oh, I shouldn't talk about the dead like this – though I must say I have never understood why we are supposed to be nice about them. What difference does being dead make to whether a person is or is not a total cunt? Sorry to use that word. I saw you flinch a couple of times the other night when my mouth got the better of me – which I am afraid it always does. When I get talking about Gerald Price, for example, I fall to cursing like a very drab. I suppose, for various reasons, which are too complicated to go into here, my relationship with Pamela was utterly unresolved when she died. I am still having those arguments we used to have in Puerto Banús. Do you remember the night she threw an entire plate of clams at me? If it hadn't been for Johnny Goldsmith I think we would have killed each other.

I didn't really talk about how she died, did I? I haven't told this story to anyone but I so much enjoyed our chat that I feel I can tell you. And writing it down – rather than telling it to your face – seems so much easier somehow. I'm in my overgrown garden, with my back to the late-September sun. For the first time in what feels like years I am starting to feel happy but I don't know why. I have no garden furniture – I got rid of it all after Pamela died. One of the many things I constantly celebrate about her death is that I will never have to go to a garden centre again. So, imagine me on one of our heavy dining-room chairs, with a pillow at my back, scribbling for dear life as, in the thick bushes that screen me from my irritating neighbours, I hear a blackbird try out aspects of its eloquence on the sun-warmed brickwork of my so-neglected suburban property.

I am wearing a figure-hugging shirt and espadrilles, which, though I say it myself, suit me rather well.

The garden was so neat the night she died. Well – she was a keen gardener.

It was a particularly warm November that year. I had gone out for a drink with a bloke called Basil, from the BBC. Not a very nice man. In fact, a gay friend of mine once said he was the kind of person who 'gave homosexuality a bad name' but for some reason he had weaselled himself into a position of authority in the Natural History Department. He knew absolutely nothing about animals – he once told me he disliked almost every species under the sun apart from some South American reptiles – but he prided himself on being what a lot of people at the Beeb used to call a 'filmmaker'. He had made a quite well-thought-of series about English insects that included a gratuitous stop-motion sequence about a group of earwigs attacking each other. I needed his help with some political issue in the department and we ended up having a meal in a grim Italian restaurant.

When I got back the house was dark. Which surprised me. Pamela usually never went to bed before midnight and it was only just after eleven. It was dark and silent in a way that made me know, as soon as I opened the front door, that something bad had happened inside. I didn't call out her name. Still don't know why. I think I knew that whatever bad thing it was had happened to her. I went, very slowly, along our narrow hall and opened the door to the sitting room.

The first thing I saw was that the french windows were open.

Oh, I remember thinking. Someone's been having a party! That was because I could smell cigarette smoke and neither Pamela nor I had ever acquired the tobacco habit. It was only then that I saw the things scattered across the carpet. There was a vase, a couple of framed photographs of the kids and, by the sofa, a half-empty bottle of red wine. It had leaked on to the carpet, spreading outwards in a blurred circle. Pamela's left hand, flung out at right angles to her body, looked as if it were still groping for the bottle.

I knew straight away that she was dead. I don't know why because I think hers was the first dead body I had ever seen. My father was still alive back then, even if the Alzheimer's had made him almost as unrecognizable as the people and things he, in his turn, failed to recognize.

I went straight over to her and, mimicking something I had seen people do in detective stories on television, put my hand to the vein in her neck. It was a totally unnecessary gesture. But it made me feel better. It was then that I saw the bottle of pills. It, too, was leaking cargo on to Pamela's pride and joy of an oatmeal carpet. There was a scattered arc of brightly coloured capsules, thrown out as carelessly as her arms, inches from her brightly painted nails.

I remember the nails, the way I remember the elaborate makeup, which she had not been wearing in the early part of the evening. I remember the earrings, too, gold, studded with diamonds. I bought them for her on our tenth wedding anniversary, but I never saw her wear them until the night she died. She had a tiny, foxy chin, and I do recall thinking how aggressive it looked, jutting up uselessly from what I suddenly saw was a very tiny neck. She was a party girl, really. She saw me as someone who would introduce her to the glamorous life of the BBC , to smart dinner parties, champagne receptions and celebrities like – God help us – David Attenborough.

She looked, I am afraid to say, pretty fucking stupid lying there dead on our – no, *her* – oatmeal carpet. Her mouth was wide open as if she was going to say something about the carpets or the curtains or how Milly was going to Oxford and why Barnaby hadn't really done what they said he had done in Thailand. But she wasn't going to say anything ever again. She had told me to empty the dishwasher for the last time.

When I had finished pretending to check her pulse I stood up. That was when I saw the cushion. It was over by the french windows. A large dark blue job. It was unusual to see anything out of place in our sitting room. Pamela drilled the fixtures and fittings every morning, and if a chair tried to step out of line, it was put on report pretty quickly. That cushion looked as if someone had thrown it down in a rage. It was dented and crumpled.

More out of habit than anything else I picked it up and tossed it back on the sofa. That was something I later regretted. Then I went to the french windows. There was no sign of their having been forced. I went out into the garden. Everything looked as neat and undisturbed as usual. The only thing that was unusual was that the door to the side passage was open.

I did all this in a kind of dream. I think I was putting off the moment when I would have to call someone and say, out loud, the words that meant I was never, ever going to see Pamela alive again; or maybe it was something else. You see, from the first I just didn't believe it. I felt, from the moment

I saw her body, as if I was being asked to accept a version of events that somebody very clever – and very nasty – had devised. I just didn't think she had committed suicide.

When the police arrived – they turned out to be even more stupid than I had feared they might be – they asked me if she had been depressed. So I told them about the not sleeping and the rages and the time she had taken herself to Putney Bridge and 'tried to throw herself off it'. How do you 'try' to throw yourself off a bridge? Put one leg over? You either jump off or you don't – in my view. She never seriously attempted suicide. Not Pamela. She loved herself far too much.

The other thing that made me think she had been murdered – and murdered by someone who knew her – was that bottle of wine by her body. Pamela never drank alone and, unless someone else was encouraging her to do so, she never drank red wine. There was only one glass. But in the cupboard where the glasses were kept, there was one goblet, matching the one by her body, which I could have sworn was put back in a different place from its accustomed one.

Someone had been there. Someone she knew. That was why the side door was open. I tried to tell them that but they were not interested. The more I tried to tell them, the more they asked me searching questions about our relationship and started to mention the screaming rows we had had over the previous six months. The neighbours were terrifically helpful there. Awfully Nice Sarah – who is nothing of the kind – said she had heard me yelling through the wall. Apparently I had said, several times, I was going to kill Pamela. If Poofy Basil hadn't given me an alibi, I swear they would have arrested me.

In the end I was almost relieved to get a verdict of suicide.

It wasn't until about nine months after she had died that I found the chain. It was a cheap man bracelet, actually, of the kind worn by very dodgy Mediterranean chaps on their hairy wrists. It was in one of the flowerbeds in the back garden. I only found it because, at the time, I had a Border terrier, which I had bought for company after Pamela died. And about the only thing that sent me out into the garden was picking up its crap. In one of the flowerbeds, right up near the fence, I found the bracelet and knew it instantly for what it was.

Maybe you remember it, Sam. Pamela bought it for Gerald when we were in that villa in Crete. It was a joke. 'I bought Gerry this in the market!' she said, at dinner one night. 'Because he is such a phoney macho Mediterranean man!' And Gerald – do you remember – said, 'The day you see me wear that, Mrs Larner, is the day I strangle you for giving it to me!' With which he pocketed the thing. I certainly never saw him wear it on that or any other holiday. But I never saw him throw it away. And it was instantly recognizable. They don't make things as distinctively vulgar as that any more – not even in Greece.

There could have been a hundred and one reasons for its being in our back garden. It could be totally unrelated to the fact that the french windows were open on the night she died or that – this is something I have never told anyone – I could have sworn I could smell Gerald Price in the room that night. His sour man smell – the acrid tang of locker rooms and bullying and all the things I so hated about school and those triumphant products of the system who, like him, now dominate the law and the Conservative Party.

Medical fucking negligence. I only hope he falls under a bus and the guy deputed to save his life is one of the people he stitched up in the Court of Appeal.

I can't believe I'm saying all these things to you. Well, writing them down anyway. Perhaps that makes it easier. Thanks again for listening, as they say. Or maybe you have already ripped up this self-pitying drivel, hurled it across the room and got on with something useful and important like – doing someone's teeth!

I really do wish I could summon up the courage to go out with you in your boat. It sounds fun. I fear I would be absolutely useless at it and you would end up screaming at me for not belaying something correctly. I do not think I would enjoy being keelhauled or given a few strokes with the cat o' nine tails! Although that would probably be not half as bad as trying to drive Pamela round the South Circular in the rush hour!

All best, Sam, and I really will remember to floss!
Mike Larner


From:
Samuel Dimmock
Dimmock Dentistry
'Because Teeth Matter'
24 Beeston Crescent
Putney
1 October

To:
Mike Larner
24 Lawson Crescent
Putney

My dear Mike,
My heart goes out to you! I have never heard such a terrible story. I am amazed you have managed to hold yourself together over the last few years and I completely understand why you

have let your teeth slip. I couldn't help noticing, by the way, when you opened your mouth to yawn that night we were in the pub that your left back molars need urgent attention. Drop round any time and I will give you a look over.

If it is any comfort to you, my marriage is in a pretty bad state. Mary and I get along but there is no real spark any more. I have been wondering, recently, if she was getting interested in another man. I am not sure I would be too bothered if she was – so long as he was my type!

Seriously, though, there are times when I feel a night out with the boys would be preferable to a night in with her! A lot of people are down on homosexuality but, really, when I look at some of the heterosexual people I know I am appalled by their selfishness and narrow-minded attitude to the 'gay community'. I think a lot of our 'gay brothers' are a deal more manly than some heterosexual men one sees about the place.

As if all this wasn't enough, Mary seems to be going through a spell of bad luck. She has been attacked several times, recently, by some prankster. She seems convinced it is a woman – although I cannot see why she should think that. A few weeks ago she was hit on the head by someone while she was walking home from rehearsal and then, about ten days since, we were sitting in the front room of our house when a brick came through the window! Can you believe it? There was glass all over the carpet, and if the cat had been sitting in her usual place she might have had a very nasty injury.

Someone had wrapped a message round the offending object. It read simply, 'DIE YOU BITCH!' And Mary swore it was intended for her. I can't think why as she is absolutely nothing like a bitch. If she has a fault it is that she is too kind and too generous to people. I tried to make a joke of it by saying it was probably intended for me and that many of my patients probably thought I was 'a right bitch' – I did what I thought was quite a funny 'camp' act as I said this, sticking the old bum out and raising the old eyebrows in what I thought was a fairly good impression of a poofter. She burst into tears and ran out of the room. Women! What can you do with them?

Funnily enough, she is convinced that the person behind all this is a woman! Well – the female of the species is more deadly than the male. I cannot think who would possibly want to hurt Mary. Apart from me, of course! That was a joke, Michael. I really respect her a lot and think she has been a wonderful mum to Elaine. I just do find I prefer masculine company these days as, from your letter, do you!

Elaine, by the way, is doing really well. She is a GP in Norwich and proving really popular with the locals. Including some bloke called Hanif, who is – as you may have guessed – a bit of a Muslim on the quiet. She seems to be quite stuck on him and he has been down to visit us once or twice. I was very diplomatic, of course, and didn't mention 9/11 once – though I think I did touch on the London bombings and that bloke Abu Whatshisname who should, in my view, be strung up, never mind sent back to Yemen or whatever Godforsaken place he comes from.

But you can always feel the tension with them, can't you? They are so self-righteous! They think they have the right to lecture us about our 'colonial past', whatever that means, although, as far as I can see, they've done pretty well out of it. This Hanif character went to Oxford (hoity-toity!) and now is involved in some rather dodgy fringe theatre in Suffolk; last time he was down he kept droning on about something called the Amritsar Massacre, of which I have never heard. From the way he went on you would have thought my uncle Arthur – who was actually in the Indian Civil Service – had personally shot up the local Islamic hordes. From what he said it sounded as if they were causing trouble in the local market and our boys were only trying to keep them in line. I wasn't alive in 1910 or whenever it happened. I do not see what the hell it has to do with me! I sometimes want to speak my mind about the Prophet Muhammad, riding around Saudi Arabia as if he owned the place and waving his sword at any passing infidel, but I suppose if I did I would have a fatwa slapped on me by the local mosque quicker than you could say 'samosa'.

Still, she's obviously keen on him. I suppose if she gets any keener we shall have to meet the parents, who are both doctors. Trained over here, of course, and, as far as I can make out, perfectly respectable people who are no keener on terrorism than me and Mary. But you never know when you're going to say the wrong thing, do you? I'll have to watch my tongue! Stay off politics and try not to air my views on the old burka or the merits and demerits of stoning people for adultery.

What did happen to Barnaby? Elaine is very much the centre of our lives. If anything happened to her I do not know what I would do. It would be so nice to meet up again and have a good old yarn. I'm going to be very persistent about getting you on the boat. It sounds like we have a lot to talk about. And an idea has occurred to me. I have just acquired a new patient – a funny little bloke called Gibbons, who is, believe it or not, a private detective. I never knew such people existed or, if they did, thought they were grubby little men in mackintoshes – a word that nowadays seems to mean a kind of computer.

Anyway – drop me a line. A weekend in a stiff breeze is just the sort of thing you need. I can do any weekend this month apart from the 24th when I suppose I'm going to have to go and see Mary give her Ophelia in St Jude's Church

113

Hall. It does not sound promising. Apparently there is a lot of nakedness and at one point Gerald AND Mary both get their kit off and chase each other round the stage. Or maybe this was just a rehearsal getting out of hand!

The 12th would be ideal if you fancied it. I wouldn't ask anyone else to crew. We could handle the *Jolly Roger* together easily. The accommodation is pretty basic. There is only one cabin in the forrard section of the aft but I normally doss down there pretty happily with a bloke called Bert, so you and I would be pretty snug, I think. I used to train people in sailoring when I was involved with the Sea Scouts and I am sure you would enjoy getting lessons from me about every aspect of life out at sea. I promise not to give you too many lashes or be too stern if I find you slacking as far as cabin duties are concerned!

Best
Sam

PS I shaved off my beard. Mary says it makes me look very sexy. But it hasn't done much for our sex life, I fear!

From:
Mike Larner
24 Lawson Crescent
Putney
6 October

To:
Samuel Dimmock
Dimmock Dentistry
'Because Teeth Matter'
24 Beeston Crescent
Putney

Dear Sam,

Isn't it weird that we both live at number twenty-four? And both our streets are crescents. Just another thing it turns out we have in common that, all those years ago, we never quite appreciated.

And the Sea Scouts! The words summon up a wonderful image of lads scurrying about in the open air, all working together under the stern command of a naval type in one of those wonderful blue uniforms. I never realized, for example, that you had ever been involved with the Sea Scouts. Although I once got a letter from a rather interesting-sounding chap who was definitely into them – if you take my meaning. I really do think we are beginning to understand each other so much better, thanks to this exchange of letters. I had always wanted to join them as a lad but my family had the usual ridiculous prejudices about the organization being full of perverts! Who is to say what is perverted and what isn't? What on earth is wrong with a few lads getting up to some pranks out on the water? And if a junior rating does something wrong he gets whacked on the bottom! I personally find it quite stimulating. There. I've said it!

Our little correspondence has totally changed my attitude to you, Sam! I think – as I may have pointed out in my last letter – I am probably one of those people who do not really pay enough attention to others.

All those years ago it may be that I struck you as rather left wing. I think I was rather left wing in those days. I was one of those comfortably off BBC producers who saw Mrs Thatcher as the enemy. I think ten years of Tony Blair cured me of all that. With his guitar and his ghastly wife and his keenness to go to war in Iraq, he finally demonstrated that socialism is simply a word people use to make them feel smug and compassionate.

More and more, these days, I see our society as simply another animal community dominated by the need to survive and moderated by the undoubtedly practical benefits associated with co-operation. I like to think of myself, these days, as someone who attempts to be compassionate in an honestly selfish way.

Gerald Price is, ultimately, not a survivor because he will always alienate those he dominates so thoroughly that there will come a point when they combine together to get rid of him. Even *Leptothorax curvispinosus* ant slave workers were observed by Hölldobler and Wilson (or maybe it was just Wilson – they did not do everything together!) to attack the mother-slavemaker-queen-of-*L. duloticus* and bite at her head and thorax. And, somehow or other, people like you and I will, in the end, expose Mr Price for what he is. A crude, self-satisfied bully who may well have murdered my wife. I might think that murdering her was not entirely a bad idea, but if anybody was going to dispose of Pamela, I would have liked it to be me.

I wonder if you would ask your private detective if he would be interested in meeting up to discuss the possibility of his investigating what happened to Pam? If you could bear it I would love you to be there at the meeting. I am not very good at asking for what I want and I suspect, somehow, that you are. There I go again!

I would like to able to tell you what happened to Barnaby but it is still just too painful. Maybe one day I will manage it. I feel that if I could talk about it to anyone, you would be that man. And, yes, I would love to go out on your boat – 12 October would be fine. I am pretty much free every day for the next ten years. Will I need to buy any special equipment? What should I wear?

All the best
Mike Larner

From:
Samuel Dimmock
Dimmock Dentistry
'Because Teeth Matter'
24 Beeston Crescent
Putney
9 October

To:
Mike Larner
24 Lawson Crescent.
Putney

Dear Mike,
Wear a mini skirt and a tank top!

Only joking. Jeans and a warm sweater would be perfect.
I thought the one you were wearing the other night was
very attractive. It brought out your figure very well indeed.
You are quite a well set-up lad, aren't you really? Although
you are always putting yourself down I think you are an
extremely good-looking fellow.

Let's meet up for a drink to finalize arrangements next
week and – well – yo ho ho and a bottle of rum, me old
shipmate!

Your friend,
Sam

PS I will fix up for us to meet Mr Gibbons in the next week
or so. It sounds as if what happened with Pamela may well
have been murder. If it turns out to be that, and if Gerry
Price was involved in any way whatsoever, we have to do
something about it.

PPS I had amazing fun in the Sea Scouts and look forward to telling you all about it when we meet up. But you will have to pay attention. I can dish out stiff punishment when at sea and everyone says I become a completely different person!

# Chapter Six

*Mrs Barbara Goldsmith sends a round robin to the surviving members of the Puerto Banús Eight. They all get back to her*

From:
Barbara Goldsmith
101 Fellen Road
Putney
25 October

To: John Goldsmith, Mike Larner, Sam Dimmock, Mary Dimmock, Gerald Price, Elizabeth Price

Dear Former Villa Inmates – John, Mike, Sam, Gerald, Elizabeth and Mary,
Think of this as one of those round-robin letters of the kind that used to be sent out by more than usually complacent suburban families so that everyone knew how well they were doing and what tremendous things they had all achieved over the last year. I even got one once addressed to the idiot

who lived in our house before we got there. I opened it, of course, and spent days cackling over the writer's attempt to sound positive about the fact that little Thomas had failed his A levels.

Maybe some idiots are still sending such things out although I am told no one apart from the Gas Board writes letters, these days. Apparently at least sixty million of them are posted in the UK every year so someone out there must still be trying to do a Madame de Sévigné; but if they are, they are certainly not practising on me. The only letter I have received in the last few months was from the man next door, asking me to turn down Bach in the early evening.

What is that awful word? Retro – that's it. This is a communication as retro as Black Forest Gâteau.

I have written it out on the word processor. You are all getting the same letter, as I do not really have anything different to say to each of you. I began to think, as last night's performance ground on through the October night, that you are all, really, the same person. And if, as Caligula dreamed of doing with the Roman people, I could behead the lot of you with one swift stroke of a sharpened axe, I would do just that.

There is nothing like a bad evening in the theatre for con-centrating the bitterness of one's thoughts. Don't you find?

Except, of course, I am talking about the last twenty or thirty years. The subject of this communication is the Goldsmiths and what has happened to them since the early 1980s. So, do not expect too much optimism. I am enclosing no photographs and am not about to tell you all about how wonderful Jas and Josh's weddings were, or how much I'm enjoying the grandchildren. Because I am not. They are about as much fun as the two sets of parents-in-law my two oafish boys have acquired. Sidney and Betty – a truly ghastly duo from Birmingham who pronounce 'broccoli' brockle-aye – are only mildly worse than Billy and Pat from Taunton, who do not seem to know any three-syllable words, even if those words belong to things you can eat. Although food is about their only topic of conversation. Very like the rest of Britain, these days. Has anyone seen those ghastly cooking programmes on television where idiots get marked out of ten for what they have done to Boeuf Bourguignon?

But, in case you all think I am going to confine myself to what has happened to John and Barbara and Jas and Josh – not to mention daughters in-law Melanie and April (yes, April) or grandchildren February, October, July and June – I shall try to give you all a progress report on how I think my other villa companions of yesteryear are doing, based on my, admittedly brief, sighting of you all at the sensationally lacklustre production of *Hamlet* mounted by the Putney Thespians at St Jude's Church Hall last night.

My God, I thought the Goldsmiths had problems!

I know that during the six or seven years when we were all seeing each other – before the children went their separate ways – I was generally reckoned to be the Group Bitch. It is a title of which I am mildly proud. At least I wasn't the Group Wet or the Group Fatty or the Group Oaf. Or, God help us, the Group Dentist or the Group Doctor. The rest of you know who you are. Do not try to deny it. These titles do not really do justice to the full banality of your various characters. Any more than the Group Bitch, who is giving you documentary evidence to support your conclusion by writing this letter, really does justice to *moi*. As Miss Piggy used to call herself.

At least I never bothered to pretend. I may be a bitch but at least I am an honest bitch. The pitiful displays you put on for each other! The drinks from six to eight, the foursomes at tennis from eleven to one on Saturday morning, the God-awful dinner parties from eight thirty to eleven forty-five on Saturday nights! The girly lunches and the boysy drinks and those frightful cycle rides out to Box Hill where the women would drive along behind, like camp followers behind a medieval army. The phoney playground bonhomie that masked the endless competitiveness over the children and, later, presumably, things like reading groups or grandchild chitchat. I missed those, thank Christ. Maybe John didn't but communication between us is at such low ebb I really wouldn't know if he had been having an affair with, say, Elizabeth Price – hi, Elizabeth! – since he always used to try to sit next to her at dinner, about the only overt sign Dr Goldsmith ever gives of sexual interest in anyone or anything.

Who was the obvious pervert playing Horatio? And why was he wearing jodhpurs for most of the proceedings? And why, at the ghastly drinks afterwards, did he keep giving furtive glances in the direction of Mrs Price, who resolutely ignored him? Are *they* having an affair? Someone told me he was a private detective – can this be true? If he is a private detective, wouldn't he make more effort not to look like one? Did Laertes fall over deliberately every time he entered? Had there, at some stage, been a plan to have Fortinbras sing – and is that why he was carrying a guitar? What was the strategy behind Gerald Price's accent? Given that he went ahead with it, could not some form of primitive subtitling have been devised to assist the audience's comprehension?

There we all were, though – were we not?

But I suppose it was accident that brought us all together. If it weren't for that loathsome Church of England school we would never have had the misfortune to meet each other in the first place. We all stood round in a circle and watched

Head Oaf Jasper and Assistant Oaf Joshua run and jump and play with Mad Conrad, Dim Julia, Mediocre Molly – or was it Milly? – Larner, Assistant Oaf to Assistant Oaf Leo and the distinctly sinister Barnaby. Whatever did happen to him by the way? Tragically Vague Elaine is, presumably, in a mental hospital by now.

Back then I suppose we thought they had a chance of growing up into mildly interesting people. As we listened to little Barnaby lisp his way through the part of the donkey that carried Baby Jesus all the way home, some of us almost certainly thought, 'Oooh! He'll be an Actor!' Although I suspect a far more complicated future lay in wait for little Barnaby. I do recall Sam Dimmock telling me, in all seriousness, that he thought Conrad was 'a naturally witty child who will do great things in science'. Conrad???? I never open a newspaper without expecting to find reports of his trial and conviction for some hideous sequence of crimes.

But, you see, we are, and were, a pretty mediocre bunch. None of us was ever likely to stumble over the contemporary equivalent of Maxwell's field equations. Some of us were almost criminally ordinary. I was amazed to see you at the play, Sam Dimmock. Do you know who Shakespeare is? I more or less assumed someone would have murdered you by now, or at very least put you into an irretrievable coma. No one can talk for so long and in such detail about teeth without being punished for it in some way. But there you were at the back, sniggering with little Mike Larner, as if you two had been best buddies for years.

Well – I will give you all your marks out of ten later in this round robin – but I should probably start by keeping you up to date with the Goldsmith family, since, as you all probably noticed, last night I was reticent on the subject, i.e. I didn't really talk to any of you, even at those ghastly drinks afterwards. John, what on earth were you talking about with Mary Dimmock?

Here goes, on the subject of my children anyway. I am sure you do all want to hear about darling Jas and darling Josh, don't you? So that then you can jump in with your ten minutes' worth about Cute Conrad or Beezer Barnaby.

We managed, somehow, to get them both into public school. I think their size helped. The headmaster at Sir Roger de Folnay had clearly never seen a nine year old who, even if he could only just read, was clearly capable of throwing him across the room. They got on rather well there. That being said, neither of them has really gained anything in language proficiency, calculating skills, manners or cultural awareness since they were six. But – yes – they have got bigger.

'Jasper got into Oxford!' is the sentence you often find in about the third paragraph of the softer version of this kind of letter and I can, with pleasure, tell you all that Jasper did just that, but he got booted out of it pretty damn quickly. Partly because he is incredibly stupid, as are many people who go to Oxford, but also because, like his father, he is incurably idle. He is very good, like John, at kicking, catching and hitting balls of all shapes and sizes, which was how he got into Oxford in the first place, but his only real interest since the age of sixteen has been in sinking pint after pint of beer and, to use his own expressive phrase, 'cocking the old leg and blowing one off'.

I am surprised that more parents do not own up to disliking their children but at least, in my case, I can argue that I am only following the general drift. The *on dit* about Jas has always been that he is the Lout Basic and I see no reason to disagree with that judgement. Early on – as I am sure you will not be surprised to learn – he showed pretty clearly that he had no aptitude whatsoever for medicine and so, of course, he decided to go into it. His father, as any of you who had the misfortune to be one of his patients will know, had – and has – no talent for it either. And that has not stopped him. But when it came to Jas, not even a public-school education and a father in the profession could save him. These days, they do actually ask awkward questions about things like the precise location of the pancreas, and if you can't answer them you are shown the door.

And Joshua? He was always supposed to be the sensitive one. I suppose, next to his brother, he was. Next to Jas, Attila the Hun would look sensitive. He also, according to his father and one or two of his teachers, 'showed some talent for English', which was probably why he ended up at Exeter reading French. He had no talent for English. He could hardly speak it. He can't really manage it now. His spoken output never amounts to more than a few dozen repetitions of the word 'whatever'.

You will all remember how, on those villa holidays we endured with such fortitude, Jas and Josh would hurl themselves on the various Lilos, rubber ducks and inflatable balls that seemed always to be lying around on the surface of the pool. And how they made a particular point of it if a vulnerable member of the party happened to be lying on the item in question. Conrad and Elaine were both nearly drowned on several occasions, greatly to Gerald's amusement, although I did think he and John were about to come to blows on the day he shouldered Jas into the deep end with a shout of 'Suck on that, wanker!'

Maybe Gerald has moved on. I somehow doubt it. Certainly Jas and Josh are still at that stage of development. Their daughters conceal their aggressive urges with the skill traditionally associated with females but, make no mistake, February, October, June and July are as viciously competitive when it comes to sticking and painting as their daddies were at contact sports. Have I got their names right? Maybe one of them is called November – she is dark, dim and gloomy enough for it to be a wholly appropriate name.

Jas did not entirely give up on medicine. He has somehow managed to wangle a position with a major pharmaceuticals company. His function, as far as I can tell, is to bribe GPs to buy his products. I am sure some of them work but they are the same outfit that recently touted a cure for diabetes that, while it was fairly effective, was also rumoured to send you blind after six months. 'How were we to know?' said Jas. 'Anyway, most of the people who went blind were in the third world so who cares? They have crap lawyers.'

He has risen up the ranks fairly fast and now drives a BMW coupé to the various hospitals and group practices, where he trades, shamelessly, on his father's profession. His brother, meanwhile, has given up on his entirely notional skills in the liberal arts for a job at a management consultancy where, so far, he has been personally responsible for firing about two thousand people. Not bad going for someone who got a third from Exeter and who has never read any book, apart from a Jamie Oliver cookbook, all the way through to the end. 'It's all bullshit!' I often hear him say; the fact that he is holding down a highly paid job seems to show that he is absolutely right.

They get on very well with each other.

'All right, Joshie?'

'Not bad, Jazzer!'

'Joshing along, are we?'

'Not so bad, Jastic!'

And so on. They haven't yet arrived at the stage of picking out each other's fleas but otherwise their interaction is about that of a couple of low-grade apes. Needless to say, although

I have absolutely nothing in common with them at all, they get on very well indeed with John.

John. John and Barbara. I was coming to that.

John – as some of you may know – is still passing on patients to people better qualified to deal with them: the traditional role of the GP, which he performs to perfection. His major speciality is reassurance. He is very good indeed at convincing people there is nothing wrong with them – even when there obviously is. Going to see him professionally, I always feel, must be a form of assisted suicide. Even in the simplest diagnosis he is almost bound to be wrong. Last year, for example, I had a problem with my knee. Well – to be precise – an agonizing pain in it for nearly two weeks. I made the mistake of asking him about it. He shook his handsome head slowly. 'We have no idea,' he said, 'what goes on inside the knee. Not really.'

That was all he would say on the subject.

'What about X-rays?' I said.

A suspicious look glinted in his oh-so-compassionate blue eyes. 'X-rays?' he said, as if he was some nineteenth-century professor trying to come to terms with this curious new invention.

'X-rays!' I squeaked. 'You shine them at the body and you can see the bones and everything!' He looked intensely doubtful. 'You know,' I went on, 'you can see what the problem is and then you cut the knee open and poke around inside it!'

He pursed his lips then, and got that sulky, childish look he always gets when the subject of illness is raised. 'You don't want to mess with knees!' he said. 'I sent some bloke with a knee problem to old Andy Boering at St Bee's and—'

'And what?' I said.

'He's dead!' said John, with what sounded like satisfaction.

It turned out the 'bloke' was ninety-two.

As far as I can make out, he has a similarly hands-off approach to the poor idiots foolish or brave enough to be his officially recognized patients. They die like flies. 'Cancer,' he said, the other day at the dinner table, 'is a total mystery, really. We have no idea what causes it or how to cure it. We are totally at a loss.'

But the problems John and I have go far deeper than his lack of talent for medicine. I suspect we are just another couple who married because they liked the look of each other. And then spent forty years and two children finding out we had absolutely nothing in common. What struck me as I looked around your faces last night – and where better to ask the existential questions than at a production of *Hamlet*? – was that the passion seemed to have gone out of all of us. The only individuals showing signs of life were little Micky Larner and Sam Dimmock – two people who, in the old days, seemed to have even less in common than those of us yoked together in marriage. Maybe they have fallen in love with each other!

But love, even love between two people who both strike me as physically repulsive, is better than nothing. We are all sixty or near to it. We shall be dead soon. As I looked around at you all, drinking warm white wine in that gloomy church hall, where we hosted parties for so many of our wretched children, I found myself thinking, What is the fucking point? What has it all been for? How can we do anything to change our destinies? Is it too late? Has any of us ever done anything brave, passionate, foolish or risky? Haven't we all just paid our mortgages and got our opinions out of the newspapers and generally behaved like middle-class sheep? Which is what we are. Isn't it? Can we not take a chance in what may well be the last decade of our lives? Can we agree not to go quietly?

Which brings me to me. Barbara Goldsmith.

Oh, I'm all right. I've been on television, haven't I? So I must be all right. I've published five novels about people with marital difficulties in south-west London and two about people with marital difficulties in nineteenth-century France. One of which contained what some idiot in the *TLS* called 'an unforgettable portrait of Gustave Flaubert'. Well – I had shagged him at the Wolverhampton Literary Festival in 2002. The critic, not Gustave Flaubert, Sam Dimmock. Gustave Flaubert is dead. I have written a 'highly praised' study of Mary Shelley. I hadn't shagged the woman who praised it but I had said nice things about *her* highly praised study of George Eliot. I have appeared on *The Review Show* with a woman called Kirsty Walk; I hope I'm spelling that right. She had, I thought, a set of opinions that seemed to have been programmed by a machine. I was even on *Desert Island Discs* where I struck the radio critic of *The Times* as 'hopelessly conceited'.

But I don't care, you see. Everything I have done seems to me of very little interest. Everything done by my contemporaries seems of even less interest. The only writers I like are dead. The only scientists I like are dead. The only musicians I like are dead. And the only living people I want to like are my friends and family. But I haven't got any friends and I can't stand my family. I last fucked my husband four months ago and it was about as interesting as the foyer at Tate Modern. The people I used to think were my friends were my friends purely out of self-interest, and I think I returned the compliment with interest. That, it seems to me, is pretty typical of most people's personal relationships.

There has been only one time in my life when I have been able to forget myself with another person. I am not, of course, going to say who that person was. Nobody, darlings, not even the Group Bitch, is going to be that frank. And yet there was a moment when even flowers seemed genuinely innocent and the world had the look of a suburban street after rain on a day when you know spring is coming. Wasn't it that miserable bastard Philip Larkin who said that what will survive of us is love? God knows what he would know about it – wretched old stick that he was. Well, the poem was about two dead people, which is about the nearest Larkin would ever get to understanding a human being, or behaving like one, for that matter. The Movement! What a horrible bunch of tossers they were, weren't they?

No, love is, or ought to be, about passion inspiring you to action; and there was a moment when I thought I had found the passion that would make me *do* something. You see, I was conscripted into the Mothers and Babies Club. I drifted into the suburbia that you all seem to think is everyone's natural destiny, but all the time I knew there was another life waiting for me. One in which every minute of every day would be a different kind of risk. One in which I would be able to turn my back on all the small decisions that, over the years, have tightened into a rope that is strangling me, into a pillow that is pressed upon my face so hard I cannot breathe. My little life hangs, like a strangled doll, in the window of a big house, empty of furniture, in which somewhere, on a yet unvisited floor, a hideous stranger waits.

I turned my back on possibility. I turned my back on love. You've all done the same. But, my God, I loved! Helplessly and hopelessly and far too late to do anything about it because I had had children by then and it was all too late. It's always too late. But it's never too late. And I do not want it to be too late. That's all I need to say. Let's be honest about the smallness and ugliness of our lives. Let's try to change – even though it is already too late.

Barbara Goldsmith

PS Who did that damage to Mary 'If I laugh loud enough no one will notice I'm fat' Dimmock's face? I thought at first it was makeup, intended to suggest Ophelia was the victim of abuse, but it became clear later that someone really has been whacking her about. Gerald Price in rehearsal, perhaps.

PPS Was the freak in the long coat Conrad? And who was the stunning girl with the long hair who was making out with the Pakistani?

PPPS Elizabeth, the beret was a mistake. You looked grey with worry. It cannot be just the marking. And where, oh, where is your edition of Propertius? Will we ever see it?

PPPPS The remains of our little group all seem to be gossiping about the death of Pamela Larner. Somebody at the interval seemed to be suggesting she had been murdered. Hard to believe that anything so interesting would ever happen to dear Pamela. If she was killed – who did it? And why did they wait so long to carry out this important public service?

From:
Michael Larner
'Chez Moi'
24 Lawson Crescent
Putney
30 October

To:
Barbara Goldsmith
101 Fellen Road
Putney

My God, Barbara!
Thank you! Thank you! Thank you!

Love! Passion! Violence of thought and feeling! Let us surrender to it! Now! I will tell you what is going on between Dimmock and Larner. It is love that is happening between us, Barbara. It is powerful and deep and crazy love – between a retired BBC wildlife-filmmaker and the best dentist in Putney. It is Tristan and Isolde, David and Jonathan, Edward VIII and Wallis Simpson and all the great loves of history rolled into one.

My life has changed. I wish I had the courage to write this letter, as you did, to more than one person. I wish I had the courage to post it on the Internet. But, of course, doing that would dilute the sense of it. Communication into a vacuum is meaningless, isn't it? Which is why those ghastly blogs people write are so lacking in form and precision and sense. Even a casual remark is defined by those who hear it as well as the person who makes it. In addressing everybody you address nobody.

I am gay. Yes, I am gay. I am gay gay gay!!! I am totally and utterly gay!!! I am so gay I think I will explode with my

133

gayness!!!! I cannot find the exclamation marks to describe quite how gay I am. I am utterly, utterly gay and I want the world to know that I am gay!!!!!!!!!!!!!!!!!

In a discreet way, of course, you understand. I do not want to parade my private life in front of a vulgar and hostile crowd. And yet...and yet...I do!!! I do!!! I do!!! It will be like Christ on the Via Whatever It Was when he was carrying the cross and people spat at him. I am pretty sure Jesus was gay. 'The disciple whom Jesus loved'! Eh? Eh??? They just didn't have the courage to write 'The disciple to whom Jesus gave a hand job'! or ' The disciple who went down on Jesus and a few Roman soldiers as well, probably because he LIKED LEATHER'! They were all gay. Pontius Pilate was clearly gay. Herod was incredibly gay. Joseph was gay, for God's sake. What other man would put up with his wife telling him she was pregnant by the 'Holy Ghost'???? Eh?? In fact, I think everyone, when you look closely, is pretty gay. President Obama is gay. I am sure of it.

And I am gay, Barbara. Your wonderful letter gave me the courage to say it. To say it out loud – well, to you anyway.

I am gay. I hope I have made myself clear.

I think I first realized I was gay when I was having sex with Sam Dimmock on board his boat the *Jolly Roger* about five nautical miles off the Dorset coast. As I was being penetrated by him – with the boat plunging and soaring through the waves – I saw, for the first time, that I was almost certainly not a fully heterosexual man. And as, later that same night, I took his penis into my mouth on the deck of his elegant sloop, I reached a new height of awareness. It was a religious experience, Barbara!

It made sense of my life at last. It explained so many things. It explained my feelings about Pamela (or the lack of them) and it explained the terrible distance between my children and me. It went some way to explaining what happened to Barnaby in Thailand – although nothing can ever fully explain that, of course. But at least now I feel empowered to begin my search for him and for what he has become. Even if it is going to be hard to reach the Burmese border and to get inside the community to which he now belongs (we have heard rumours they have all gone to Cambodia although some say Dr Robert is in La Gomera in the Canary Islands), I am going to make that journey, make that trip. Oh, Barnaby, I am coming for you. I am going to tell you I am gay and we are going to really communicate!

I am not afraid of leprosy. I am not afraid of anything.

The boat was rocking and swaying through the waves and yet nothing seemed to put me off my stroke. As I tasted the essence of Sam, as his salty masculinity began to course through me, like blood through the veins of a newborn child, we laughed for sheer joy. What did it matter where his semen went? In my ear, on my hair, across my windcheater? It can go up my arse for all I care!

And, yes, Barbara, love makes you ready to do the work you have to do in the world. I left the BBC nine years ago, driven out by petty in-fighting and John Birt – never a man who understood wild animals since they showed a remarkable lack of interest in focus groups and all the other management bollocks he introduced to the Beeb. A bloke called Bleistein, who accused me of fiddling my expenses and being 'unproductive', cruelly persecuted me. Oh. Sorry, Mr Bleistein, but filming gudgeon just doesn't come cheap!!! And since I left I have watched public-service broadcasting degenerate into a ragbag of food programmes and ludicrous reality shows. No names, no pack drill, but David Attenborough is not the only man on the planet who understands it.

Yes, I was bitter. But I am no longer bitter. I know what I

have to do and know it is going to be very important work. No one has tried to do it because it is hard. It is going to be hard. I will be spat on and accused of prejudice when, of course, my detractors will be hiding behind their prejudices.

*Homosexuality in the Animal Kingdom* will be a massive landmark series following gay animals, literally, from the very smallest to the enormous – and deservedly celebrated – gay rhinos of northern Botswana. We will film extensively in communities of the homosexual ant species *Pheidilliata macerata* and shine light – at last – on bisexuality among the British earwigs. We will explore, for the first time, the vivid and sometimes painful homosexual life of the Cypriot viper and study the explosion of gay behaviour in captive animals, including Gus, the justly celebrated masturbating polar bear in Central Park Zoo. The great apes, of course, will feature heavily and we will penetrate into the heart of the Borneo jungle to report on homosexual courtship in the lesser orangutan and we will expose the anti-gay prejudice rife in the heron colonies of Twickenham. It is going to be very, very exciting. At last I have a purpose in life.

Thanks, Barbara, for your wake-up call. It was as refreshing as a double espresso. We all needed to hear it. I only hope the rest of the sad sixsome, who spent so many summers pretending to feel things they did not really feel, will listen to you and find themselves, in the way that Sam Dimmock and I have done.

Right on, Barbie. We all need a good bitch and you are a Good Bitch!

Who was the man you truly loved? Or was it a woman???? I somehow suspect it was!!!!

Your friend in gayness,
Micky Larner

PS We are sure that Pamela's death was murder. We do not yet know for certain who killed her. Though we have our suspicions. And Sam and I are going to find out. I am hiring a brilliant private detective.


From:
Elizabeth Price
112 Heathland Avenue
Putney, SW15 3LE
30 October


To:
Barbara Goldsmith
101 Fellen Road
Putney


Dear Barbara,

My letter arrived at the same time as Gerald's. I am assuming they are exactly the same but would never, of course, think of opening one of his letters any more than he would open mine. We have all sorts of ways of abusing each other but that is not one of them. Oh, marriage marriage marriage. We have all been married too long – you are quite right, Barbara. We are too frightened to change but we need to change, nonetheless.

We neither of us have discussed it; I know he will be hurt by it. He is more vulnerable than most people think. I don't even know if he has opened his. Would he recognize your handwriting on the envelope? I did, of course. How could I ever forget it after our memorable exchange of letters back in the nineties? We were so good at hurting each other, I still want to say hurtful things to you but I am simply not as good at it as you are. The beret, by the way, is to hide the fact that I have developed alopecia. But you had probably spotted that.

So – as he almost certainly won't tell you – perhaps I should start by letting you know how Gerald is bearing up under the complicated burden of becoming a sixtysomething.

He is rather distracted at the moment. He is defending a surgeon who, it is alleged, went out to telephone his bookmaker in the middle of a heart operation. Gerald seems rather vague about whether the patient survived, from which I deduce that he or she is almost certainly dead. He is also recovering from the avalanche of insincerity that greeted his perf in the geriatric version of *Hamlet*. Apart from your contribution, of course – and, by the way, as usual, I find myself in complete agreement with your artistic judgement. The Putney Thesps are always saying they are looking for 'young blood', but if they are doing so, it is only in the hopes of drinking it. They are a band of classic baby boomers, all utterly convinced that no one apart from them ever had the experience of being young.

Yes, wasn't it a shocker? I thought it bid fair to be the worst ever, almost eclipsing the 2003 open-air production of *King Lear*. Putney Heath is not an ideal place to do Shakespeare, and if you are going to use it, it would probably be better not to choose a venue quite so near to the bus depot. I have never forgotten Gerry's rendition of the 'Plate sin with gold' speech. Just as he got to the bit about a Pygmy's straw piercing it, a number seventy-three got into serious difficulties with its clutch and Gerald abandoned ship, going off into some improvised blank-verse ramble about how 'great machines did murder sleep hereabouts'. The tragic thing was that nobody seemed to notice.

Why was it, by the way, that everyone turned up the other night? We have not seen each other for twenty years and, for some reason, there we all were, horrified at what age has done to us and unable to recognize each other's children. Yes, the weird-looking boy in the long coat was indeed Conrad. He has been living at home throughout his twenties, writing an immense novel about the Spanish Civil War. I have not read any of it but I know as surely as I know that summer follows spring that nobody will publish it. All he will say about it is that the central character is called Juan – which is not a promising sign.

He will never recover from having Gerald as a father. That is all there is to it.

But I did not write to complain about my marriage, although there is plenty to complain about on that front. It is as much my fault as Gerald's. I picked up my pen in the hope that the two of us might, perhaps, one day, manage to be friends again. Perhaps my scrawl will remind you of happier times we spent together, chatting about literature in those curious villas we all used to hire.

I want to say, first, how sorry I was to hear about you and John. I had rather gathered, way back in the year we all went to Spain, that things between you were not quite as they should be. I think it was when you described him to me as 'an incorrigible meathead'. At first I thought this was just one of those things that wives say about their husbands. We are much ruder about them than they are about us, aren't we? But as you talked on I realized this was a more permanent conviction.

I am not sure it is a completely fair description of Dr Goldsmith.

I know about meatheads, Barbara. I am married to a man who, though highly intelligent, spends his life pretending to be one. And John is not, by any stretch of the imagination, a meathead. He is an averagely intelligent, averagely decent person stuck, like many of us, in the wrong job and cursed with a range of expressions that make him look as if he is more intelligent and sensitive than he actually is. Those wonderful blue eyes of his could make any woman believe he is thinking only of her when, in fact, he is actually agonizing about the prospects for Arsenal Football Club.

I suspect your real problem with him is that you will never be able to have him completely to yourself. Men as good looking as John Goldsmith are, quite simply, public property. I had always assumed he was having an affair with the desperately needy Pamela Larner.

Not that Pamela was the only one obviously drawn to your husband. Poor Mary Dimmock made her passion for him so pathetically obvious. Do you remember that night she 'got something in her eye'? I can still see her proffering her great moon of a face for John's inspection; somebody should tell dear Mary that when you are thirteen stone you shouldn't try to do girlish.

As for Pamela, what can I say?

There were moments during one of our villa holidays when I was sure that John and she were having an affair. But maybe I am wrong. He certainly did try very hard to look uninterested in her, didn't he? Even to the extent of not passing her the milk at breakfast – most unusual for such a punctiliously polite person as your husband. I suspect we both disliked her simply because she was one of those women who manage to keep their figures after having had children – in her case three, although she always managed to make it sound as if there were four of them. She was a great one for the trouser suit, wasn't she? Never a successful outfit, I feel. It always makes women look as if they are a salesperson in the perfume department of some upmarket store.

And, Jesus, was she competitive! Even about her own education, or the lack of it. She stubbornly insisted to both you and me, Oxford and Cambridge both, that she had been to Oxford when we suspected she was at the ghastly secretarial college that my contemporaries always called the Ox and Cow. I am sure there was something similar at Cambridge. Someone told me she couldn't even get her typing speeds up, which was why the scissors and the shampoo started calling to her. Oh, the hairdressing! Oh, the hairdressing of her! God! Do you remember the day she offered to do John and Gerald's hair? And kept going on about the shape of their heads? I don't think I have ever paid any attention to the shape of Gerald's head, except to notice that it is vaguely square.

Gerald told me that Mike Larner had told him he thought dear Pamela was murdered. I can think of at least five women in Putney who would have been delighted to do the deed. I am afraid I would number myself among the women of Putney who can't really mourn Pamela. That laugh! She laughed as a way of marking territory, didn't she? And, oh, dear God, she was so brisk! Unbearably brisk.

We hadn't really seen each other for nearly twenty years. There was something that happened with Milly (or was it Molly?), who, for some unknown reason, ended up at Dame Veronica's for a brief period. She had absolutely no aptitude for academic study and I am afraid I told her mother so.

I was supposed to dislike you, of course. Everyone always assumed I did; but I didn't. We are far too similar. Which is, as I think I said, why I am writing this letter. I really do want your marriage to succeed.

Together you were such a handsome couple. Him with his tennis and his golf and his running and his wonderful profile, and you with that amazing figure and the long, striking black hair and the smile, like a cat's, so private and sensual and mocking. And he was genuinely in love with you. I can still see the two of you at that table on the terrace in the villa in Corsica – you filling up his silences with such craft and energy, and him looking at you with such quiet adoration.

You say in your letter that we all have to take control of our lives and dare to do something new and unusual and that our marriages are stale and frightened. But I suspect, Barbara, that the really serious adventure, for people like us, is growing old together. Is not keeping faith with the feelings that brought us together in the first place the only way to give meaning to our lives? There is, as you point out so vividly, not much of them left. Should we not try to be happy with what we have? How else can we ever possibly hope to do good?

I am sorry you seem to dislike your children – even if the pair of them did once land on my head in one of those swimming pools we all shared. I am sure they have given you plenty of reasons to do so. Certainly Conrad, in what Gerald and I still talk of as the Cider Years, was unspeakable. I lay most of the blame on his tutor at Oxford, although Jacques Derrida, the French phoney to whom his tutor introduced him, must take some of the responsibility.

By the way – something rather interesting was happening between the Boy and Elaine at *Hamlet* the other night. Did you notice? You were so busy looking at no one in particular I expect you did not, but my unemployed son looked to me as if he was chatting up his former primary-school playmate. I do recall them both at Barnaby Larner's eighth chasing each other round that peculiar little hall near the bus station. I am almost sure Elaine Dimmock said she was going to marry him.

Her Indian friend didn't look too pleased, did he? Sulky little beast he was, I thought. Somebody told me he was trying to convert the Dimmock girl to Islam, a religion even more pointlessly simple than Christianity I've always thought, and from what I heard of their conversation Conrad was doing a rather good demolition job on the *hadith* of the Prophet – blessings be upon his camel. It's funny, he never shows any sign of wit or originality around us, but if ever I eavesdrop on him in mixed company, I think, What a clever and original son I have produced!

So – children do change. I am sure Jas and Josh do not always show you their sensitive sides and I am sure their wives seem dull. What mother of sons can ever really like the women they marry? They can do a good job of pretending to but if they really give them their hearts there is likely to be some sinister motive, in my view. And it may be that your view of John will change as he changes. Why do we always have to change partners instead of trying to effect change *in* our partners?

I really do feel there is hope for the two of us, at least in regard to the men we have chosen for ourselves. We both married The Other, didn't we? In my view both our relationships are living proof of Blake's idea that in opposition is true friendship. If one can ever say that Blake has ideas. I don't suppose he does. Crazy convictions, more like. I must say, I sometimes wonder if Gerald isn't The Alien rather than The Other but there is a side to him that very few people, apart from Julia and I, ever see. I know I haven't talked about Julia much but there is never anything much to say about her, is there? Did you ever realize that Gerry is addicted to the music of Bruckner? Or rather good at knitting? He reads medieval French poetry for pleasure and can recite by heart most of the work of Ronsard.

By the way, I did enjoy your last novel. Or was it the one before last? I can never keep up with you. I enjoyed bits of it, anyway. It reminded me of the less interesting bits of Margaret Drabble, although her novels are rather made up of bits that are less than interesting, aren't they? Yours started a bit slowly, got a bit lost in the middle and didn't really deliver a satisfactory conclusion but it was about something, wasn't it? Even if I couldn't quite work out what the something was. There is no earthly reason, by the way, that middle-class people in Putney should be any less interesting than working-class people in Leeds or Chinese migrant workers in Hong Kong – even if that stupid man on the radio seemed to think that there was something intrinsically dull about the Makepeace family. Was it called *The Castaway*? Or was that the one before last?

And, no, I will never finish the work on Propertius. About the only thing I have in common with A. E. Housman is that both of us become incurably dull when engaged in classical scholarship. Let us meet up soon and we can bitch to each other's faces rather behind each other's backs or to the blank page, something both of us, I suspect, face far too often these days.

All my best
Elizabeth Price

From:
Samuel Dimmock
Dimmock Dentistry
'Because Teeth Matter'
24 Beeston Crescent
Putney
30 October

To:
Barbara Goldsmith
101 Fellen Road,
Putney

Dear Barbara,

Well – really! I am glad I am only Sam the humble dentist and not an 'arty' person like you. If this is how arty people behave – well – may their teeth fall out before their time!

I received your round robin and noted that you had sent a similar one to Mary, which I took the liberty of opening. I never open her mail, unless I think it might contain something that may upset her. If I recognize the handwriting, of course, I sometimes have a peep, especially in respect of her mother who used to write quite regularly when she was alive and from time to time say some unpleasant things about me, which I really needed to know about. I also tend to open any letters she gets from abroad as a Dutch man once tried to seduce her at a dental conference and still bothers her with his problems.

I have not shown your letter to her as I think it would upset her. I have hidden it in my desk drawer – where I keep my private collection of photographs and illustrations. I also put in there any other things that I think will cause distress to my dear Mary. It is, as you can imagine, quite full! I cut anything out of the newspapers that I think she should not see. Some things, like 9/11 for example, are gloated over by the media so extensively that it is impossible to avoid them. But I certainly try to keep from her anything unpleasant that has happened in the Putney area. And that keeps me quite busy enough! I have, for example, removed all the photographs of Elaine's second boyfriend from the family album and kept them in there. Chris was a very disturbed boy indeed. I liked him a lot, actually, and offered to take him sailing on several occasions; but although he was a fit young lad with a good physique, I could not interest him in a life on the ocean wave. He was not a good partner for Elaine. Cutting up her underclothes was not, as he seemed to think it was, a way of getting her to love him!

May I say this, Barbara? Mary and I have a good marriage. It is based on mutual respect. Mary has her painting and her writing and her dance and, of course, her acting. I am sure, as a published author, you found much to criticize in the production of *Hamlet*. It is a very long play and not always easy to understand, but I have to say I thought Mary was superb. Seeing her naked was a little shocking. It is not a sight with which I am overly familiar. Marriage is about a lot more than nudity. But I thought it was obviously necessary for the production in order to show the desperation of the characters and their need to display their love in public. Not a thing I approve of – but, then, these people are theatrical types.

You were cruel about it, Barbara. It is never necessary to be cruel. Sometimes as a dentist I have to inflict pain. I do not enjoy it and wherever possible I try to avoid doing so.

While we are on that subject, I thought your remarks about myself and little Micky Larner were ill judged in the extreme. I am, as I am sure you know, a man's man. I am not the type of chap who brings Mary red roses or hauls her off to the opera. I am the kind of guy who gets a kick out of large blokes kicking hell out of each other on the rugby field. I like to be among men, Barbara, especially at the weekend. Yes – Micky has become a pal of mine. I took him over to Cherbourg on the *Jolly Roger* the other weekend and we had a whale of a time! But to make the kind of sneering remark you did about two happily married men, especially when one of them had a wife who died in tragic circumstances ten years ago, was tasteless and unnecessary. My marriage is very important to me. Some of my happiest times have been spent sitting by the fire with Mary, holding hands and talking about our dear Elaine – who is the centre of our world even if she has got mixed up with one of the Mad Mullahs.

Mary is, like Micky, my pal. In fact, when we first met, before we met any of the West Putney Highbrow Set, as I call you lot, she was very much one of the boys. She loved to watch us row and often joined us big, hearty masculine blokes as we nipped into the Duke's Head by Putney Bridge after practice to 'put back the sweat', as we say. I think what I liked about her was her delicate femininity. She is like some Greek statue that I worship from afar, even if I am only in the next room. Back in the day, she came to watch the guys arm-wrestling, putting the shot, boxing and cage-fighting, which we did quite a lot of, and I was known as Mad Mick, although that is not my name. She was known, in the long ago, as 'Flower' among us lads.

Motherhood changed her. I have, at times, been slightly shocked by the sheer force of the femininity I seem to have aroused in her. With her floral dresses and her lovely lilting laugh and her wonderfully prominent bosoms, she is all woman. There is now no trace of the delicate creature

I remember watching me as I chucked up in the alley next to the Spotted Cow after six pints of Young's Extra Strong Lager. You never knew her, Barbara. I did, and she still has a special place in my heart. Yes, I do miss the Judy Garland grace of her as us boys lounged around lighting our own farts, smoking small cigars and trying to throw knives blindfolded. But people change, for God's sake. It sounds as if you have not. You are bitter, Barbara. All those years ago I know you looked down on me, the humble dentist, while you were up there with Jeffrey Archer and Antonia Drabble and that bloke who writes about the Lake District and used to be on the television.

Love is not a free ticket, Barbara. Love is the light that draws us on through the immense tunnel that leads from the cradle to the grave. Love is tough, and we have to be tough to reap its rewards. You have given up on things and that is not good. You have given up on your husband, John, who is a marvellous bloke and a first-class doctor. Most sadly of all, you have given up on those boys of yours. They are wonderful young men, Babs. I have not seen them for nigh on twenty years but I know, from your description of them, jaded as it is, that they are the kind of blokes I would be glad to count as friends. How I long to play a game of footie with them out on a muddy field and then, in the light of a winter afternoon, with thighs and shoulders aching from the contact, hearts lifted in victory or lowered in defeat, to walk, as pals, arm in arm, to the pavvy and to joke with each other in the steam of the showers, as we towel down, totally and naturally naked by the grey lockers and wooden benches that stand, like sentinels, on guard over the joyous, sacred, intimate moments of a man's life. No, Barbara, don't sneer because sneering does not become you! Learn to trust. Learn to give. Learn a bit of humility, damn it!

And do not give up on Jas and Josh. They need your love. They need John's love. They need my love, for God's sake. Do say to them that if they ever fancy going out on the water, the *Jolly Roger* is at their disposal!

Harsh words I know – but this needed saying.


Sam Dimmock



From:
Mary 'Only the Wife Not on the Notepaper' Dimmock
But still care of
Samuel Dimmock
Dimmock Dentistry
'Because Teeth Matter'
24 Beeston Crescent
Putney
30 October

To:
Barbara Goldsmith
101 Fellen Road,
Putney


Dear Barbara and John,
I am writing to you both, although Barbara wrote her 'letter' to me and to Sam separately. I don't believe in trying to split off married couples, which is clearly what Barbara is trying to do. It gave me especial pleasure to write DR and MRS JOHN GOLDSMITH, which was what we always used to write in the old days when letters were addressed correctly and people could spell and didn't use the Internet all the time and Google, which tells you

everything, though you never remember it afterwards, like Chinese food making you hungry an hour after you have eaten it.

You are a 'married couple', whether you like it or not, Barbara. You are a team.

The whole point of marriage is that you know everything about the other person even the things they do not want you to know. Sam took the letter addressed to me by Barbara and hid it in a special drawer where he keeps things he thinks I shouldn't know about, including a magazine of his called *Men in Thongs*, which, as you might guess, is a magazine with a lot of pictures of men in thongs in it.

It may be that Sam is a homosexual. I have often thought so over the years. But I just cannot see it somehow. If being interested in naked men makes you a homosexual, then what of Leonardo da Vinci or Michelangelo? I am pretty sure one of them was interested in naked men. Whichever one it was did that statue in St Peter's, didn't he? That was pretty naked. For God's sake! I like looking at pictures of naked men and I am not a homosexual. Sam is just a guy who likes extreme sport and he keeps plenty of things in that drawer apart from pictures of naked men. There are a lot of pictures of boys on cross-country runs, for example, all of whom are fully clothed, also – is this a sign that he is 'gay'? – many of the rejection letters sent to me, which he has very sweetly intercepted. For the last few years I have been writing a book about a frog that accidentally gets on the Eurostar to Brussels. It is a comedy.

I have occasionally sent out selected chapters to publishers who, I think, might have the courage to get behind it. It is at least 100,000 words long and still growing! I must say I had been puzzled as to why I had not received any response to the many letters I had sent out, but when I saw the answers that dear, dear Sam had hidden from me, I was very glad I had been kept in the dark. 'Predictable', 'coy', 'badly written', and many other hurtful things. One letter simply read, 'Dear Mrs Dimmock, We do not want any more books about frogs.' And that was it! Is that literary criticism? I don't think so.

Sam keeps many hurtful things from me. I didn't find out about the tragic events at the World Trade Center until three o'clock on the following afternoon, and I did not realize Diana, Princess of Wales, was dead for three days! Mind you, I think he was helped there by the fact that I went in for an appendectomy almost at the very moment her car collided with that underpass wall in Paris.

He wants me to be happy, Babs. To be the happy, happy girl who ran and played with you and the children in those villas in France, Spain, Italy and Brittany, which is in France although it isn't quite the same, is it? Do you remember how Elaine and Conrad painted Jas and Josh green? Wasn't it fun? And now they are management consultants and GPs (yes, Elaine is a highly successful GP!!!) and high-powered sales people.

And yet – and this is what I think you are saying in your often very hurtful and cruel letter – things are not really as they should be. There is a lot of pain and misery behind the net curtains. I know nobody has net curtains any more but people still write as if they do, don't they? You are clearly not a happy woman and I, though I love and respect my husband more than you obviously do John – I cannot understand how you can so underestimate a man who is so widely regarded, locally, as a saint – I am, also, still not contented and fulfilled. I do not seem to find my child as offensive as you clearly find your two boys but I do wish Elaine would find the right man. She was involved with a not-very-nice Spanish sociologist, who stole some of her furniture and then wrote her a horrible letter about it. I could not find it in my heart to weep for him when he was electrocuted on holiday in the Costa Brava. Mercifully Elaine was not with him at the time. She is now with a very nice (Pakistani) man called Hanif but I feel things between them are not as they should be.

And Sam and I, Babs, have come to the end of the road.

As you were so frank with me I will be equally frank with you. I have had an affair with Gerald Price. I expect you will be a bit surprised by that. I think you always rather liked the look of him yourself – but it was me he chose, Barbara, even though I have not published eight (or is it nine?) 'highly praised' novels. I found them all unreadable, actually. They have none of the narrative sweep of Margaret Drabble or Melvyn Bragg. He found me sexually very desirable and I felt the same about him. Gerald Price, that is – not Melvyn Bragg. However loud my laugh and however 'fat' (your word) my body. We had sex in the open air many, many times – which might also surprise you. Not bad for a fat woman with a loud laugh, eh? I have already told your husband and, actually, he has been very helpful about it. I have also told Sam – as the affair has now ended and we are remaking our lives. Things are changing. Sam wants to be alone. I, too, need to be alone. Although I am not fully alone . . . Intrigued, Barbara?

But I do not write in order to be bitchy and gloat about my sexual success with a man you clearly fancied. I will leave that to you. I write to let you know that, ironically, I rather agree with the conclusions of your letter. It is time for a change in Putney and, unlike you, Babs, I have actually made some big, big changes in my life, fat or not.

Gerald, as you probably do not know, since you and he never really got beyond the stage of you ogling him, is a very dark character indeed. I believe him to be, possibly, a murderer and he is certainly violent towards women – and to me in particular. I have also been attacked by someone I think may have been his wife – hence the bruising commented on by you, which was not in any way part of my makeup but the product of several frightening and potentially life-threatening attacks perpetrated on me during the autumn, which are being investigated, as I write, by a fully trained and qualified private eye, who was the one in the jodhpurs playing Horatio.

Sneer away, Barbara. He is the man I love. Roland O. Gibbons. It is an anagram of Orlando Gibbons, the Jacobean composer, after whom he was named and he changed it because he felt embarrassed by the *soubriquette*, if that is the right word, and if it isn't, I am sure you will let me know by return post. He is multi-talented but not musical. Yes. The man I love – although you do not seem to know the meaning of the word.

Sam does not know yet but I am being completely open with everyone else so he will find out very soon. I don't think he would pay much attention even if he walked in on me and Roland actually doing it. All Sam can talk about these days is his new 'pal' Micky Larner, whom he is teaching to sail. He says he is a very willing and talented pupil.

Roland (or Orlando, as I like to call him) is inclined to corpulence, too, and our relationship began when we both discovered we had been to WeightWatchers. I first got to know him when he came to our surgery. You find out a lot about people when they are sitting in the dentist's chair. I am not talking about their susceptibility to pain, though that may be part of it, but – it is what interests me about the job – you have the chance to watch someone very intensely, at close quarters, without their being aware of you. A good dental nurse is like a good waiter – almost invisible. The moment

I like is when Sam is busying himself about the surgery and the patient is sitting back, staring at the ceiling, waiting for him to start work.

At first I didn't really like Orlando. When he was sitting in the chair his eyes never stopped moving. Most people waiting for the dentist to begin do not seem to be looking or, at least, do not seem to be seeing what they are looking at. Mr Gibbons, as, of course, I called him then, flicked his gaze this way and that, like a bird looking for worms. It was as if he was expecting some predator to leap out at him from behind one of the gleaming white cupboards, but he did not seem to be afraid. He just looked as if there was some secret in our rather ordinary little room, and he wanted to uncover it, even if there were people determined to stop him doing so.

I found it very unsettling. There was one occasion, when I had sex with Gerald while Sam was watching the Sailing Channel, during which I could have sworn Orlando had crept into the waiting room and was listening. Now, of course, I know that was not the case, but at the time I thought he might be an undercover policeman investigating the murder of Pamela Larner. As I am sure you know, Babs, being a real gossip, many people are now saying that Pamela Larner was murdered. Yes, murdered. I can't say whom we suspect, of course, but it is almost certainly Gerald Price. He was having an affair with her as well! Really, it seems you were about the only person on those villa parties that he didn't 'pork'. Too classy, I suspect. Old slappers like me and Pam were a snack before dinner for him. Excuse the vulgarity of my turn of phrase but I have become a much freer person of late, due to the open-air sex, I think.

Orlando will shoot me for saying all this. The murder business is supposed to be totally confidential. But people do talk, don't they? You cannot stop them. And I've said it, so there. And, really, after working with and sleeping with Gerald Price for two or three months I have to say I think he is a really unpleasant person. He is constantly moving downstage of you when you have a big speech and waggling his bottom at the audience in order to get the attention. He is more than capable of murder. The German accent – something to do with Hamlet having been at university in Wittenberg, I think – was frankly ludicrous, wasn't it?

Where was I? Oh, yes, Orlando, as I now know him.

Well, I think on his third visit Sam said to him something about Twix bars. It was a dental point. As it is usually is with Sam. And Orlando said, in a tone I recognized, 'Ah – I save my points!' To which I responded, in a flash, 'Four Plus Points in a finger of Twix!' Anyone who has ever been to a WeightWatchers' meeting and spent a few happy hours debating how many calories there are in a slice of lean bacon will understand. He shot me a quick look of sympathy (Sam was totally oblivious, of course) and later, as I was sorting out his bill, he suggested we meet for lunch in a very 'points friendly' spot called the Fish and Grill in the Lower Richmond Road.

That was quite a lunch, Babs.

'Shall we start with a few langoustines?' he said. We were sitting out on the pavement in the late-autumn sunshine and it felt as if we were in France. Quite a few of the lorries that roared past us up the Putney Bridge Road were actually French; and although the waiter was Polish, he had recently worked in France. So I felt quite *sur le tapis* (if that is the right phrase). We discussed, at some length, the amount of Plus Points there were in the average langoustine (they do vary in size quite a lot), and when the waiter insisted on offering us both mayonnaise, we smiled very politely and told him we were on a diet. After we had finished the langoustines, Orlando said, 'Will that be all we're having?' I must have looked a bit doubtful because he went on to say, 'Oysters?' I said I loved oysters, which I do, and we discussed whether to have them raw or cooked. We both agreed that if they were cooked they were sometimes wrapped in batter as opposed to Oysters Rockefeller, which is when they are fried with spinach, which is delicious but not as delicious as with batter, like the Chinese do, and that batter obviously made them more fattening but we both agreed that we much preferred oysters deep fried in batter and the Chinese are not a particularly fat people, so we ordered twelve. And then we ordered another twelve.

I think the moment when we first realized we had bonded in a really intense and serious way was when we had finished the oysters and decided to order just a small crab – well, two, actually – and Orlando said, 'Shall we have some mayonnaise with that?' I laughed in a manner I am sure you might have thought offensive, Babs, and said, 'Mayonnaise! Why not?'

We both realized we had broken through to yet another level when we agreed we needed a bottle of Sancerre with the crab. We had, up to that point, been drinking mineral water. Sancerre is a very variable wine, isn't it? Like Chablis, the name covers a multitude of sins. Saying you've just drunk a glass of Sancerre is like saying you've just met a girl. What kind of girl? Where is she from? What kind of Sancerre? Who made it and how? We ordered a bottle of Sancerre from a producer called Guy Louis who, Orlando said, was a very fine maker of very fine wines. That made us both laugh and we drank it very quickly. We then had a bottle of Macon Villages to finish off the crab, and then I said, 'Do you like turbot?' It turned out Orlando *loves* turbot. So we each had a grilled turbot, and, although we had decided not to order chips, we ordered chips.

Spinach and chips are a good combination, aren't they? We polished off the turbot fairly quickly and found we were ordering a *fritto misto di mare* with some fennel as a side dish, which we thought would be enough but seemed to provoke a need for a meat course and it turned out they did meat as well so we had two T-bone steaks with some mashed potatoes and buttered cabbage, which we washed down with a really very good Malbec.

Orlando had been writing something as we got through the steak and when I asked him what it was he said he had been working out the Plus Points for the meal so far. He said he thought it came to over half a million, and I said that couldn't be right so I added it up and it came to over two thousand, which just set us both laughing like idiots. So we had to have pudding, of course, which we did, and when we had each had our puddings (two each) and a bottle of Beaumes de Venise we went back to Orlando's flat in Keswick Road and had sex. We had a lot of sex but I don't want to talk about it, as it was private and personal and very beautiful. I will say, though, that he is a better-endowed man than the Butch Barrister – as I know you all called Gerry – and he brought me to a pitch of ecstasy that I had never previously experienced. In fact, at one point his neighbour started banging on the wall. Stupid woman! She is Vietnamese apparently.

Yes, Babs, things are changing in Putney. I am going to tell Sam about me and Orlando very soon and we will probably separate. I think Elaine will understand. What I am writing to say is that I do not think you and John have reached the point yet where you should part. I think if you were nicer to him, indeed, if you were a nicer person, Babs, which seems unlikely but must be possible, you could have quite a decent marriage.

I do wish you all the best,

from the Fat Woman with the Annoying Laugh
Mary Dimmock-Weston

From:
Dr John Goldsmith MRCGP, DRCOG
101 Fellen Road
Putney
30 October

To:
His Bitch of a Wife
At the Same Address
Unfortunately

Dear Barbara,

I always knew the end for us would come when we started writing notes to each other. So, I suppose this is the end. You've added an extra twist by publicizing our marital difficulties to a group of people I had rather hoped never to see again. The friends you make when your children are small have a special quality, don't you think? And they go sour so painfully. They remind you of the time when parenthood was such a passionate, simple joy. A time I am reliving with Jas and Josh's beautiful children, to whose names I am now almost accustomed.

We will get on to Jas and Josh. Oh, you bitch, Barbara – you absolutely hateful bitch!

But I suppose you wanted to trash that, along with everything else we have shared over the last thirty or forty years. You have always liked parading your opinions and have made a habit of publishing novels in order to do so. They certainly weren't about the story, were they? It was always the same story. Woman shags man and gets bored. Enough to get you talked of for the Orange Prize several times, I'm sure, but not, for me, a really satisfying reworking of the world in which we live. I don't think I ever quite forgave you for the character called Gordon, a stressed GP with 'a fine profile and limited intelligence', who cropped up in *The Day Kate Walked Out*. You could have changed the colour of his fucking hair. I remember asking you if he *had* to have 'late-flowering blond curls that made him look a little like Grabber, the Head Prefect and Star Athlete in the Molesworth books'.

'That,' you replied, 'is just the way the character is!'

Is it, Barbara? It is roughly the way *I* am, on superficial inspection anyway. It certainly allowed our friends to ask, coyly, whether the novel was autobiographical and for you to answer airily, 'Oh, no – fiction isn't like that!' Well, your kind of fiction is, darling. It certainly isn't *Anna* fucking *Karenina*, is it? It is, like most of those other novels you like or don't like, simply a chunk of Higher Gossip for the Middle Classes. Or your particular bit of them.

You did it because it made you feel superior. You like feeling superior to people. It is why you write novels and appear on television and get your name in the papers. Oh, the horrible sham modesty you put on when they mention your birthday in *The Times*. I really thought I would throw up when you bothered to pretend it irritated you last year. I live with you, Barbara. I could see the smirk on your cat-like face.

What makes it all the more horrible, of course, is the fact that I love you. I have always loved you. Ever since I first saw you at that party of Gerry Price's all those years ago, before any of our children were born. When Gerald was a halfway decent human being. Do you remember? We had a small flat in Heathland Avenue and I had met Gerald in a pub up near there. We talked about sport. We talked, enthusiastically, about our wives. I think I thought I liked him. And then there you were, across the other side of the room, and you had known him since Oxford, it seemed. Back in those days, before we had all blended into the suburb of our choice, you both seemed to me impossibly glamorous. You talked about parties on the river and the wonderful light in the quad at Christchurch. The only quads at the hospital where I trained were associated with the obstetrics department.

I thought, at first, that the differences between us were political. You got very excited about the women at Greenham Common. Excited enough to go there for a day. Not excited enough to live in one of those *yurts* or whatever it was they built to show the power of ordinary lesbians to influence the largest military nation on the planet. But excited enough to go for a day and make me feel guilty about it. When the kids were born you were one of those women who stood outside Mothercare (remember Mothercare, Barbara?) and shouted, 'Mothercare out! Fathercare in!' A little later you graduated quickly from mother-and-baby groups to what I called disenchanted mothers' groups but which weren't that at all. They were actually celebrations of female power; as if, among the English suburban middle classes there had ever been any doubt that women were in control of everything. They were all about empowering women, letting women ramble on about how terrible their husbands were – something you're still good at – and how your feelings were constantly being thwarted by our refusal to communicate. Well, Barbara, I was a little bit busy. I was sitting at a desk, trying to help people with cancer and heart disease. It wasn't all tennis, although, from the way you carried on, you would have thought it was.

I don't think, though, that politics was the real quarrel between us. I think it was that you never thought I was good enough for you. A feeling made even more intense when you started to become a novelist and a TV personality – but one that had begun a long way back. Do you know? I often thought you had always been in love with someone else. God knows who. Yourself most likely. You do say in your letter that there was one person with whom you 'managed to forget yourself' but, you do not mention his (or her) name. Perhaps you were talking about your adolescence, when sexual attraction made almost all of us feel like that. Or perhaps – the thought has only just occurred to me but I have a horrible feeling it may be true – that was a lie. Just another fiction you made up to hurt me. Because you can't really feel anything at all, can you? You can't even love your children.

For a while I thought if there was anyone you really loved it might have been your father, that most elegant of estate agents, whose speech at our wedding still remains, for me, a masterpiece of the calculated insult. He managed to stay just inside the limits, didn't he?

'We have had a lot of problems with John's skiing!' he began – well, he had won medals for bloody skiing. 'But we are gradually getting him in order! We have had problems with his time-keeping and his handwriting, a doctor's privilege, and if any of us is ill he has promised not to try to look after us!' So your hoary old jokes about medicine and me are really a re-run of Elliot's wedding speech. I remember at the end he seemed to be threatening me physically if I ever dared to look at another woman.

And, yes, I have done that. There is simply no more to say on that subject. I'm sorry. I don't think any man on the planet has apologized for a single marital indiscretion as much as I have. It wasn't an apology, Barbara. It was ten years of crawling round the kitchen on my hands and knees. I'm sure you're telling the truth when you say you've never looked at another man all the years of our married life but then, by your own analysis, I am the most dumb, unobservant, emotionally stunted creep who ever crawled out of medical school so how would I ever have noticed if you *had* cheated on me? You could probably have fucked half of Putney and I would still have been so busy apologizing I wouldn't have noticed.

As for Jas and Josh – I don't know what to say, but I will say it.

You were always jealous of my relationship with them. You resented the fact that you had never given birth to a girl. That was my fault too, of course. A chance to publicly criticize my sperm! A chance you took with great enthusiasm. 'All John ever wanted was a football team!' was your line, and I was supposed to look rueful and apologetic over having produced two strong, good-looking boys, who were not unlike me. If you had ever really bothered to notice them, instead of simply calibrating how far they conformed to your negative view of males in general, you might have noticed that they are a couple of intelligent, reasonably sensitive, hard-working young men, who occasionally make farting jokes. For God's sake, Barbara!

Images from our married life keep coming back to me. You lying in bed with Jas in that hospital, looking up at me as you held him in your arms and saying, in such a sweet, unabrasive voice, 'What shall we call him?' You and I stepping out on the dance floor at our twentieth wedding anniversary, held in the tennis club because I am a conventional man and do things like that. You and I kissing in the back of that MG I had, on a summer night, down by the river. You and I sitting by your mother's bed in the hospice as she looked at us, so pale and wan, and held my hand and thanked me for taking care of you. What would she say if she could see us now? How has this happened so quickly?

All these once precious images now seem sinister and unreal. It is as if I merely dreamed them. As if they were some trick played on me by my own sentimentality. I am, of course, a sentimental person. You always told me I was full of false feeling. The fact that I imagined my emotions were real was of no account. And now, of course, you are proved right and I am proved utterly, utterly wrong about what I thought and felt. A ludicrous middle-class stereotype (rather like your picture of me in that awful novel), who doesn't really have an independent existence of his own. Who was wrong, wrong, wrong about politics, about class, about his chosen profession and, most especially, about the woman he thought he loved and who, he was foolish enough to imagine, loved him.

You always called my job, with that slight sneer you do so well, one of the 'caring professions', putting inverted commas round those words as if to make it clear that nobody ever really cares about anyone else, least of all the people who say they do. Heroism and decency are not options for the human race. At least, not in a comfortable middle-class suburb. So you, who have a comfortable position in what I might call one of the 'uncaring professions', felt justified in being totally and utterly selfish. Because that was how we all were. Really.

I don't believe people are like that. I believe the large mass of people are decent, caring individuals who want to help others. I have spent much of my life trying to help people who are afraid or in pain. I am not under any illusions about why I do what I do. I am sure it is as self-interested as the pursuit of women or money or power. There is, of course, a great deal of rational selfishness about the quest to be good. It makes it much less likely that people will be nasty to you for a start. It has worked that way for me throughout much of my life. But it does not seem to have been much of a success as far as my wife is concerned.

What is really going on, Barbara? Are you having a nervous breakdown? Are you having an affair with someone? And, if so, can I be allowed to know who it is? I might, then, be able to make a more coherent defence of my position than this letter, which, now I have read through it, sounds rather pathetic. The work of a man whose 'major speciality is reassurance' but can't quite manage to reassure himself. Who is 'very good indeed at convincing people there is nothing wrong with them' but not quite good enough at convincing himself he is an adequate human being. Who, even in the profession he loves and worked so hard to join, is 'almost bound to be wrong'.

I don't think I can bear to be in the same house as you. I am going to stay with one of the boys. We can all cock our legs up and make farting noises.

John


From:
Hell
Gerry
Writing this by hand on
30 October at 9 p.m.

To:

Darling Barbara,
I am writing this in my car. I am parked about twenty-five yards down the street from you.

If I had the nerve I would get out my cock and trace its outline on this piece of paper, like that convict did in the Genet novel when writing to his boyfriend back home. If

164

it would fit on the paper. Ha ha ha ha. Such a funny guy, Gerry. Always full of laughs. Really good down the pub. Doesn't funk his tackles. Tough guy. 'Hello, mate!' That's me! Big bloke. Not afraid of anything. Fantastically big penis. Yowzers! Girls? Shagged them all. Look, mate. Look! I mean...look!

And what a chopper on him. Practically smoking with suppressed power. Betcha he fishes it out right now and amazes the neighbours. Just the kind of thing old Gezza would do, eh? His todger's knocking at the old denim trousers like the NKVD making a midnight call in 1930s Russia. That's the general idea with Gerald. The Beastly Barrister, or whatever they call me.

Except, of course, that isn't me. You know that. I know that. But no one else knows that. Which is why I love you. Have always loved you. Have loved you since the first day I saw you walking across the Oriel quad on your way to see some other lucky bastard. Your dress was only just below your crotch and your black hair was halfway down your back and, yes, you did actually have flowers in it. Because it was 1968 and people did things like that then. Not me, I hasten to say. But I rather liked people who did. I was always the unstraight straight man. The buttoned-down lawyer with a crazy hooligan locked up inside him.

I loved you but I did nothing about it. There was nothing to be done. I can't remember who you were with then. Some idiot in a kaftan, I think. People did wear such things in 1968. Dominic Barker-Wentworth did. Of course I knew his name. I know the name of every man who has ever touched you or tried to touch you. Which, taken together, probably amounts to about half the population of Wiltshire. But I love you more than all or any of them. I love you as salt loves meat. I love you as the river loves the sea. I love you as F sharp loves G major. I love you as water loves whisky and gin loves tonic and the French love abstract nouns. I love you the way flowers love the rain, Welshmen singing and sailors a following wind.

Some people, Barbara, see me as a crude person. They can go and fuck themselves up the arsehole with a baseball bat, as far as I'm concerned. There is a great delicacy in me, Barbara. There fucking is.

No one has a clue about us, do they? I don't think my delicacy has ever been so beautifully expressed as in the way I have concealed our affair from the prying eyes of the women of Putney. I have done such a good job that there have been times when I have wondered whether we were actually having an affair. I have done such a good job on my own memories of the times we have made love – which have been so few and so hedged about with difficult circumstances – that I can't remember now whether we actually kissed in that ridiculous summerhouse in the garden of the villa in Corsica or whether I did agree to meet you by the bus stop opposite the old Putney Hospital and waited for an hour in the rain but still you did not come.

What I really remember is that first kiss. That one kiss.

Yes. 'Affair' suggests all the things people usually associate with Gerald Price, i.e. being wanked off in the back of a hired car on the way to St-Martin-sous-le-Bois. We didn't actually do that. I mean, I know we didn't do that. Which isn't to say I haven't often fantasized about our doing it but, unusually for Gerry, I had the delicacy, with you, not to suggest it at an inappropriate moment simply because it had always been something I would have liked to achieve. All that being said because, although there is great delicacy in me, Barbara, waiting to emerge from fifteen and a half stone of muscle and this neck that I have not been able to move since my last rugby injury, I do, from time to time, find myself entertained by the image of you folding your fingers neatly over my cock, pulling it with the skill of a housewife polishing a kitchen table until my sperm jets out of the vas deferens, heads for the steering wheel and, perhaps, oops, my white linen trousers, which, as you may remember, I wore almost every day in that ghastly place in Brittany.

Am I being crude? Me? Gerald Price? Gerry fucking Price crude? Carm off of it. I should fucking coco.

Behind these cold, narrow, heartless eyes, which have been telling whoppers for profit ever since the day I was called to the bar, there is a soul that only you have seen. Fuck off, you know you have. Inside, I am a thing of gossamer, old bean, as finely spun as sugar in the hands of Raymond Blanc, as yielding as the grass in a Japanese movie.

Perhaps.

If there is an ounce of sensitivity in me, you are the only one to know it, Barbara.

Although – since we are being honest here – let us admit that Elizabeth knows it. She knows it and she uses it against me. Which you don't. You understand me completely. You are the only person who has ever done so. With you, I am not the person the world knows as Gerald Price QC. Thanks be to God! He is an appalling person. I don't want to be him any more.

If we had decided not to be delicate, I suppose I might, just possibly, have fucked you from behind in those woods behind Santa Maria della Rucola – or whatever the place was called. I might, in this alternative world in which we had the courage of our convictions, have ground my knees into the pine needles, with my trousers rucked up round my shoes, and, mesmerized by the one really dirty bit of you, poked at your extraordinary arse like a conductor in the middle of the slow movement of Bruckner's Fourth. Which, of course, I never did. I am not sure, even, that there were any pine trees near Santa Maria della Rucola or that, during that holiday, or, indeed, any of the others, you and I ever did anything but look at each other in that dangerous way people do when they want something from one another that isn't friendship or hatred, exactly, and yet has a little in common with both of those things, that is need, probably, of a kind neither of them really understands and don't, in one sense, want, but cannot do without.

We didn't do any of those things because we knew the damage it would cause. We both wanted to but we didn't. Not in forty-odd years, Barbara. Not really. Which is why that one kiss seems to mean so much. Of course, I hear you say, there were a lot of other things as well; and I suppose you could say that there were. I see I used the words 'made love' back there and that is as good a way as any other to describe what has been going on between us for the last forty years.

Yes, there was more than one kiss. But there is only that one kiss that I remember. That's it. And it was as if, with that kiss, we had both admitted how much we needed each other. And how much that scared us. Maybe that was it. Maybe we've just been frightened all this time.

So – were we being moral? Is that it? I'm not sure. I was – I still am – terrified of Elizabeth. Her virtue scares the pants off me. She is like the RSM at my old public school urging me over the assault course. 'Come on, Price! Go! Go! Go!' There are things I feel guilty about – such as the children. Of which, more later. Yet I am not entirely sure that we acted the way we did out of morality or respect for the other people in our lives. There are few things more curious than you

168

and me, Barbara, apart, of course, from every other fucked-up relationship between human beings on this planet. It is a story of abstinence and indulgence that makes Jane Austen seem extreme.

Do you remember that conversation we had in the Duke's Head by Putney Bridge, just before the whole team shipped out for Corsica? A risky place to meet, of course, but we were good at that. If anyone had come in we would have had our stories straight. We were just a mummy and a daddy from St Jude's discussing the sponsored cycle ride or the school quiz night or – even better – hey, we'd just run into each other as you do if you've lived in the same suburb for twenty or thirty years.

It seemed to me, at the time, that that was when we said our goodbyes. It wasn't, of course. We had more farewells than an elderly diva. But I think of it as our last meeting because it was the moment when we realized how much we loved each other and how we didn't want to become another of those couples who met furtively, for a while, and then parted because what they were doing made them feel dirty and ashamed. We did not want to be the kind of illicit couple who drop the kids at judo with the perverted Mr Wallington and then sprint back to whoever's house is empty to screw on the carpet just before the retreat home in all innocence for tea with the children and a drink with the wife and the nightly tussle over the TV remote.

We were sitting at a table by the window. It was, as it is now, late autumn. We looked out at Putney Pier and Putney Bridge, with the fancy lamps and big red buses stuck on its slow curve as the whorls of water on the dark Thames were sucked east to Vauxhall and Tower Bridge, Rotherhithe and Deptford and, beyond, Gravesend and the wide, bird-haunted estuary.

You reached over to the table next to us to take a pack of cigarettes that was lying there and I think I said, 'Are those yours?' You blushed violently and said, 'I don't believe they are. I think they belong to that man who just went to the bar. I'm always picking up things that aren't mine.' And I said, 'Like me, eh?' You looked at me for a long time with those big black eyes of yours and I remember, as always, being fascinated by your white, freckled, not quite tomboy skin, more like some brindled cat slinking in from the street to do the house no good. I shiver now, as I realize that we did not do what I now can see was the right thing. We did not up and run from this stupid suburban shit – the dinner parties and the wedding parties and the children's marriages, stretching ahead of us, like grim carnivals in praise of death, lining a long, dark street, leading nowhere. We should have walked out of both our lives that afternoon, Barbara. We should have made a break for it. Gone somewhere where no one knew us or our all too familiar history.

But we did not. And it was on that Corsica trip that Pamela Larner happened.

You, of course, were the only one who suspected anything. Well, let's say you'd spotted that I fancied her. You were the only one I was afraid would find out, but I'm fairly sure we managed to fool you as well as everyone else. We were very careful in Corsica. There was one afternoon when everyone apart from Pamela and I went to the beach. She – if you remember – had a migraine. She had a lot of tactical migraines, did Pamela. That afternoon was a very quick fuck. I do remember she smelt of cheap shampoo and musk – a common sort of smell, mixed with scents I still don't recognize even though I like to write down the words that might represent them – sandalwood, spikenard. She made little mewing noises, like a cat. She didn't reach orgasm. She never did. Like a lot of people who have sex with a lot of people I don't think she enjoyed it much; but the early stages were always entertaining.

The serious screwing only really got started when we were back in Putney. That was how, I think, Elizabeth began to suspect something. There were afternoons at her house when Mike was away on location, stalking stickleback. Or was it gudgeon? There was an elaborately set-up weekend away in a Hampshire hotel. There was an awful lot of fucking in almost every position from the *Gourmet Guide to Sex* but there wasn't much conversation and there certainly wasn't any love – not as I understand the word. I don't think Pamela had any idea what 'love' meant. It was just another thing women were supposed to be good at – like hair care or flower arranging.

I heard she had died but I never went near the funeral. It was like she had just disappeared, like someone in Pinochet's Chile or Stalin's Russia. It was only recently I found out that Mike Larner seems to think she was murdered. I don't think that's very likely. She was exactly the sort of person who commits suicide, and that seems to have been the verdict in the case, but people in Putney will gossip about each other. I even heard, from a source I don't think I want to reveal, that Larner is saying he thinks I did it!

I didn't, Barbara. I have done many appalling things in my life but murder does not happen to be one of them. There were many times when I felt like strangling Pamela Larner. There was a moment when I dropped in on her at a time when I knew no one else was at home and she looked at me, put her pointy little head on one side and said, with a sort of triumphal negativity, 'You want sex, don't you?' On that occasion I could have fastened my hands round her throat and squeezed until her blue eyes popped out on stalks and that cheeky schoolgirl tongue swivelled its way out of her dry little lips and lolled, for the first time in genuine abandon, across her elfin little chin.

But I didn't.

Jesus – maybe Elizabeth killed her. I think Elizabeth would cheerfully have strangled her even if she hadn't found out we were having an affair. Or, rather, had been able to prove it. She never spoke about it to me, but she had many motives for doing away with the 'Mother of Four', as she always called Pam. Her use of the word 'fantabulosa'. Her lip gloss. Her nail varnish. Her habit of telling us all that Molly (or was it Milly?) was a genius. And her unhealthy, all-encompassing love for the deeply sinister Barnaby.

Not that Elizabeth would have told me, even if she'd had photographic evidence to prove I was doing little Pamela. For the last ten years, Elizabeth and I have hardly spoken about anything except the whereabouts and general health, well or ill, of our children.

What's been haunting me about *la* Larner is that, as far as I could gather from a brief exchange of letters I had with Mike, who seems fairly well on the way to being clinically insane, Pamela died of what looked like an overdose of sleeping tablets on an evening in early November. Around the time I finally dumped her. Maybe that pushed her over the edge. I don't know. I don't really want to know.

I think, in her own limited way, Pamela was in love with me. She wasn't very keen on my ending it. I had tried before, but however many times I said, 'I don't want to go on with this!' she still did not seem to grasp the meaning of the words. They became, as the row developed, even simpler and more direct: 'I have had enough'; 'I fucking hate you'; 'I am bored out of my mind with you'; 'I wish you were dead.' And so on. She still did not get it.

Whatever you may think of my Hamlet, and I know there are some who found it 'a unique blend of the wooden and the melodramatic', to use Elizabeth's words, I think I have something of a way with the theatrical gesture. It's part of being a barrister, a way of impressing the invisible jury that is never far from my left shoulder. I had brought along a cheap man-bracelet that Pam had given me as a joke on one of our villa holidays. It was supposed to look like something of an insult. 'This is for Macho Man!' she had squeaked, as she gave it to me at the dinner table. And – because she loved those little games – as something to 'throw people off the scent', I always felt *la* Larner enjoyed the deception more than the affair itself.

I pulled it out of my pocket at a crucial moment – I think I had found it at the back of a drawer some days earlier – and held it in front of her face. 'This,' I said, 'is about all I ever had from you. Cheap and tasteless. Like you. And that was what the whole affair was.' At which she grabbed it off me, walked to the french windows, opened them and hurled it out into the darkness. Sobbing as she did so. She, too, was fond of the theatrical gesture but I always felt hers were lower rent than mine. I remember thinking at the time, 'What happens if young Michael finds that on his lawn? Will it be a problem?' And then I realized I really didn't care if it alerted her fucking fish-film-director hubby to what was going on. I didn't care if she and her appalling husband rang Elizabeth and told her the whole story.

After that she stopped crying and did a bit of dignified acting. Never her strong point. 'You never loved me!'; 'I always knew you thought I was boring!'; 'You think I'm a stupid little hairdresser!' I said I was pretty much in agreement with the general drift of all those statements. I think, as I left, she was threatening suicide. She was always threatening suicide.

I think Mike once told me she had once swallowed a whole packet of aspirin. It turned out they were junior aspirin.

I expected a phone call the next morning. I expected a nasty letter at any time during the following week. I expected something. But nothing happened. I never heard from her again. I must admit that I couldn't believe my luck. I had got away scot-free. As the weeks turned to months and the months to years and I still didn't hear from her, I think I just assumed she, too, had decided to forget the whole thing. It was only later I heard she had died; and then, recently, I ran into old Norman Staines in the Green Man and heard this first talk of suspicious circumstances surrounding her death.

I only mention her now because, of course, the only reason I ever looked at her was because I couldn't have you. She was just someone I took up with in order to hurt you. When I got your letter I realized you, too, were beginning to regret what we never had the courage to do. Unless, of course, that mysterious person you dare to mention so openly in your letter wasn't me at all. Which I suppose may be a possibility. But I don't think it's a serious one.

We were both frightened by the intensity of it, Barbara, that was the truth. We couldn't handle all that wanting each other. We couldn't handle not being able to live with each other, so, of course, we decided to live without each other. Because that is how human beings behave. They are not rational in any degree, even though they like to pretend they are. They fall out of love with each other and decide to have a baby because perhaps the baby will bring them together. I think that was how poor invisible Julia got born – although both Elizabeth and I are far too clever to own up to doing such a thing. Two people fall in love, in a way in which neither has ever done before, in a way that makes each word or gesture or thought of the loved one the most wonderful and exquisite thing that either has ever seen, and what do they do? 'Stop it before something terrible happens.'

That terrible something has already happened, Barbara. It is why I am sitting in a car thirty yards from your house, feeling that the whole of the rest of my life is in jeopardy if you don't come out to me and tell me we'll be together for the rest of our lives.

I certainly do not want to be with Elizabeth any more. In fact, I can't think why it is I have spent so many years of my life with a woman I have never really loved. Unbelievable as it seems. It may be that when I walked down the aisle or, rather, shambled into the register office with her I genuinely deluded myself into thinking I was in love; but now I look back I cannot think I could possibly have been so stupid. I suppose, to be fair to my younger self, she had not yet done the things she was about to do over the next few decades. The same goes for her, of course. Age makes personality clearer and what she dislikes about late-middle-aged *moi* is, clearly, the melancholy, the self-obsession and the indifference to surroundings that she must have spotted at the Oriel summer ball in 1968 – about two months after I first saw you.

Why have I stayed with her for so long?

Fear. She is a very frightening woman. I was frightened of her bad temper. I was frightened of her constant disapproval. I was frightened by her astonishing ability to occupy the moral high ground. She even managed to make me think, for years, that she was always putting my interests first. She did this in a very simple manner. Every day, morning, afternoon and evening, she said, and sometimes screamed, 'I am putting your interests first!' She also followed a classically successful female strategy, that of staying so close to me for so long that I grew, inevitably, terrified of her possible absence.

Sex. She fooled me, somehow, into thinking I was having enough sex. I still do not know quite how she managed this.

Intellect. She spotted, quite early on, that the only sure way to my heart is to disagree with me. This she did, as a matter of principle, on almost every topic that came up between us. She also said, and sometimes screamed, every day, morning, afternoon and evening, 'I am an intellectual!' I have only just realized that she is, actually, not an intellectual at all. What she really likes are the carpets and the curtains, the lawn that I have to mow and the Aga that I have never really grown to like, and the holidays in France and Spain and Portugal where, unknown to her, I fell even more in love with her nemesis, i.e. you. She pretends to be an intellectual but, of course, no teacher has the time to be an intellectual. Elizabeth is 90 per cent housewife.

The children. Oh, God, the children. 'We stayed together because of the children'; 'We were driven apart by the children.' The children are the perfect expression of what we are. And of what we have failed to become.

You are the only one I have ever been able to talk to about my children. You are the only one who understands how I feel about them, and how passionately I want to be able to feel differently. I suspect all that stuff about Jas and Josh was there to make me see that. For you and me, only leaving will ever make us able to face up to what we feel – or do not feel – about them. And, perhaps, to do something about it.

Conrad took nearly twenty hours to get out of her womb. He has always been a cautious individual but on that occasion I really thought he might have decided to stay up there for good. When he finally emerged he was grey in colour and covered with the kind of hair you might see on the average house rat. 'There you are, Mr Price!' said the midwife. 'Another rugby player!' I took one look at him, gasping like a fish on Elizabeth's ribcage, and thought, No way! He has never shown any aptitude whatsoever for any kind of ball game.

What I didn't like about him was that he was there. He hadn't been there before. What the fuck was he doing there now? And what made it worse was that he didn't seem to want to be there either. He cried when he was hungry. He cried when you tried to feed him. He cried when he did it in his pants and he cried when you tried to take them off and he cried when you put on new ones. He screamed blue murder when he was trying to go to sleep and he screamed blue murder when he found he was awake again, although he hardly ever seemed to sleep for more than about three minutes every twenty-four hours.

This was the seventies, remember. We were all supposed to be New Men. We were supposed to sling babies round our necks and walk along like idiots with them bumping against our chests. We were supposed to go to natural-childbirth classes and push strained carrot into our toddlers' faces while looking as if we enjoyed doing something so moronically simple. I didn't. I'm sure John embraced it all with total fervour. I'm sure, from things you have said, that he cut you out of their lives as surely as Elizabeth cut me out of Conrad's.

I can remember, one night, having the little bastard spread out in front of me on a plastic mat. He was kicking his legs wildly as yet more yellow stuff oozed out of his arse and all over my fucking hands.

'Listen, you little bastard!' I said, pinning him down with slightly more force than was necessary. 'Fuck off, if you don't like it! Just fuck off out of it! Or if you're going to stay – and at the moment I don't see any alternative – please shut the fuck up!'

177

But he just kept on making that noise. He couldn't talk. He couldn't walk. He couldn't focus his eyes or control his bowels or bladder. He had no teeth. He had no memory. He had no idea who he was or who I was or why I was telling him, with some urgency, to keep his fucking mouth shut. All he could do was keep making that noise. And as I stood there, in the early hours of the morning, I began to wonder more and more at that one thing he could do. It was an incredible noise for a thing of that size to make. It didn't go up or down the scale. It didn't get louder or softer. It started at what seemed maximum intensity, went on until his tiny lungs were empty, and then, with the briefest of pauses for the taking in of more air, started again. He was putting absolutely all of his eight pounds and fourteen ounces into it. His little face, wrinkled with bad temper, was dark red and, for a moment, I thought something was going to burst in that minuscule frame.

But he did not give up. What he was saying, what he is still saying, was 'I can keep this up for longer than you, you cunt!' It was the message I got from Conrad the toddler, in his Osh Kosh dungarees, and it was the message I got from Conrad in his St Jude's school uniform. It was the message I got from Conrad the ten-year-old terror, and Conrad the teenager, with the haircut that made him look like a mad scientist, and the unexpected talent for shoplifting. It was the message I got from him in the Cider Years and it is the message I get from him now.

I haven't said anything about Julia because there is nothing to say about Julia. Elizabeth made sure of that.

I am going to post this at your house now. I know you are there because I saw you go in. And I know John is not there because I saw him come out. If you love me at all, come out and sit next to me and maybe we'll kiss and maybe we won't, but at least I'll know we've decided to do away with all these horrible suburban lies and start again. And maybe I can work on being a halfway decent human being.

Gerald

# PART THREE

# Chapter Seven

*Mr Gibbons continues to use the post office*

From:
Roland O. Gibbons
Gibbons Detective Agency
12 The Alley
Putney, SW15
5 November

To:
Elizabeth Price
PO Box 132
Putney

Dear Mrs Price,
I have not heard from you since 10 September and am writing to keep you up to date with developments in regard to my surveillance of your husband Gerald Price.

I find taking up my pen to write to you makes me extremely nervous. I hope you will not be offended if I tell you that. In Putney you are generally known as a 'scary lady'! And when I actually caught sight of you at the performance of *Hamlet* I did not know how to behave. I hope you felt I was sufficiently discreet. Mrs Dimmock said that when we were introduced by Gerald I was 'blatantly rude' but I felt that it was time to 'play old Stone Face' and that was what I did. I am sorry.

Wasn't it a wonderful production by the way? Didn't you think that Mrs Dimmock somehow caught the spirit of Ophelia? She is, as some unkind people pointed out, at least thirty years too old for the part – but that is not the point, is it? I am not exactly the 'Horatio type' and felt inhibited by the jodhpurs. It was a bit of fun. I think it is always best to treat Shakespeare as a bit of fun and not take it too seriously even though *Hamlet* is obviously a tragedy and everyone dies. The fact that some people were openly laughing at the moment when Hamlet and Gertrude and Claudius and Laertes all died, was not, in my view, a bad thing. It is pretty funny, isn't it? I mean, they all die at practically the same time! Who was Shakespeare trying to fool?

I am obviously keen to know your feelings as to your 'next move'. As I think I said in my last letter, I do hope the revelations with which I have provided you have not been distressing or – even more importantly – prompted you to 'take the law into your own hands'.

Let me know if you wish to commence legal proceedings against your husband. Some people object to my filming them having sex when they have not given me permission to do so. It is a tricky area. Although, of course, Mrs Dimmock did do what she did with your husband. You may well say that if people don't want to be filmed having sex with people, they should choose their partners more carefully.

Perhaps you could write to me as soon as convenient at the above address. I am enclosing my bill for your kind attention. I have not, obviously, included time spent in rehearsals for *Hamlet* or my attendances at Sam Dimmock's surgery; quite often, as I became more deeply involved in the case, these were things I actually took pleasure in doing. That might be a strange thing to say about visits to the dentist but Sam is really good at his job and Mrs Dimmock, in spite of her deplorable behaviour with your husband, is a very sweet and compassionate person, who was never less than a perfect dental nurse as far I was concerned.

After payment of my bill I shall assume – unless I hear from you to the contrary – that our professional relationship is terminated and that you now have sufficient evidence of your husband's deception. As to the matter of the unfortunate death of Pamela Larner, I should also let you know that I have been asked by another party to investigate this on a full-time basis. It might be that I should request an interview with you about the late Mrs Larner but would obviously not touch on our entirely confidential relationship at that or any other time.

I can say no more at the moment. My investigation is not a murder inquiry although I could not definitively say, either in my private or professional capacity, that it might not, at some stage, turn into one. In pursuit of that end it might be necessary for me to visit your home in Heathland Avenue. It would obviously be more convenient for me if Mr Price was not aware that I was the same man who has been filming him having sex with Mrs Dimmock! I might not even say that that is what I have come to interview him about.

I am not saying that he definitively is a suspect but he might become one. Or might, indeed, already be one, even if I am not at liberty to say that he actually is. Or that I have any evidence to suggest that he might be. Although that might well be possible.

If it is any comfort to you, I have discovered that Mrs Dimmock seems now to be involved with another man. I will not name him but, from what I hear, he is a decent sort. I, personally, feel she was as much a victim in all this as you, and hope it will not be necessary to 'drag her name through the mud'.

I await your response and assure you of my good attention at all times. I do hope your marital difficulties are resolved satisfactorily,

Yours with deep respect,
Roland O. Gibbons


From:
Roland O. Gibbons
Gibbons Detective Agency
12 The Alley
Putney, SW15
10 November

To:
Elizabeth Price
PO Box 132
Putney

Dear Mrs Price,
I am sorry not to have received a reply to my letter of 5 November. It is possible that my letter did not reach you so I am going myself, personally, to the local sorting office to make sure you receive this.

I do feel that now our professional relationship has ended, and I have acted in a manner that totally and utterly safeguarded your privacy in regard to the question of your husband's adultery, there is no logical reason why we cannot have a 'face-to-face' meeting. Indeed, we have already had one! Even though, of course, we had to pretend we had never met. You get to know someone just as well, however, by correspondence as by meeting them physically in person. The way people write, if you will forgive me saying so, expresses their personality – which is perhaps why my first wife described me as a completely inadequate human being.

Ooops!

May I say, while I am on the subject of being in the room with you, how foolish it seems of your husband to ignore the charms of such a beautiful and commanding woman as you so clearly are. When I met you I got a real charge! You are physically intense, and your dry, drawling 'upper-class' voice gives you a steely edge that made me think of the films of the 1940s in which stylish women behave badly. Your beret really suited you!

I know I am expressing myself badly. I am nervous. I cannot think why you have not answered my earlier letter. I am worried in case you think I behaved improperly in the course of the investigation. I do assure you I did not.

If I do not receive an answer to this letter within five working days I will present myself at 112 Heathland Avenue at 1430 hours on the afternoon of 16 November. I am being precise about this time because it may be possible for you to arrange for your husband not to be on the premises when I call. If it is not, I would suggest we meet on 'neutral ground' either the 'Duke's Head' by Putney Bridge at the same time or, if a 'pub' does not seem suitable, the Caffè Nero near to the junction of Disraeli Road and the Lower Richmond Road at the same time. I believe you have my email address, my mobile and landline numbers. There cannot have been many periods of history, Mrs Price, when there have been so many methods of communication available to those wishing to make contact. It really does seem almost barbaric that I should be writing this letter by hand, then sending it by 'snail mail' to a post-office box address and I feel it is time to 'break through' the entirely artificial barriers you seem to wish to put between us.

Two and a half thousand pounds, Mrs Price, is, to someone in my position, a very great deal of money. It may not seem a great deal to you. I have seen the outside of your house and I would estimate its value at upwards of £2.5 million. I admire the flowering cherry tree. I like what you have done with the iron railings and the white wall. I have noted the ADT security system and the Range Rover. Olive trees in tubs – of which there are four on the front paved area – give the place a 'Mediterranean feel'. My humble flat in Keswick Road seems, next to your 'mansion', almost squalid. I did not go to Oxford. Or to Cambridge. But I want my money, Mrs Price. And I want it now.

I look forward to our next meeting. If it has to be 'face-to-face' I hope it is a pleasant one. I feel I have given you sufficient 'leeway' and that now we will be able to communicate more directly on the question of your husband's adultery and, indeed, on many other matters.

This is no longer the age of the letter, Mrs Price. This is no longer the time of Lord Chesterfield or Horace Walpole! You see, I have read some books in my time, even if my 'writing style' leaves a little to be desired!

Yours truly,
Roland O. Gibbons

From:
Orlando Gibbons
Flat 12, Woodvale Mansions
Keswick Road
Putney
17 November

To:
'Mrs Price'
PO Box 132
Putney

Dear 'Mrs Price',

This is an occasion when my use of inverted commas is completely and utterly justified. You are not – whoever you are – Mrs Price, are you? You are 'Mrs Price'. Inverted commas. You are a person who has deliberately adopted the identity of an innocent woman in order to practise some kind of hoax on an innocent private investigator who has been 'done up like a turkey' by your vile deceitfulness. You may not be a woman at all, 'Mrs Price'. You may not even be English.

Are you a psychopath? Is that it? Are you one of those people who gets pleasure out of creating torment and misery in those around them?

I think you probably are a psychopath. At least, for the moment, I cannot see what possible motive you have for assuming the identity of a perfectly innocent woman whose only crime seems to be that she is married to a man who may be a murderer. Maybe you are that murderer. Maybe you are the person who killed Pamela Larner.

Perhaps – and stranger things have happened to me during my career as a private detective – you are a pervert who simply wishes to get hold of live video and still photographs of people having intercourse. I have supplied you with plenty of that, haven't I? But if you are a pervert, you are a pervert who knows a great deal about the private life of the real Mrs Price. I am writing this letter to let you know that I am going to track you down and find your real identity. I am a private detective, 'Mrs Price'. It is my job.

How do I know you are a fake? Well – I finally paid a call on the real Mrs Price and I am absolutely positive she is not the woman who has been writing to me.

I rang her doorbell – a little nervous at the thought of having to confront her about money.

'Oh!' she said, her face brightening into a smile, as soon as she saw me. 'It's Horatio!' For a moment I thought she had simply mistaken me for someone of that name, but then she said, 'I thought you were terribly good. Even though I had my doubts about the jodhpurs!' I realized, at once, that she was talking about my recent performance with the Putney Thespians.

'I've come,' I said, 'about the letter.'

She looked completely blank. 'What letter?' she said.

'A Mrs Price,' I said, 'has been writing to me. And...I thought ...'

'I'm so sorry,' she said. 'If a Mrs Price has been writing to you, I'm afraid it wasn't me!'

I didn't know what to say. I will admit that, at first, I thought she might be lying. I have known perfectly respectable people – with plenty of money – lie through their teeth just to get out of paying a few thousand quid, but somehow I think I knew from the first that this wasn't the case.

She sat on the large sofa and, after offering me a drink, which I refused, asked what she could do to help me. 'Who is this Mrs Price who has been writing to you?' she said.

'Well,' I said, 'this is very difficult to talk about but it is someone who has been ... er ... claiming ... that ...'

Then, as I sat there, wondering how best to continue, she burst into tears.

I did not know quite where to look: she was shaken by sobs and, burying her head in her hands, she must have cried for nearly a minute. Eventually I said, 'Mrs Price? Are you all right?'

In the end she looked up. 'I am so sorry,' she said, still with her head in her hands. 'My husband has just left me and I thought I could cope with it but I can't and it just all got too much at that moment. I don't know why.'

She lifted up her face to me, then, and, in a reasonably steady voice, said, 'I loved him. I loved Gerald. I don't know why. In many ways he was an absolutely appalling person.'

I think I was sure from that moment that this was not the woman who had hired me to spy on Mr Price. I think I had known it as soon as she opened the door. This was absolutely not someone who had paid a private detective to spy on her husband. It was clear that his leaving her had come as a horrible surprise.

I waited for quite some time, watching her very carefully, before I said, 'Is there anyone else involved?'

'He says not!' said Mrs Price. 'But there is. There always is.'

Indeed, I thought, there usually is, and in your case there certainly has been. I suppose at that point I should have told her the whole story, but I honestly could not face doing so. This was a woman in genuine distress. She was clearly not my client. If she was, she was an actress of world-class stature with a very weird way of keeping herself amused.

At that moment a rather good-looking young man in his early thirties walked into the room, carrying a very large wodge of A4 paper. I recognized him from the party after the opening night of *Hamlet* as Conrad, Mrs Price's son. He is a tall, open-faced lad with blond hair, worn longer than is usual in young people nowadays, and a large walrus moustache, an unusual and not completely successful fashion decision. The rest of him, however, looked absolutely nothing like his father's negative descriptions. 'Bit of a weasel', 'hopelessly unemployed tosser' and 'cider-sodden loser' are some of the phrases he has applied to his son when in conversation with me.

In fact, young Conrad, apart from looking like a member of a west coast rock group in the late sixties, was a very personable young man indeed. It was also clear that he and his mother have a very intense and satisfying relationship. Mrs Price's face suddenly lit up and, as he waved his wodge of A4, she beamed proudly at me. 'Conrad,' she said, 'has just sold his novel for a six-figure sum. It is about the Spanish Civil War!'

'This is it!' said the young author, with a charming, slightly sheepish grin. 'I'm afraid it's about two hundred and fifty thousand words long. It may need cutting!' Then he announced he was out tonight and would his mother be all right? She said she was fine. He said he knew she wasn't fine. Then she asked him if Elaine was fine and he said Elaine was very fine, although Hanif might well be coming after him with a knife. That made his mother laugh. I wondered, for a moment, whether they were talking about Mrs Dimmock's daughter – but I didn't like to ask. I suppose I felt I ought to go but it looked to me as if Mrs Price wanted me to stay. When Conrad had gone she offered me another drink and this time I accepted.

'Have you any idea where he is?' I asked, as she poured me a glass of white wine.

'There was just a message on the machine,' she said. 'About two weeks ago. He said he was leaving me. He sounded quite upset about it and not nearly as horrible as he can be sometimes. He's very good at being horrible. He said he was going away somewhere to "think" and he would write to me. Write to me! Isn't that how we used to dump people when we were twenty? We have been married for over forty years, Mr Gibbons.'

Then she started crying again. I went over to the sofa and, very quietly and gently, I put my arm around her. 'Have you no idea where he might be?' I said.

'No,' she said, crying even harder now. 'I have no idea at all. He has just disappeared. Apparently he took three weeks off from work. They thought he was going on holiday. With me.'

This set her off again. I found myself wondering how it could be that someone so obviously odious as Gerald Price could inspire this kind of uncomplicated affection. The woman really does love him. Unlike you, 'Mrs Price', who, whoever you are, seem to have got the little bastard about bang to rights. Love really is blind, isn't it?

'I don't quite understand,' she said, when she was a little calmer, 'why you thought I might have been writing to you. Did this person use this address? What did they want?'

'I think,' I said, 'there has been some mistake. I really do not want to bother you with it.'

I decided to introduce the subject of Pamela Larner. 'Tell me,' I said, as casually as I could, 'did you know Pamela Larner well?'

For the first time in our conversation she looked troubled. I had the impression, too, that she might be concealing something from me. I could not say quite why I thought that. 'Detective instinct', I suppose. She looked away and started to twist her fingers to and fro. She has rather lovely hands. Very fine white fingers, with black ink staining her nails. From marking I suppose. It was only then I noticed that, although we were indoors and it was a mild day, she was still wearing the beret she had worn to the première of *Hamlet*.

It was the first trace of affectation I had found in her. I felt it was rather touching.

'Pamela Larner...I hadn't thought about her for years,' she said, in a puzzled voice. 'And then...suddenly...it seems...' Her voice died away. 'Why,' she went on, 'are you asking about her?'

What was the expression on her face? If I hadn't thought she had no reason whatsoever to feel guilty about Mrs Larner, I would have said she looked guilty. I could not think why that should be the case. I was not even sure, at this stage, whether she knew the woman was dead.

'There seems to be something not quite right about the way she died,' I said. 'The police said it was suicide, but Mr Larner seems to think it might have been murder. I'm not sure yet.'

She continued to look shocked but, for the first time since I had come into the house, I wasn't sure I trusted her completely. I was still absolutely sure she was not the woman who had been writing to me. If there was a doubt in my mind, it was connected to the Pamela Larner business.

We had both drunk a glass of wine. She offered me another one, which I accepted. New Zealand Sauvignon, I think, with that fresh, lemony flavour. I always think the Enzedders do it better than the French. She sat, in silence, for some minutes, staring out at her garden, as if it was all she had left in the world.

'I was faithful to him,' she said, 'for all of my life. I met him at Oxford and I fell in love with him and I thought he fell in love with me. A few people have tried it on over the years, but I was never interested. I'm a one-man woman sort of thing. He is a very unhappy person. His father was quite horrible. Because, I suppose, Gerry's grandfather was horrible to him. He was a very bad-tempered judge. And so the misery is handed on, Mr Gibbons. I suppose you see a lot of it in your business.'

I presumed she must know I was a private detective. I wasn't sure how she knew this. I didn't think I had told her. 'I do,' I said. 'I do quite a bit of divorce.'

She turned and looked me full in the face then. 'Well,' she said, 'I'm sure it's not always easy to outwit the locals when it comes to marital deception. Although you may think you are adept at snooping, Mr Gibbons, you have no idea of the talents of the women of Putney in this area. Very little escapes their notice.'

She smiled slightly as she said this, keeping her eyes on my face. I recognized the sentence immediately. It is in the first paragraph of your letter to me of 17 June. For a moment I was, suddenly, convinced that I might have made a mistake. That this might actually be the woman who had been writing to me. That everything she had said was a lie. That it was her (you) who had first approached me about Gerald Price. I was almost tempted to tell her about the letters, then decided that would be foolish. If you are 'Mrs Price' as well as Mrs Price, I shouldn't even be telling you I suspect you, should I?

And, anyway, I was still, without quite knowing why, assured of her innocence. Maybe you – whoever you are – slipped in that phrase because you knew it was the kind of thing she often said. People repeat themselves, especially when they're over sixty. Maybe it was the beret – the one piece of vanity in a woman who had, otherwise, lost all confidence in her power to attract.

I went out into the street. I thought I could still hear her crying as I made for my car. I know I couldn't, of course, but, because it's only in my imagination, I still think I hear her tears, as I sit here, writing this to you, my unknown reader.

Roland O. Gibbons

# Chapter Eight

*Dr John Goldsmith sends a long letter
from the Languedoc*

From:
John Goldsmith
c/o Hôtel du Levant
Rue Gobineau
Béziers
France
14 November

To:
Elizabeth Price
112 Heathland Avenue
Putney, SW15 3LE

Dear Elizabeth,
You will probably be very surprised to get this letter from
me; and even more so when you see where I seem to be
staying. The Languedoc is not a number-one destination in
November. And this hotel is the sort of place most people
avoid, even in high season. One of those French hotels with
hard, sausage-like bolsters under the pillows, and locks

on the room doors that are wound slowly backwards and forwards on a ratchet that looks like something from a piece of Victorian machinery.

Wi-Fi is not a word they know or understand. There are no telephones by your bedside. I have not seen a television anywhere on the property. It is just what I need. I have not brought a mobile, laptop, iPad, iPhone or i-anything with me and am, therefore, very well placed to say that none of these devices has added anything to the sum of human happiness.

What I have brought with me is something probably only the sixtysomething bothers with at all. An address book. I have had it more than twenty years. It is a green-leather affair with pages that you are supposed to take out and put in at will and, in order to make this sort of thing easier, there are holes in the pages and two rings that bind your contacts together.

So old am I, darling Elizabeth, that I do not think I can remember the word we used to describe these things when they were new all those years ago. Filofax. That's it. I'm not dead yet. I can still find the words. Just. It isn't a Filofax but it's like a Filofax and, instead of pulling out pages and adding new ones, I have just allowed certain pages to fray and wander or disappear altogether so, for example, absolutely no one at all is listed under K. I must have known someone whose name began with K. Surely.

As I leaf through it, the first thing I cannot help but notice is that quite a few of people listed in my Time Organizer, that is how it describes itself on the inside front cover, are dead. There is absolutely no point in my calling Polly Jackson whose number, like almost everyone else's, has the now defunct London prefix of 0171. I happen to know she committed suicide nine years ago. I never went to her funeral. I never sent a letter of condolence. I didn't really know her very well. If I had known her better, I'm not sure I would have liked her. She liked a man I thought I liked and then realized I didn't.

Your name is there. You are not listed under P for Price but under E for Elizabeth. You do not even have an 0181 prefix to your number so that suggests you have been there well before April 2000. I wondered, with a touch of sentimental nostalgia for the old codes, whether I ever knew you when London exchanges were MACaulay (Nine Elms) or HILlside (Finchley.) There is just the one number there. Some people, with whom I have quarrelled or for whom I never really cared seem to have about ten numbers. Mobiles crossed out, new ones added, new addresses put in next to the new numbers. Your number seems always to have been there. Your address in Heathland Avenue, too, is a reminder of the old days. There is no postcode.

It is to that address I am writing. What I want to say to you cannot be said in a phone call – even assuming I can find a phone in this very strange hotel. I am not even quite sure what it is I want to say. I am groping my way towards it as I write. I have been going back over my life, trying to make sense of the things I did, and failing, of course, as we all do, but what has become clear to me is that whenever I try to summon up the times when I have been happy, you are always in the picture.

We met first, if you remember, in the playground of St Jude's Primary School. We had worked out, along with the other middle-class people in the area, that it was a seriously good place, run by a very strict Welshwoman called Myfanwy Jones. Do you remember the day the improbably named Lucy Lockett went crazy and ran across Putney Common to the school in her nightgown? Once there, she started pulling all the plugs out of the walls, because, she said, she thought the electricity would harm the children. 'It was a bit of a shock!' Myfanwy lilted, at a few concerned parents later. 'She is a very well set-up woman!'

Later, Mrs Lockett became convinced that tiny little Stephen Lockett was Jesus Christ and threw him into the deep end of Putney Swimming Pool to see if he would walk on water. He only just escaped with his life.

When I met you, though, none of us knew how crazy the other parents were. We were new parents, standing by the wire fence around the school, as very small children wobbled their way towards the door still marked with the stone letters that read 'INFANTS'. It was the first day and, before they were all taken away, each mummy or daddy or, in the case of the Dimmocks, both Mummy and Daddy, leaned over their charges and whispered words of solace.

Afterwards some of the mummies looked as if they needed solace. I think Mary Dimmock burst into floods of tears while Pamela Larner was heard to mutter, 'Pull yourself together, woman!' but you and I were of the stoical 'Let them get on with it' breed, were we not?

Barbara, of course, was never there. She was never there for rugby matches or school plays or one-to-one chats with Miss Pimm or Mrs Hughes about whether Jas and Josh could be prevented from excessively competitive behaviour on the sports field. 'All they want to do,' I remember Mrs Hughes saying plaintively, 'is win! There is more to sport than that!'

So it was always me and you in the line outside Myfanwy's office or on those hideously uncomfortable chairs in the school hall, watching Elaine Dimmock hammer her way through some basic Mozart. We became friends, I suppose, without really realizing it; and though, later, the eight of us became the Goldsmiths, the Larners, the Prices and the

Dimmocks, we were always, somehow, slightly apart from all that camaraderie.

Is it Barbara's appalling letter that is making all this clear to me? Or have I always known it? I think I must always have known it but it is only now, as I write, that I really understand what I think and feel. You discover these things by trying to describe them and, though I am no writer – one in a family is enough – I think I can now say, no, write, with complete confidence, something that I never knew before I began this sentence. That I love you. Have always loved you. In a hopeless, hopeless way.

I can recall the precise moment when it started.

It was at a nativity play at St Jude's. Always an occasion to get the hard-nosed lawyers, surgeons and bankers blubbing like babies. 'Little don-kee . . . little don-kee on the dusty road . . .' Jas and Josh were Israelites. They spent the whole performance thumping each other and trying to take the tea towel off Herbie Rosenbaum's head. Conrad was a Roman soldier. Well – *the* Roman soldier, actually. The only one who spoke.

'I am Marthelluth!' he began – his lisp was terrible in those days, 'and I have thped to Jewuthalem to thlay thith Thon of the Jooth, the Thaviour ath they thay – Jethuth Chwitht! Where ith he?'

No one seemed to know.

The Baby Jesus, a jumble of old face flannels and dish-cloths, wrapped in a piece cut off one of Mrs Hughes's old cardigans, was, in fact, being hastily assembled offstage by Miss Pratt and Tallulah Fanshawe, who had been chosen to play the Virgin Mary because, in Mrs Hughes's own words, 'It might make her feel better about herself.' I had never quite understood why Tallulah should have benefited from stepping, so soon, into the role that was clearly waiting for her in the world outside St Jude's, i.e. Eternal Virgin.

Conrad glared about him and started to wave his plastic sword in the air.

'Where ith thith Jethuth?' he snarled. 'Thaethar theekth the Thon of the God of the Jooth!' There was still no answer. 'I want him!' Conrad went on. 'Right now!'

People started to laugh. Conrad, clearly, thought this was a very good thing. 'Thtop mething awound!' he continued, moving now into what sounded like a pretty good impression of Mr Loop, the games master. 'I will not thtand for mething awound, you thtupid Jooth! I am going to thlithe Jethuth into thmall pietheth!'

By now the laughter was becoming more general. At first, I could see, you were worrying the poor little bloke might burst into tears or run off the stage to hide his shame but, in fact, he was buoyed up by the audience's laughter. As his gestures became wilder and you could see he was courting the attention, enjoying his role as clown, I saw your expression lift gracefully and your eyes start to shine with pleasure. You have a lovely smile, Elizabeth, and it wasn't often that Conrad was the cause of it.

Jesus – imagine having Gerry as a father. No offence. But it must have been hard.

'I am going to count to ten, Jethuth,' said Conrad, moving on from his Mr Loop impression to an even better one of the headmistress, 'and then I am thlithing! I am thlithing you into thmall pietheth! I am going to thtart with your legth!'

Prolonged laughter. Conrad does a bit more sword-waving. Even more laughter.

'Nectht cometh the toeth and all the bitth that thtick out!' More laughter. 'And then I will thtick my thword in hith thtomach! And hith ... hith ...'

Expectant giggles from the audience.

'Hith bowelth!'

Prolonged laughter and applause gracefully acknowledged by Conrad. He was now working the audience like a stand-up comedian. The more serious he looked the more they laughed; but they knew the seriousness was only a pose. They were allowed to laugh. They were not laughing at him, they were laughing with him.

You were laughing, now, too. As Conrad went into a sort of gorilla mating dance around the stage, waving his sword and putting one small hand on his paper helmet in order to make sure it stayed in place, you laughed for sheer joy that your boy had shown that he, too, had a talent, even if he was so frightened of his father he had never dared to show it in public before.

I think I fell in love with the love I saw in your face that day. I fell in love with your kindness and your tolerance and your ability to take pleasure in the world. I watched you later as the four of us – you, me, Gerry and Barbara were the centre of the group in those days – became closer.

When our three boys were at prep school, I remember standing at the school gates, waiting for Jas and Josh. It must have been some time in the late eighties. I think Margaret Thatcher was in power. There are brown leaves heaped up in the gutter and the sodium streetlamps have come on as Jas and Josh and Conrad emerge in their bright black blazers. Orchestra for Conrad, I imagine, and football for Jas and Josh. Jas's hair flops forward over his eyes and he looks, as always, contained and amused by it all. Conrad looks like a man weighed down by the troubles of the world. When he sees you he bites his lip. I wonder whether someone at the school is bullying him. I wonder whether it might be Jas.

It's impossible to tell with children. What happens between them is something we will never know. They will not even remember much of it themselves.

You move towards him and I can see you want to put your arms around him, but that isn't done. Not at the gates of the Royal Collegiate School, Putney, anyway.

'How was school?' you say.

'It wath all wight!' said Conrad. His lisp is one of the many endearing things about him but I don't imagine it goes down too well at the Royal Collegiate School, Putney.

He is not going to say any more than that. You put your head to one side. You have long, auburn hair in those days, like a forties film star. You have big blue eyes and your eyes betray you. You love him too much. You are so frightened for him, and for all of us. In your eyes I see something that is in short supply at home – tenderness. Perhaps, in the still gloom of that autumn evening, my face, too, betrays me. Jas is looking at me oddly.

'You comin'?' he says. He loses the ends of words in those days. It is supposed to be cool and Jas is good at being cool. Josh is bent over some early draft of the computer game. Game Boy, perhaps.

(I don't remember. All I recall is the way the children looked and the way you looked and the way I felt, which was that I had married the wrong person and it was too late to do anything about it because it was not something I could ever dream of saying to you.)

'Of course!' I say, because, like you, my first loyalty is always to the children. So we go to the car and he tells me how he *smashed* Roger Frayne when he tackled him in second-eleven practice, and I drive off, but as I turn the corner I look back and you are stooped over little Conrad and your arms are going round him and he is standing quite stiff, like a good soldier on parade, and I think how much you love him and how much I love you and how hopeless it all is, and then I ask Jas about the game and he tells me.

I am sorry I am saying all this. I probably wouldn't be even thinking these things, let alone writing them down, if it were not all over between Barbara and me, which it is, but I have faced that now and I can say what I like and what I feel honestly and freely. If you want to write back, even if it is only to tell me to stop bothering you, the above address will find me. I am doing nothing apart from taking long walks, reading books and lying on my bed staring at the ceiling. I have told the practice I will not be back for a month. I have not told Barbara where I am and I do not want her to know.

Love
John Goldsmith


From:
Elizabeth Price
112 Heathland Avenue
Putney, SW15 3LE
18 November

To:
John Goldsmith
Hôtel du Levant
Rue Gobineau
Béziers
France

My dear John,
I cannot tell you how nice it was to get your letter.

Gerald left me around two weeks ago. I had had no warning whatsoever that anything like this was about to take place. There are have been times in our marriage – I think, overall, a period of, say, eight or nine years out of the forty – when each of us viewed the other with almost total contempt, but for the last year or so I had thought we were getting on fairly well. He just failed to return one evening and left me a message saying he had 'gone away to think about our relationship'. Why one needs to go away to think about anything I really do not understand.

He had seemed rather upset to learn about the death of Pamela Larner. I couldn't really understand why. That sounds callous, but she was widely disliked when alive. I fail to see why death should improve a person's character. Mike Larner, he told me, seems to think she was murdered; I am sure there was no shortage of candidates for the role of ending the Putney Supermother's life.

I was fairly sure she was having an affair with Sam Dimmock. The way she howled with laughter every time he started on one of his funny stories about gum disease. The way she propped that odiously small chin of hers on one of her tiny fists and looked up into his face when he started on why it was that Maggie Thatcher was a good thing and we were all effete Londoners who knew nothing about life whereas he was a West Country lad in touch with the sea and the soil.

She was a woman who in spite, or perhaps because of, the lip gloss and the nail varnish was a byword for malevolence and the worst kind of competitive mothering. I seem to remember, one evening in San Marco di Stefano, Barbara and I playing a game in which we had to count the number of sentences she spoke that began with 'Barnaby'. She seemed, as far as I recall, to have embraced almost every subservient role offered to women apart from that of air hostess. And that perky little walk! And the tiny, tiny bottom! And, oh,

God, the trouser suit! And the way she shrieked on receipt of the most trivial kind of information!

She couldn't spell, either. I don't know why that should have irritated me so much – but it did.

His hearing about her death seemed to cast him into gloom. He kept gnawing his fingers and muttering about how we none of us had got that long and he should have been nicer to her. 'You haven't seen her for years!' I said. 'And when you did know her I don't think you could possibly have been nicer to her. I am assuming you drew the line at sexual intercourse.'

He didn't say anything to that. I have always assumed that Gerald went off and screwed people from time to time. His testosterone level has always been way off the scale. Whenever he stopped trying to bamboozle me into having anal intercourse and started bringing flowers home, I assumed he had found someone else to penetrate. So long as he didn't bother me with the details it didn't really worry me.

He said, in his phone message, that there wasn't anyone else; and, for some reason, I am inclined to believe him. Unless, of course, he has found someone young. That thought does give me a chill. I don't think I could bear to watch him prance around with someone of Julia's age. Older men are such fools, aren't they? Except you, of course.

I can't say that what you said in your sweet letter came as a surprise. I think we all pretty much know what everyone is thinking about everyone else for most of the time, don't we? We have to pretend we don't, of course. The world would be an orgy of sex and recrimination if we admitted or listened to or – God help us – acted on our awareness of this very simple fact; but I do remember so many times with you, as our children were growing up, when I found myself thinking, Suppose I wasn't with Gerry. Suppose John wasn't with Barbara.

And now that seems to be the case; and I don't know what I think about it.

Well, I'm glad it's out in the open. I am glad about that. I'm glad, too, that you spoke so eloquently in your letter about a subject that is dearer to me than any other. Children, as an American writer says somewhere, are all, and yet our society persists in treating them as an alien species. For me the greatest joy in life has been watching my children develop. I can hear Gerry's voice in my head as I write that: 'Develop? Is that the right word for what Conrad did? Develop?'

My own parents, both of whom were teachers, often muttered dark things about the basically evil nature of humanity – especially when you were talking about eight-year-olds – my mum, as I think I once told you, ended as a primary-school headmistress in Salford. As a teacher myself, I never felt that. Perhaps because the girls at Dame Veronica's came from nice homes and their parents paid thousands of pounds a year for the privilege of being taught Tacitus by the likes of me – but I don't think it was just that. Virtue is not only the ornament of the poor, whatever the Marxists may say. My middle-class pupils amaze me every day with their capacity for joy and charity; perhaps I should be surprised to find such charm among the daughters of estate agents, bankers and high-powered solicitors, but I am not. I'm simply grateful for it and every day, for me, it is a privilege to be facing the young, with their energy, their endless questions and their capacity to look at things in a different way from me.

We think the same about life, you and I. I've felt, at times, writing this letter, that we had never really met at all and we had made contact with each other through a dating agency.

Maybe writing letters teaches you that you do not really know your correspondent, even if they are someone with whom you have been reasonably intimate for years. This oldest and most trusted path to communication, perhaps because it allows us time to consider our thoughts before trying to make sense of them for other people, allows us to remake our relationships, even with friends of long standing, as we grope our way through each sentence.

What do I feel for you?

Well, that we have allowed each other to see our good sides, I suppose. I am not in front of you so you do not have to look at the cast in my left eye, the unfortunate hair that is the colour of a British battleship, or listen to that terrible upper-class drawl that I learned at Oxford as a defence against all those posh girls and am now unable to lose. Oh and the smoking. You can't smell the tobacco on me. That must, perhaps, mean that we were only meant to write love letters to each other, never to do the things that lovers are supposed to do, even as they crawl so horribly close to threescore and ten.

There is one thing I have to tell about me that I have never told anyone. Curiously enough, I got close to confiding it to a total stranger the other day – a funny little man called Gibbons, who is, of all things, a private detective. He called on me – quite why I do not know – and looked as if he was about to tell me something of terrible importance; he asked me a great many questions about Pamela Larner and seems sure that she was murdered. I really can't believe Mrs Larner was capable of doing anything as interesting as getting murdered.

I did start to tell him about Julia – but I could see he wasn't interested. People are never interested in Julia. That, in a sense, is why I am writing this letter.

You never saw much of how Julia and I were together.

Not, anyway, after primary school and, if you remember, she left St Jude's very early. She was one of those children who, everyone agreed, would be 'better off at a private school'. They didn't say this in a tone that implied that only there would her natural talents be recognized. It was much more that well-informed people thought that that might be the only scholastic environment in which she would not have the shit kicked out of her until she was old enough to leave.

I never liked Julia.

I know you have just written me a sweet letter in which you seem to be saying that you fell in love with me because of my wonderful talent for mothering but the fact of the matter is that I have never really liked my daughter. I don't think I have ever admitted that to anyone before.

I didn't really notice her at first. Conrad was a very demanding baby. He cried almost all the time for the first four years of his life. We never really found out why. General disenchantment, I think. Julia was a very quiet and easy baby. She slept through the night from the beginning, and even when she was awake she did not seem very interested in the world around her. Music seemed to puzzle her. Small objects hung over her cot – giraffes, lions and smiling teddy bears – only produced a slow, suspicious look. She seemed to prefer sleeping face down and when she first smiled – at about eleven months – it was more a slight twist of the mouth that never really reached her eyes.

You are supposed to bond with babies if you breastfeed them successfully, and Julia was quite efficient at milking me, but it certainly didn't bring us closer. I think I felt slightly exploited by her. She was surprisingly aggressive about the whole thing, and occasionally she would grab at my tits with such force while she was feeding that I found myself wincing. She always went to sleep immediately afterwards –

something Gerry always did after we had had sex. She also snored from a very early age.

I don't know why but I was abnormally aware of this noise. I could hear it even if I was downstairs in the kitchen and she was upstairs in her cot. I remember once passing her nursery – she must have been about eighteen months – and peering in to check on her. Most parents do that because they are worried their loved one might have stopped breathing. It wasn't like that. I really did think she might secretly be doing something she was not supposed to be doing. It's a crazy thing to say, I know, but there were times when I felt she was deliberately concealing new developmental skills from me – that, when I wasn't there, she was walking and practising phonemes.

She actually didn't walk until she was nearly two and scarcely said a word until she was well on the way to being three years old.

It was about this time of the year, in dull November when there is neither morning nor afternoon but only a dismal grey followed by total darkness. She was lying on her back. Her eyes were wide open. She wasn't looking at anything when I opened the door but when she saw me her eyes slowly focused on my face. She just stared at me – as if to say, 'Who the fuck are you?' She didn't smile. I tried to smile but the smile froze on my face. She was thinking something – but I was never going to find out what it was. Then I tried one of those encouraging, high-pitched sentences that mothers try on babies, although, I have to admit, they were never my strong point. 'Hel –o-*oh*-oh-oh!'

Julia just continued to stare at me. There was no one else in the house. I stood there, looking at her. I didn't try any more cheerful mummy stuff. I found myself wondering what it would be like to walk slowly over to the cot and hold a pillow over her face. She wouldn't struggle much. You would

hardly notice. It would be as if she had never been there –
but, then, that was how it was anyway. She won't be happy,
I thought. She won't find anyone to love her because I can't
love her enough and Gerald can only think about himself. So
why don't I? Why don't I save us all the trouble?

I am told mothers quite often have murderous feelings
about their children. What was particularly frightening
about this urge of mine was that I knew I was lying to myself.
I didn't really want to get rid of her because I was worried
about her future. There was no genuine concern in the desire
I had to hold a tiny pillow over her face and press it down
until she stopped moving. There was nothing crazy about it
either. It was a cold, rational sort of feeling. I just didn't like
her. I didn't want her there. She bothered me.

Julia lay there, looking at me, her face blank; after a
while, without even bothering to pretend to talk to her, I
went on upstairs.

I was very correct to her after that. All through St Jude's
when, as you will remember, she hung at the corner of the
playground, whispering quietly to the kind of girl she always
befriended – Smelly Annie (as she was called), Lonely Lorna
or Spiteful Sarah Smith – I was as impartially polite to her
as I was to the Swedish au pair or the man who came to
look at the drains. She always did what she was told. She
never shouted or lost her temper. She hardly ever argued
with Conrad. But she was always there, in the corner of the
room, looking at me with those big blank eyes of hers, and
I could never forget that afternoon when I had stared at her
in her cot and thought, seriously, about what it would be like
to kill her.

I sent her to Dame Veronica's pre-school, as I said, against
my will. That was Gerald. I couldn't bear the idea of having
her anywhere near the building where I was teaching. Later,

when she passed the exam for the senior school, without any real help from me, I was terrified she would end up in a class of mine; but by this time she knew what I thought of her and had got very good at letting me know she reciprocated the feeling. 'I don't want to do Latin,' she said, in that frozen little voice of hers. 'There is no point in Latin. Why would anyone want to do Latin? It's for stupid people.'

'Mummy does Latin!' said Gerald, in the laborious voice he always uses for children.

She just looked at him.

'I noticed!' she said, in those grim, flat tones that always made her sound as if she had been taken over by an alien intelligence.

I tried not to notice her adolescence. It was impossible to avoid it completely. Think she gave a party once. Not many people came – mainly girls of about fifteen. She was nearly eighteen at the time. I think there was a boy but he didn't make much of an impact. She spent much of the evening looking at me reproachfully. 'You didn't buy enough wine, Mummy!' she said, when it was all over, although she had not drunk anything but Coca-Cola all night. I hated being called 'Mummy', but she seemed to enjoy using the word. She put a babyish lilt into it that always made me feel slightly sick.

Then there was university. Exeter 'Probably the Best University in the World', said the car-window sticker in a fairly effective parody of the advert that claimed Carlsberg had achieved a similar status in the world of lager. It was about the wittiest thing that ever came out of Exeter University as far as I could see. The lecturers communicated by email and seemed incapable of writing a decent sentence. Julia found a boy called Stephen but lost him shortly before her finals. She got a 2.2 in English. She works as a secretary in a law firm (Gerald found her the job) and lives with a girl called Philippa in a flat near London Bridge. I have never liked anyone I have ever met – no matter for how short a time – who was called Philippa. This one is a pretty standard Philippa. Thinks she is prettier and cleverer than she actually is. Overworks her boyish charm horribly and manages to make Julia even more invisible than she is already.

I never see her. She usually manages to avoid Christmas. If she comes, she sits in the corner with her head hung low and her ridiculously long blonde hair drooping over her face. She looks at me reproachfully from time to time but rarely says anything at all – apart from 'Happy Christmas, everyone!' in tones that suggest she is announcing a death in the family. She has got a pair of glasses that make her look like a low-grade worker in the People's Republic of China. She has taken to wearing dungarees, which enhance the Gang of Four look. Maybe she is a lesbian. It would, at least, be a sign of initiative.

So – there it is, John. I may look as if I have a heart of gold but I am afraid I don't. We are all supposed to have hearts of gold, aren't we? I am a naturally cautious person and caution has made me somewhat cold. I am afraid of being carried away by emotion. I am intolerant, too – much more so than I seem in public. I find it very easy to withdraw my affection if I think I'm going to get hurt. Perhaps that is the real reason why Gerald has left me.

I am lonely without him. I am frightened of getting old and spending Christmas alone. I sit in this big empty house and think that, if you could stand it, it would be nice if you called when you get back to London. I am assuming you are coming back, John; and, if you do, there is a room here where you could stay if things between you and Barbara are impossibly awkward.

With all my imperfections, dear John, I am waiting for a letter or a phone call or, even better, for you to call without warning one day and for me to open the door and see you smiling there on the doorstep. We used to call on people, didn't we, when we were younger, and didn't feel the need to warn them that they might have company?

With much love
Elizabeth

# Chapter Nine

*Mike Larner looks for a different kind of
private dick*

From:
Michaela Larner
'Chez Moi'
24 Lawson Crescent
Putney
19 November

To:
Orlando Gibbons
The Great Detective
12 That Funny Little Road in
Putney

Dear Orlando,
I know, from talking to Mary, that you have at last come to
terms with your first name. I do understand. I had a similar
problem about coming to terms with the fact that I was gay.

I will not always be Michaela but felt like Michaela this
morning, so here I am!

You never seemed like a Roland to me. Rolands are

phlegmatic and thoughtful and quite dark. They have a dash of chivalry, of course, and always make me think of chainmail and those brooding woods above Valdemossa but you are lighter, more nimble. I have never seen you as someone who has to watch their weight – although I know, from talking so intensely to Mary, as I have done over the last few weeks – that it is something that concerns you!

Isn't it amazing how we have all sort of blended? How my deep love for Sam and your similar feelings about Mary have brought us all together so that we can share those feelings with each other and our children and with anyone who will listen. Although we may be running out of people who come into that category!

Sam says I am a bit of a bore about being gay and would prefer I did not advertise it quite as much as I do but I am afraid I feel like doing just that. People should be told. Most of them are so horribly prejudiced, they should be forced to confront it, even if they do not want to do that. Political speech over.

Anyway, the purpose of this letter is not to drone on about my new-found sexuality. Although it is amazing how it has totally transformed my view of the world and my attitude to music, for example, especially my fondness for the music of the 1920s – no, not all gays like Barbra Streisand, *actually*, although I do not *dislike* her. I suppose working on my big new project about gay animals has focused my mind in that direction and I cannot these days, look at a squirrel without thinking, Is he one of us? and have spotted an Alsatian in Richmond Park that is obviously struggling to come to terms with his feelings for a dachshund called Victor that has serious issues and just needs to own up to what he is but ... But.

Ididntcomeheretotalkaboutbeinggay.

I am writing because you said that before you began your

enquiries into the death of my late wife, Pamela, you would need a formal letter setting out my desire to have you go forward with this investigation. I appreciate, too, that as you are not formally licensed to investigate murder this is, perforce (don't you love that word?), an informal inquiry. I am also, as you requested, using this letter as an opportunity to re-state some of the circumstances surrounding Pamela's demise.

As a gay man I am obviously very aware of the difficulties she faced in her later years, especially in respect of my need to wipe the surfaces in our home. I have always been a devil with the Hoover (who was, by the way, also gay), even in the days when I was deluding myself that I was a heterosexual, something that obviously came about because of the intense conditioning in our society, which is reflected in such words as 'poof', 'fairy' and other terms so offensive I will not even bother to repeat them here, although 'light on the carpet' and 'bowls from the gasworks end' come to mind as phrases that are constantly in casual use by people who ought to know better. Gerald Price – that murdering adulterous bastard – to name but three!

I think I have already gone over the details of the evening with you and know you are already beavering away on my behalf. Did you know, by the way, that 82 per cent of all beavers in the Continental United States are homosexual?

But.

I have gone over and over that evening and I have thought of one detail I had overlooked that might, perhaps, help you in your search. I think I already told you that one of the things that seemed strange to me, when I found Pamela's body, was that there was a half-empty bottle of red wine next to her. She very rarely drank red wine – and never, never on her own.

I think I also told you I was fairly sure that, although there was only one glass on the coffee table, one of the goblets in the cabinet where the glasses are kept had been moved. Someone, I thought, had been anxious to remove all trace of their presence in the house that night; but, now I think about it, what struck me about the position of the glasses in the cabinet was the precision with which they had been rearranged.

I don't know why but I think I saw a woman's hand in this. Maybe it is being gay and being very sensitive to how women feel. Maybe it is just that Gerald, if he is a murderer, is liable to be a clumsy murderer. In fact, a cushion over the face seems a little subtle for him. I am surprised he didn't come at her with a pickaxe or blow her head off at short range with a double-barrelled shotgun. More importantly, if he was being so careful about moving the glass, why did he leave the cushion where it was?

My own theory – and I know private detectives do not like the general public to have theories – is that Gerald had an accomplice. I know we are all supposed to think that Elizabeth Price is a kind of saint, but I, personally, favour Elizabeth Price as the guilty party. She is very good at suggesting she is a nice person but, believe you me, Orlando, when you are locked up in a villa in Corsica with her for two weeks, you soon see the seamy side. She is a tremendous intellectual snob with very little feeling for animals.

And she worships the ground that bastard walks on. Excuse my French, but she would crawl down Putney High Street on broken glass for Gerald. If he was having an affair and he wanted the woman out of the way she'd be right behind him. She pretends she's not interested in where he parks his penis but when we were *en Bretagne* she clocked every single move my late wife made in Gerald's direction –

and, believe you me, she made a few. She was utterly obsessed with where he was and what he was doing – and I do not imagine she's changed, for all she pretends to be interested only in the Silver Age of Latin Poetry.

Mrs Goody Two Shoes, as Pam and I used to call her, was also very, very down on Milly, whom we sent to Dame Veronica's. She and Pam had a most terrible bust-up about it and, though it was more than twenty years ago, I can still remember it with horrifying clarity. Pam pulled out some of her hair. Quite a lot of it, actually.

Well – that's my tip for the day, Orlando. I must say I never thought that you and me and Sam and Mary Dimmock would all hit it off so well. I think the arrangement of Sam staying with me at weekends and visiting me for the odd night of passion (he's an amazing lover, Orlando, with an intuitive understanding of what my body needs) seems to be working well. I am still trying to get him to come out to his patients. I suggested a sort of informal wine and cheese party at which I might make a short speech – but he seems opposed to this.

So looking forward to taking you and Mary out on the boat. Beware of Sam when he is skippering, however. He is gloriously dominating but it may not be to everyone's taste. I rather like it but, then, as I may have said earlier in this letter, I am a gay man and have a totally different attitude to power and control than you will find in many straight males, obsessed as they are with the existing structures of a society that is, let's face it, more or less committed to wiping homosexuals off the map!

I have got huge interest in my new documentary series from Holland, and a group of gay Dutch filmmakers are keen on collaborating with me on it. Jens and Burgwaal will be over in the next few weeks and I would love you to meet them. They want to visit the Lake District and, if possible, sleep naked on one of the mountains. I also want to tell you more about some very exciting developments on the Barnaby front. I came out to him via the British embassy and I think we are more or less reconciled. Milly and Leo have been terrific! Leo said, 'I always knew you were a poof, Dad!' Isn't that marvellous?

Onwards and upwards!


Ever your
Mike


(Not Really Michaela – I Like My Dick Too Much!)


From:
Orlando Gibbons
Detectives Are Us
12 The Alley
Putney
21 November

To:
Micky Larner
'Chez Toi'
24 Lawson Crescent
Putney


Dear Mike,
How nice to hear from you. I am totally with you on the issue of confronting prejudice against those who have different sexual tastes from our own. I have very different sexual priorities from, say, Sam. I like going to bed with his wife

for a start! But this does not mean I do not respect him as a man – in fact, he is one of the most masculine men I know and I have often admired his physique, stamina and ability to stay at sea for long periods.

This does not mean, by the way, that I am in any way attracted to him sexually.

My rates, as I think I said when we met in the pub, are £200 a day – but, as I think of you as a personal friend, on this occasion I would offer an 'all-in' price of £1,500 – 40 per cent of which is refundable if I do not come to a credible conclusion. I have known 'private eyes' who wander around for a few weeks and then, rather like the police, say they are 'baffled'. You do not pay me to be baffled. You want to know what happened to your wife, to the mother of your children. It was not, as you have made clear, a good relationship. You are much happier now you are living, on a part-time basis, with a man for whom I have the highest regard purely as a friend and dentist; but you need to know how Pamela died. She was not an easy woman. She was widely disliked. She obviously did something terrible to Barnaby and he took his revenge in his own way but, even if she lied about the number of children she had brought into the world, the university she had attended and, clearly, was financially dishonest in quite a major way, she was a person. She had a right to live. Well, a right not to be brutally murdered, anyway. If I can 'track down' her killer, I will, it seems to me, be doing the world a service. And also learning something. I have never done a murder inquiry before and am not in any way qualified to begin one. I can only say I am deeply grateful for your confidence in me and will try to justify it even though that seems, at the moment, unlikely.

I did have the chance to speak with Gerald Price, as it happens, and learned much of interest in regard to the death of your late wife. It was about a week ago and he seemed slightly more communicative than usual. When I asked him whether he was on his way to 'chambers', he said, 'Fucking chambers can fucking whistle for me!' Which is not typical behaviour for him at all.

I was not surprised to find him changed. I had heard from Mrs Price that he has recently left her and is no longer living at the marital home. I thought I would try to find out where he was living, and, if possible, with whom. Although he has told Mrs Price that there is no 'other woman', in my experience there generally is. In his case there are probably two or three, with a few young Malaysian boys thrown in for good measure.

I hope you did not find that remark in 'bad taste'. It is simply that Gerald Price is a man whose sexuality knows no bounds whatsoever and his urge to have intercourse is not, in my view, sex or even species specific. There is, obviously, nothing wrong with having sex with young Malaysian boys, provided the boys are old enough to have sex legally and provided, of course, they are consenting adults and not simply 'doing it for money', although that, too, is obviously, in many cases, not a bad thing since we all need to earn money and I understand there is much poverty in Malaysia and, you know, why not?

He was not dressed, as he usually is, in a conservative dark suit but in stonewashed jeans and a bright red cardigan, which would have suggested to me, even if I did not already know it, that he is going through some life-changing emotional experience. His shirt, too, seemed to be a 'cry for help'. It was dark blue with spots on it and had a very large collar. When I asked him what he was 'up to', he said he was 'going away'. I asked where he was going. He said he did not know but wherever it was it would be 'for a very long time'.

I then asked after his wife, without letting him know that I had talked to her and knew of his situation. He said, 'She is probably lurking behind a pillar somewhere in the vicinity.' I asked him what exactly he meant by that and he went on to say that he thought Mrs Price was following him. 'She is always following me,' he said, looking around him in a somewhat hunted fashion. 'She always thinks I have got my dick into some other woman. Which is ridiculous. I keep my dick in my trousers, Mr Gibbons, as I am sure do you!'

I was familiar with his way of talking, and, in our time rehearsing *Hamlet*, had almost got used to it, but I must say I was shocked by the deliberate crudity of his language. Partly to change the subject and partly because I wanted to see how he would react, I said I had recently taken instruction from you to investigate the death of Pamela Larner and would welcome the chance to come and talk to him about the case. I said I was now aware he had been having an affair with her and that he had ended it around the time of her death.

'I have no desire to keep any of that secret!' he said. 'I don't care what the old rat thinks any more!'

I took him to be referring to Mrs Price. He started to peer about him again. We were in the Putney Shopping Centre, just at the bottom of the escalators, opposite to Waterstone's Bookshop. A woman with a black beret was coming out of that shop. I thought for a moment it was his wife and so, obviously, did he. He began to twitch like Fagin in the condemned cell.

'Yes, I was having an affair with Mike's wife,' he said, as soon as he was sure it was not Mrs Price. 'I don't mind saying that. It's the truth. If he doesn't like it he can come and thump me. Or, rather, try to thump me. I'd like to see the little tosser try.' He then went on make some very ill-informed remarks about your sexuality – which I will not repeat here. Then he grabbed me by the lapels and stared deep into my eyes. 'I like you, Gibbo!' he said. 'You're a funny little bloke. The jodhpurs were a fucking disaster. But I like you. I know people think I'm some kind of monster but I'm not. I know Larner's been telling people I killed her but I certainly do not go around killing women – even women as unpleasant and boring as Pamela Larner.'

I stood very still. A fat man waddled towards us wheeling a Waitrose trolley. A woman stood listlessly by the flower stall, the only sign of real life in the place. The impartially white light of the mall illuminated Gerald's face in a way I had never seen before. He was a man, Michael, in the grip of something, and I did not know what it was.

'I had a row with her and told her it was over and buggered off. I did not want to fuck her any more. It was a nightmare. It was like dipping it into a knife sharpener. She screamed at me and did all those girly things they do. But when I was walking away from her house, I had this weird feeling. I'd had it all night in fact.'

I kept my eyes on his face. I knew it was important not to break the line of communication between us. He grabbed my arm and I realized, once again, how extraordinarily strong he is. If medical-negligence cases ever dry up he could almost certainly find work as a circus strong-man.

'I was being followed, Gibbo!' he said. 'Someone was following me. They had been following me for days. They followed me to Pam's house and they were watching me when I came out. I know they were.'

He looked around him again. 'People think she's nice,' he said, 'but she isn't. I'm sure it was a woman following me. You get a feeling about these things.'

'How,' I said slowly, 'do you know there was someone following you that night?'

'A kind of prickling in the back of the neck!' said Gerald.

I did not like to point out that this was not really going to count as evidence in a court of law. I asked him if he had heard footsteps or turned to see anyone flitting behind a lamppost immediately his gaze switched in their direction. As a private detective I think I can claim to be something of an expert in the field of following people.

'It was just a feeling,' he said, 'but I know she was there!'

'Who was there?' I said.

'The wife, of course,' he replied. 'I'm leaving her so as I can say what I like now, and I'm telling you she makes the Stasi look like the Putney Sea Scouts after they've been buggered senseless by the Dodgy Dentist.' I am sorry to have to report these offensive remarks but I think it important to give the 'flavour' of the speech of a man who is, after all, our principal suspect. 'If you ask me,' he went on, 'the old rat did her in if she was done in. I would look no further. Do not, for God's sake, tell her you've seen me. I'm not here. I've left her by the way. I have had enough of her perverted little ways!'

I will never cease to wonder at human beings and how they view each other. I do not think I have ever met anyone less likely to have acquired 'perverted little ways' than Mrs Elizabeth Price, but Mr Price clearly saw her very differently from me. Perhaps you and he are steering me in a direction in which I am 'become blind' and I must take Mrs Price more seriously as a possible suspect.

'Pamela took pills, didn't she?' went on Gerald. 'Isn't that what happened? Maybe the old rat forced them down her throat after getting her drunk.'

This, without in any way being planned, was turning into a very useful interview. Detective work is like this, Michael. I have been accused of getting 'too close' to my subjects; on one occasion I actually became engaged to a woman who, it subsequently turned out, had poisoned thirteen people in Raynes Park, but I do not regret it. I am now as deeply involved in the group I like to call, privately, the Puerto Banús Eight.

'I am sure we can clear up Mike's problem with this,' I said to him, keeping my voice as unthreatening as possible, 'and if you wouldn't mind me asking you a few questions we might be able to sort it out very quickly.'

'I'm not supposed to be here,' said Gerald. 'I'm at a secret address in Norfolk.'

'Oh!' I said.

He was still darting those paranoid glances to right and left of him. A woman wandered out of Gap, carrying a large plastic bag, and looked round her with that dazed look people get when they are shopping. I realized that it would not be long before he disappeared completely, probably with whatever woman he is currently 'doing'.

'It's ten years ago,' I said. 'What I have to do is discover the sequence of events on the night she died. Which was the third of November 2000.'

He was looking edgy again. Was there something significant about this date for him? Or was it something else? The woman with the plastic bag, who was obviously not Mrs Price unless she had taken to going out in very elaborate disguise, seemed to be engaging an unhealthily large amount of his attention. Perhaps, I decided, she was yet another of the women of Putney with whom this insatiable man had had sexual intercourse.

'Actually,' said Gerald, managing to drag his eyes away from the rather attractive creature with the plastic Gap bag, 'that date sounds familiar to me. I can tell you very precisely the exact time I left the house. I keep a very detailed diary and also preserve back numbers of the volumes that tell the world and yours truly What Gerald Has Been Up To. I tell you, Gibbo, when you have shagged as many women as I have and have lied so enthusiastically about your whereabouts for the last thirty years, you bloody do need a reminder of where you actually were as opposed to the fictional location you handed over to the wife or the girlfriend.'

'And,' I said slowly, 'you have been looking through this "diary" of yours recently, have you?'

'Because,' said Gerald, with elaborate patience, 'I had heard Larner was saying all this stuff about me and I wanted to check. There is nothing sinister in the fact, Gibbo.'

I just stared at him. Then I nodded with what I hoped looked like sympathy. He was, I must admit, a man greatly changed since my last encounter with him. There were moments when I thought he might almost be trying to be honest. Emboldened by my sympathetic nods (an indispensable 'tool of the trade' for all private detectives), Master Gerald drew closer to me. Although it was only about eleven in the morning, he smelt strongly of alcohol.

'I looked it up only the other day,' he went on, 'and I can tell you I left the Premises of Doom at twenty-two fourteen precisely.' I considered this. Gerald, as if he had complete access to my innermost thoughts, gave me the kind of rumpled grin that went a long way to explaining the power he has over women. And men, too, probably, Michael.

'If you don't believe me,' he said, 'you can always check out KGB Katharine at number thirty-three.'

I was about to ask him who KGB Katharine might be, when he told me.

'She's an old bat who lives opposite. I noticed she was still at the upper window when I went round to try and shake Poofy Boy out of his tree the other day!'

Once again, Michael, I do apologize for this man. He makes me ashamed to be a member of the human race and has little understanding of the highly complex nature of our sexual needs and the obvious necessity of tolerance and sympathy for those who are 'wired' differently from us. Not that I am suggesting there is anything mechanical about your feeling for that rugged dentist of yours. Which I have had the opportunity to observe at close hand and, as far as I am concerned, is a vindication of the beautiful principle that love blossoms in the strangest places and can transform and enhance lives in a manner that is nothing short of miraculous.

My feelings for Sam's soon-to-be-ex-wife are, as far as I am concerned, in the same category.

'What,' I said, 'does she have to do with the murder – or suicide – of Mr Larner's wife?'

Gerald grabbed my arm again. It was, if possible, an even more painful experience than the last time he had tried it. 'She is always at the window,' he said, 'staring down at the street. I noticed she was there the last night I saw Pamela. KGB Kathy always has the look of someone who is about to report you to the police. My worry was that she would find a way of letting the old Fish Faggot know that I had been round, trying to get out of the tiresome responsibility of poking his missus!'

I said I did not doubt his word but was not sure that this person would be able to be precise about the time of something that had happened ten years ago. Something that was, after all, not of particular significance or, at least, probably did not seem as if it was when it occurred. Gerald became very animated indeed at this remark. For a moment I thought he was about to attack me, which I have always been anxious to avoid where he is concerned.

'Listen,' he said, 'these people have nothing else to think

about apart from what their neighbours get up to. Their entire horizons are blotted out by things like parking permits and whether you have taken an inch of their garden or who owns the fucking fence. This is Putney, mate, not ancient Athens. Nobody considers the higher things of life. This is the suburbs, Gibbo, where no one gives a fuck about the meaning of life or about anything that does not directly affect their own comfort. They do not give a monkey's about the starving or the tortured or the mentally ill or the politically abused. Which is why I am getting as far away from it all as possible.'

He had started to look around him again. This time it was a woman in her early sixties who was walking away from us, in the direction of Waitrose. It was curious. I had never, in all the time I had known him, heard Gerald express any interest whatsoever in those less fortunate than himself. What had caused this 'volte-face'? Was he, at last, going to develop into an approximation of a human being?

I thought, but did not say, that Norfolk was, perhaps, not as far from Putney as all that, and that the people there were liable to be no more interested in the Dialogues of Plato than his or my or, indeed, Mrs Larner's neighbours. Once again he seemed to have a very good idea of what was in my mind. In a curious gesture, he stretched out his hand and ruffled my hair – or, at least, what is left of my hair.

'Gibbo,' he said, 'this may well be the last you see of me. I'm in love.'

I asked him, politely, to explain the connection between these two statements. He smiled and I saw a look in his eyes I had never seen before. I have never actually been to Darien or run across the peak on which stout Cortés is supposed to have experienced wild surmise but here, in the more humble surroundings of the Putney Shopping Centre, I thought I might have glimpsed, for the first time, a pretty good example of the kind of gazing around oneself that might well make a strong man, such as Gerald, or indeed Cortés, grow strangely silent.

'Love, Gibbo,' he said dreamily, 'is not just a question of winching the old leg across a nice piece of tail. I thought it was – but it isn't. It is not just a matter of fishing out the old penis and shoving it up the nearest bit of slippery. You can squeeze their behinds all you like. You can get down and dirty on the Bournville Boulevard if that is what takes your fancy. You can clamp your teeth on to as many tits as you choose – and I am a tit man, Gibbo!'

For reasons I do not really wish to go into here – I knew this to be the case.

'You can shag an entire girls' school in the open air, old boy. You can stick it in and waggle it about and unload as much white stuff as there is in a jumbo bottle of hair conditioner but it isn't necessarily love. Love is amazing, Gibbo. Love is something that... you know... I mean... love is ...'

'What,' I said, realizing it was a question that many had asked before me, 'is love?'

He patted my arm gently. 'I'll tell you one day, Gibbo!' he said, and vanished into the crowd of morning shoppers with the grace and speed of a much lighter man.

Well, Michael, the game's afoot. You may well see a great deal of me in the next few days. I shall be round to visit 'KGB Kathy' – although, as I do not plan to address her by that name, I would be very grateful if you could give me a 'steer' as to what I might call her. I shall be going back to talk once again with Mrs Price. Although her husband is still my prime suspect, there is no doubt that this seemingly innocent woman had a definite motive for doing away with your late wife. The *modus operandi* of the crime (if it was a crime) is much more that of a woman than of a violent male like Gerald Price. It may be that Elizabeth, whom I find a deeply sympathetic and moral person, is a possible candidate for the role of your wife's assassin. I would be very upset indeed to find out that this was the case but we have to face the possibility. Even though I find the idea of Mrs Price spending twenty years in Holloway very difficult to accept! But the truth is what counts! I shall leave no stone unturned and – God willing – I shall have a 'result' for you as soon as possible.

I am looking forward so much to our 'seafaring trip'. Your new partner said to me, only last week in the Coat and Badge on Lacy Road, that we would have 'plenty of rum, bum and concertina'! I do not quite know what he meant by that but I shall enjoy whatever is on offer and once again I assure you of my best professional attention at all times. I do hope your documentary is going well. I don't know whether it would be of any interest but I once had a female guinea pig who, quite clearly, was more interested in her 'girlfriends' than any mere male! I am not sure she was an active lesbian but I think that if she had been given the opportunity that is the path she would have chosen for herself!

Best,
Orlando Gibbons

# Chapter Ten

## *In which Orlando Gibbons gets stuck in a Post Office Box*

From:
Roland O. Gibbons
Gibbons Detective Agency
12 The Alley
Putney, SW15
23 November

To:
'Mrs Price'
PO Box 132
Putney

Dear 'Mrs Price',
Or should that be Mrs Price? Are you who you have been pretending to be? Is any of us who we pretend to be? It is a major question.

I went down to the Putney sorting office the other day and was able to discover that someone had, indeed, picked up my last letter to PO Box 132. So you read what I write to you. I don't think I have ever had that before. The chance to address the Unknown Criminal, to say exactly what I think to the person I am pursuing before the chase is over and the banality of the solution is revealed.

I think whoever hired me has something very important to conceal and that that 'something' is connected to the murder of Pamela Larner. I think I am probably talking to the person who killed Mike Larner's wife. I don't know how you did it. I don't know why you did it; but I am pretty sure you are one of the Puerto Banús Eight.

I am following lines of enquiry that may soon lead me to the person who wrote me those letters. Be warned.

Apart from Gerald – who is still in the frame – the three women who, with Mrs Larner, formed the core of the 'Puerto Banús Eight' had the strongest motives for doing away with Pamela. Let me think aloud – for your benefit, 'Mrs Price'.

Let us start by assuming it was you, the real Mrs Price, who committed the crime. Yes, you, the nice lady teacher in the house with the olive trees, your motive being sexual jealousy. Gerald was having an affair with Pamela. You told me when I called on you – if it is indeed you – that you had no idea, until he left you, that he was involved with anyone seriously. I was 'taken in' by what you said. For whatever complex series of reasons I believed you.

That doesn't, I now realize, mean that you are not a murderer.

But – and it is a big 'but' – if you really did kill Pamela Larner for reasons of sexual jealousy I do not see why you would want to hire a private detective in order to find evidence that you presumably already knew about and that had, anyway, caused you to commit homicide and was therefore liable to lead to the uncovering of your crime.

Maybe that is it, Mrs Price. Maybe, like many murderers, you want to be caught.

Actually, I am not sure that is true. I have never met a murderer who wanted to be caught. In my experience they are all pretty keen to get away with it. What I am trying to say, Mrs Price, if you really are 'Mrs Price' and I am writing to you and not someone else, is that you are a much deeper and more complex character than I had first suspected.

I have never seen anyone speak with such venom as Mr Price when he was talking of you. Mary Dimmock, with whom, as I have admitted, I am having an affair, loathes you with a passion. She has described you as 'a nasty old toad', 'cat's arse', 'wrinkly bum', 'the Witch of Endor', 'the Madwoman of Chaillot' and 'Loopy Liz'.

It is one of the few things I do not like about Mary. Perhaps she only says these horrible things because she suspects how fond I am of you. Women are very quick to find out where their men's affections lie and they do not extend much tolerance to women they think might 'steal' their property. Mary would be overjoyed to find out you had killed Mrs Larner. And yet – oh, I hate saying this even in a uniquely secret letter – you, Elizabeth Price, if you are Elizabeth Price, are a strong suspect. Of all of the other three women who went on those holidays, you must have hated Mrs Larner most.

It may not be Elizabeth Price to whom I am talking, however. There are other possibilities even more frightening to contemplate. Perhaps I am really writing to Mary Dimmock. My Mary. My God! Mary Dimmock – you and I have become lovers. And yet – do we really know each other? You are, Mary, a woman whom I have stalked. A woman whom I have filmed having anal intercourse behind a tree in Richmond Park! I have not behaved well towards you; by the same token, you may be not the person I think you are at all. You may be a murderer. How could you do this to me, Mary? If you are Mary.

But, again, how could I do this to you? I am no better than you, am I? Even if you are the woman posing as Mrs Price and the woman who, probably, murdered Pamela Larner, I am in no position to sit in judgement on you. I have not, of course, told you that for a period of nearly three weeks I watched you and Gerald Price 'at it' and that, even now, when we have become lovers, images from my surveillance of you often surface when we are reaching the climax of our lovemaking. Last week, for example, when we joined so beautifully together in my humble bed in my humble flat in Keswick Road, I had a sudden vision of Gerald whacking your naked behind with a large branch in a secluded area of Putney Heath. This was something I had not only filmed but also, from time to time, replayed for my own private pleasure on my home computer.

That isn't right, is it? What I do is not right, Mary, if you are Mary. I am, as you insinuated in that first fateful exchange of letters back at the end of the summer, a grubby little man in a 'mac'. Or, at the moment, actually a grubby little man *on* a Mac. And yet, if you are you, which you may be, and probably a far sicker and more complex person than I had imagined, there may be a sense in which you can see that even if I have masturbated over an image of you being beaten on the bottom by Gerald Price, that is, in a way, a compliment to the love I have for you. There is nothing ugly or sordid about it – even though some people might find it offensive, it is not something I am proposing to do in front of 'some people'. It is something I do in the privacy of my room in Keswick Avenue, making sure that I close the doors and windows, draw the blinds and disconnect the telephone in case anyone should see or hear the revolting thing I am about to embark on.

And yet is it 'revolting'? I fail to see why yanking one's

penis in front of a secret video recording (obtained without her consent) of the woman one loves is 'revolting'. Why do we use such words so easily about things like that?

It is revolting, Mary. I am sorry. It is revolting and wrong, and yet I love you in my own twisted way. Even if you are a murderer and an impostor and a pervert in your own right, as it were, I love you and want to be with you. Let us be perverted together! Let us murder together, if necessary! I love the way you eat langoustines, for example. I love the way you look at a menu with such care and intensity. I love the way you speak. I love your poetry – such of it as I have heard. I especially like the one about the tsunami, the Shakespearian sonnet about Shakespeare and the very powerful prose poem inspired by your finding the pictures of naked men in Sam's drawer.

This murder, in my view, has all the hallmarks of a 'crime passionelle' committed by 'une femme extrêmement passionelle', which you undoubtedly are as I found out last Wednesday when we had that bath together. Maybe you were so disgusted with yourself and with Gerald that you decided to alert his wife, by a complicated route, to what was going on. It might seem improbable that you would impersonate Mrs Price and send a private detective to spy on you and her husband having sex but, believe me, stranger things have happened in my business! And one thing is certain: if I had not been employed to spy on your illicit affair I would not have fallen in love with you so utterly and completely.

I am hoping against hope, though, Mary, that this letter is not addressed to you.

It may well be that I am addressing the only one of these women whom I do not really know – although I hope to remedy that state of affairs very soon. I am talking, of course, about Barbara Goldsmith.

I have only seen you once, Barbara, across that crowded church hall. As a published author who has been on television interviewed by Kirsty Wark – although I hear she was not very nice about your book – you looked as if you thought ordinary people in Putney were beneath your attention. I have to say I once tried to read one of your books and was not impressed. I did not like the descriptions of the weather and I was not convinced by your thinly disguised portrait of the bus depot outside the Green Man.

And, while we are on the subject, who are you to go on about the 'oppression of women'? From what I hear, you live very nicely off the earnings of your very hard-working GP husband while you swan around talking conceitedly about your 'novels', which hardly anyone reads.

You are a mystery, Barbara. I do not know what is going on in your mind but I do know, from my now extensive knowledge of the Puerto Banús Eight that you disliked Pamela Larner as much as any of them – and, indeed, more than some. You are, Mary Dimmock tells me, a very malicious person indeed. I have seen the letter you wrote. It is, in my view, the work of a psychopath. Many of the 'literary set' have distorted ideas of morality and think it is perfectly acceptable to go around having intercourse with anyone they fancy, irrespective of marital status. If Jonathan Cape says it's all right – then it's all right!

I am not built like that, Barbara. I know, as you will realize from this letter, that I have done things that are wrong. I do not mind admitting them. But I know what is right and what is wrong; and I am not sure that you do. So it may well be, Miss Famous Novelist, that you are the one for whom I am looking.

There is a very good reason for my writing this letter and for my being so convinced that one of you – and *not* my prime suspect Gerald Price – is the guilty party. Yesterday I went to visit the woman known locally as KGB Katharine. She really is a world expert on what goes on in and around the patch of pavement immediately opposite 24 Lawson Crescent. I do not think she has moved for the last ten years (apart from a few snatched hours of necessary sleep) and, as far as I can see, she has been taking notes for much of that time.

She was certainly very excited indeed to learn that I was investigating the events of 3 November 2000, the night that Mrs Larner met her unfortunate end. 'She took pills, didn't she?' she said, with unmistakable relish. 'Serves her right! Her garden was filthy!' After I had listened to her account of the crimes committed by young Barnaby Larner (in this case, if even half of what she said was true, she may have had a point) and a ten-minute tirade on the subject of the late Mrs Larner's inability to reverse her 'show-off car' when parking, she did tell me a fact of vital importance.

I know from Mike exactly when Mrs Larner died and I will confirm the precise hour (22.14) at which Gerald Price left the house; and I now know that *an as yet unidentified woman* left the house at least half an hour after he did. I am going back there very soon to show her photographs of all three of you, and if she identifies one of you, I am coming for you, madam. I may be weak. I may be corrupt. I may be a despicable human being. But I believe in justice and I will do proper service to my profession before the month is out.

Orlando (formerly Roland O.) Gibbons

# Chapter Eleven

*In which Gerald Price tries to let his wife down easily, while the Goldsmiths and the Prices find writing home more complicated than usual*

From:
Gerry Price – who is
Somewhere in Norfolk
On or Around 25 November

To:
His Wife
In the Ancestral Home
Château Heathland and All That

Dear Elizabeth,
This is not an easy letter to write, old thing. We have been married an awfully long time. I know I keep forgetting the date and, because of my damned lawyer's habit of always having to be right, frequently have forced you to celebrate on what we both have realized to be the wrong day, but I am aware that it is something of an achievement to have been

spliced for forty years even if most of them, from my point of view anyway, were absolute fucking torment.

I think it's forty years anyway. It might be forty-one. It feels like three hundred and forty-five, actually.

I am, I know, a bit of an oaf. People have often called me that to my face, although if and when they do I tend to wind back the old right arm and give them a bunch of fives right smack in the gob; so it is not something normally sized people do frequently.

I am trying, Elizabeth, to be a better person. Have you noticed that when people want you to think they are being sincere they lob in your Christian name at a totally inappropriate point of the sentence in hand? Ironically, although that use of the name bestowed on you by the pompous bastard who was so inexplicably proud of being your father might seem to be another example of Gerald being a total cunt, the fact is that, in this letter, I am trying, for the first time in our marriage, to be completely honest.

All headmasters are pompous – it goes with the territory – but George was a world-class pompous git. I know we were all supposed to feel sorry for him. I know Haflinger's Syndrome is not a nice disease to have, especially in the form in which he acquired it. I know terrible things happened to his arsehole but, admit it, Lizzie, he was a world-class jerk.

As a result, of being honest, of course, I realize I will come over as a bit of a cunt. I mean, no one is totally honest for that very reason, but the time has come to make the attempt. I do appreciate that I haven't said this before. There have been many occasions when I have let you know how I was feeling – most notably the night I made a half-hearted attempt to strangle you in that hotel in Bordeaux – but I feel I do now need to clue you in on the whole emotional thing between us as tactfully as I can. I want to get it off the old chest in a way that doesn't make this one of those 'dump the old rat' sort of letters because you haven't got the guts to do it face to face.

It seems a bit hurtful to say this to you directly, however, so perhaps a letter is better, and I think I owe it to you to say, having thought it over quite carefully, that I really dislike you.

It has happened gradually. There must have been a time when I found you bearable, although I really cannot remember when that might have been. We did manage to produce two children, although I really cannot remember how or why that happened. I have it in my head, for some reason, that Conrad was conceived in the Lake District. I think both of us agreed that Julia was, in all senses of the word, a mistake. I seem to remember you saying it publicly quite a lot. Another of those things that got you your undeserved reputation as a wit. Putney dinner parties were never complete without your looking down your nose, puffing on a fag and saying something clever-sounding about Catullus or Lucretius or some other complete wanker ending in -us.

Everyone was terrified of you, weren't they?

Do you know? I think I was terrified of you. I think that was why I hung on for so long. You somehow managed to convince me that, without you, I would be an even bigger mess than I already was. Like all the best forms of advertising, your self-publicity managed to subtly undermine its target audience. You also managed to be savagely dismissive of almost everything I ever tried to do in public or in private for the entire time we have known each other, which, if you count the time we spent in Oxford and the wretched few years immediately after it when you somehow managed to convince me that marriage might be a good idea, comes to forty-two fucking years.

Forty-two fucking years, 'Mrs Price'. Having twisted my arm to get yourself that title, you then decided you didn't want it, didn't you? And, after a swift stroke of the pen on your birth certificate, you became Ms Smaillie. I have to say I thought the original spelling was much more to the point.

We have been constantly in each other's company, Elizabeth, for more than five hundred months or fourteen thousand one hundred and twelve days. And when I took five minutes out to ask myself, 'Why?' I could not come up with a satisfactory answer. You have probably told me I am a selfish bastard nearly thirty thousand times – given that that is something you usually manage to say to me at least twice in every day. Well, if I am, isn't it about time I started living up to my stereotype and began to make some moves towards self-protection?

Protection from you – which is what I am talking about – is not easily achieved. What is really required is some kind of FBI witness programme where I could be relocated, permanently, to Omaha or Duluth, Minnesota, but long-suffering husbands are not offered this kind of support. Thousands of women who have only been thumped a few times, by men who have been driven past the point of endurance with their whining at them about leaving things on the lavatory floor, are spirited away by dedicated teams of lesbians to 'battered refuges' up and down the country. For us men, who have been given the female version of the Chinese water torture for fourteen thousand nine hundred and sixty-five days, there is no such service available. Which is why I am reduced to hiding out in Norfolk for a short period. No, I am not going to tell you where I am. No, I do not want a conversation. No, I do not want to see you. I do not want to see you ever again, which is why I am writing this letter and am not obliged to listen to your hideously unpleasant silence over the phone or look at your face, twitching with fury, while you tell me what a despicable little cunt I am.

How do I not love you? Let me count the ways.

I do not love the way you do not want sex. I do not love the way you manage to make me feel as if this lack of libido on your part is, somehow, my fault. I think the most favoured phrase over the years of our long stalemate is probably 'the way you make me feel'. How about taking some responsibility for the way you feel? Is it my fault you never managed to finish the definitive edition of Vindictivius, or whatever he was called? Is it my fault your sister stole your first three boyfriends? Is it my fault you have legs that look as if they have been severed from a large Victorian dining-room table? Is it my fault your hair is falling out and mine isn't?

I do not like the way you look at me – out of the corner of your eye. I do not like the way you ignore me when you come into the house, instead of saying 'Hello, dear, I'm home!' like normal people. I do not like the way you pretend to offer me the TV remote and pretend to ask me what I want to watch, while we both know that what you really want to do is to blame me for the fact there is nothing on the television. I do not like the way you put your hands over your face when you laugh.

I do not like the things you say – and I have heard almost all of them, at least twice, by now. 'I'm rather against football!' for example – which was something your mother used to say and now, to make up for the fact that the old bat is no longer here to give me a hard time, you repeat it at least twice a week. 'I want Elgar's *Dream of Gerontius* played at my funeral!' That, apart from coming into the category of Remarks You Make About Your Funeral and therefore, by definition, managing to be attention-seeking, offensive and dull all at the same time, is also meaningless. I have never bothered to ask you this before but now seems an appropriate moment for discussing What We Do When You Are Dead. Do you mean *all* of *The Dream of Gerontius*? It's about three hours long. If the congregation aren't already dropping in their seats after an endless line of speakers have droned on about your classical scholarship, your endless compassion for the daughters of fee-paying parents and the grace and charm you brought to the task of mothering two totally inadequate children, this might well tip them into open revolt. If you mean a *bit* of *The Dream of Gerontius* – which bit?

While we are on the subject of your funeral, no, I cannot 'guarantee that awful little man from Oriel will not be there' or that Julia will not want to read that awful bit of schlocky prose about you not being dead really but just nipped round the corner for a packet of fags. It's a funeral. You won't be there. OK? And don't get me started on you and tobacco.

It's the urge for control I can't take, Elizabeth. It's the way you want to manage everything and everybody – from how we lay the table to what kind of prepositions we do or do not end a sentence with; and, most of all, I suspect, it is the way you are with our children. I think it is just possible that before they arrived I quite liked you. Don't, by the way, assume that this thought is going to lead me in the direction of being positive about our relationship. I do not want any part of this letter to somehow give you the illusion there is anything worth preserving in our marriage or that there might be some point in our meeting to discuss the fact that we have been wasting each other's time for nearly half a century.

This is a rejection letter, Elizabeth, and one I am trying to make as thorough as I can. So let us start with Conrad.

I think you began winking at him when he was about three. I don't think, at the time, he even knew what a wink meant. I think I had said something you regarded as foolish or self-aggrandizing – so almost any remark of mine would have done, I imagine. I looked across and saw you giving him a sort of musical-comedy twitch of the left eye. It cannot be that this was actually the case, but I could have sworn that he gave you a saucy wink in return. I certainly felt, from the very beginning, that he was on your side rather than mine; and there were sides in our house, Elizabeth, from very early on. Weren't there?

He was about eight when he started to refer to himself in the third person. 'Conrad is tying his shoes!' 'Conrad doesn't like cheese!' 'Conrad is bored of skiing!' From the very first you seemed to find this hugely amusing. In fact, as I recall, you started to do it yourself. 'Elizabeth is distressed to hear Conrad does not like cheese!' To which the little ponce would reply, 'Conrad is concerned to hear Elizabeth is distressed that Conrad does not like cheese!' He used words like 'concerned' from about the age of four.

I think the moment I snapped was when I heard you say something along the lines of 'Elizabeth was interested to learn that Conrad was irritated to discover that Gerald was not amused to notice that Conrad always referred to himself in the third person.' I think I said I thought you were both beginning to sound like psychiatric patients. I may even have made one of my many pleas for you and me to be called Mummy and Daddy, as opposed to Elizabeth and Gerald, but that, too, fell on deaf ears.

'I don't think of myself,' you said, tapping fag ash all over the carpet, 'as a mummy. Aren't they the things in the third room on the left in the British Museum?'

'That,' I should have answered, 'is exactly the kind of mummy you are like. You are certainly not a warm-smells-of-baking-bread-jam-on-the-apron-let's-make-potato-paintings-and-do-animal-impressions kind of mummy. Only that is the kind of mummy I would like to have in charge of my children. Not some fucking Martian who keeps quoting Greek verse at them.'

I never said those things, though, did I? I know everyone thinks I always say what I feel because, so much of the time, the things I say are crude or unacceptable so they assume they must come from the heart. They do not come from my heart, Elizabeth. That is not the person I am. I wanted to have a nice, normal family who called each other 'Mummy' and 'Daddy' and 'son' and 'darling precious girlie', a family where my boy played football with me on Saturdays and my daughter wore pretty dresses and sat on my knee and asked me if she was my princess, but I didn't get that kind of family, did I? I got a mad, twitching freak, who referred to himself in the third person, and a daughter who looked and sounded like someone who had been rejected by the Addams Family as too weird.

Don't start me on Julia. I think we both know what happened with Julia. I know that wasn't my fault, Elizabeth.

I thought I was going to enjoy writing this letter but, of course, I haven't. I can't bear to write any more. It reminds me of what a total fuck-up our marriage was. I thought I was going to say all the things I have never dared to say to you but, now I look at them, I can see they don't, any of them, really express what went wrong or, rather, never got started between the two of us. Most importantly, I suspect, it was about me not having the courage to admit I never really loved you, but I have found that courage now. That's sad. That it has got to the point where it is easier to say these hurtful things than not to say them. Of course it makes me sad, but there is nothing I can do about it. There isn't anyone else – well, if there is, they are not the reason for my writing this letter. I am going away for a while and I think we should sell the house and split the proceeds. There is enough money for both of us. There just isn't any use in pretending any more. That's all I am saying.

Gerald

From:
John Goldsmith MRCGP, DRCOG
Writing from the desk of
Gerald Price QC
112 Heathland Avenue
Putney
29 November

To:
Said Gerald, Sad Wanker that He Is

Hi, Gerry,
This is not your family doctor speaking, John Goldsmith.
Come out wherever you are so as I can punch you on the
nose. I have just read your letter to Elizabeth. I am writing in
reply as she doesn't really want to go to the bother of writing
to you herself. Having read your little effort, I can quite
understand her position. Bloody hell, Gerry – I always knew
you were a shit but I never realized quite how much of a
shit you actually are until I wrested your last communication
from her trembling fingers and, on her instruction, read every
line of it – twice.

Why do people imagine their letters are private? Nothing
else is, these days, is it? My brother once wrote my mother
a letter in which he referred to me as 'a loathsomely creepy
member of the shiny-shoes brigade' and he seemed surprised
to find that she had shown it to me, that I had read it and I
was standing on his front porch preparing to whack him on
his horrible little beatnik jaw.

I haven't ever told you about my brother, have I, Gerry?
But, then, you never listen to anything anyone ever says to
you so there would not have been much point, would there?

You may be equally surprised to learn that I am writing

this letter to you from your own house. Yes, Gerry, I am sitting in your chair as I write this. I am looking at your horrible Russell Flint watercolours and sitting at your carefully restored Victorian escritoire and using one of your large collection of Montblanc fountain pens. Your taste in music is shocking. All you have on offer is CDs of Bruckner. What happened to the Tamla Motown, Gerald? Have you no life in you at all?

Last night, Gerry, I slept, very peacefully, in your immaculate Hülsta bed with its high-quality Vi-Spring mattress. I was lying next to your very attractive, sweet-natured, intelligent, moral and highly sexed wife, and we both enjoyed a very good night together. I made love to her four times, Gerald, which, she tells me, is more than you could manage in six months. She has also told me, Gerald, something I had always suspected but had never quite been able to put myself to the trouble of verifying: that you have a very small penis.

Who are you 'doing' up there in Norfolk, Gerry? That is the kind of word you would use, isn't it? If it is, indeed, Norfolk where you are hiding. You are probably lying about that as well. 'There isn't anyone else – well, if there is they are not the reason for my writing this letter.' Hmm. So there is someone else but you haven't got the guts to tell Elizabeth who it is. A thirteen-year-old Thai hostess, perhaps? Mrs Dimmock? You were 'doing' her, weren't you?

I have left Barbara by the way. You may as well know that. I haven't communicated with her since I walked out after reading that letter of hers.

Barbara was always going on about something called 'the unreliable narrator'. I must say, I could never see the point of reading a story told by someone who was supposed to be unreliable – unless the reader was supposed to flatter him- or herself by working out where the narrator was on the money and where he or she was not. What is, or is not, interesting about a story is the story itself – not our attitude to it. Unreliability, in physics or in storytelling, is not helpful, and in life it is downright disgusting.

I just did not recognize the woman you described in your letter. That is not Elizabeth. All you have done is pick on a few of her mannerisms, exaggerate them and then take issue with them. I simply do not believe you have been in any kind of torment as far as your marriage is concerned – ever. All that has happened is that you have decided to leave Elizabeth for someone who has managed to flatter you into believing that you love her. I am sure she makes all the right noises, Gerald, in and out of the bedroom. What you couldn't take about Elizabeth was that, from time to time, she told the truth about you to your face. You have no idea, Gerald, how lucky you were to have been loved by a woman like that. If you want to know what people are really like, Gerald, look at what they do, not at what they say about themselves. Elizabeth has loved you faithfully. She has been true to you. She has supported you when other people – such as myself – touched on the fact that you are a reprehensible little cunt. She has tried to pass on her love of the thing she loves most in the world – Latin and Greek literature – to her pupils. This, Gerald, seems a rather more useful way of passing the time than making money out of the sometimes inevitable errors of judgement committed by people like me. What you do Gerald, professionally and privately, is disgusting. You cheat on your wife. You bully people who are supposed to be your friends, unless they are people like me, because you know I am capable of pushing your teeth back down your throat – 6–4, 6–3, 6–0, wasn't it, Gerald?

What do you do that allows you to pronounce on Elizabeth's love of classical languages or, indeed, the teaching of them? You present a version of the truth in open court that often you know to be false, even if it makes perfectly decent people miserable. While Elizabeth feels mortified at her inability to love Julia as she feels she should – something you have never helped her with at all – you think it amusing to make a cutting remark about either of your children without appearing to realize that you have any responsibility for them at all.

Oh, sorry, Gerald, I'm being 'pompous'. You use that word about me quite a lot, don't you?

*'Don't start me on Julia. I think we both know what happened with Julia. I know that wasn't my fault, Elizabeth.'*

What on earth is that supposed to mean? Don't you take responsibility for anything that happens in this house, Gerald? She's your daughter as well. You do not seem to have grasped that simple point. I have been having quite lengthy conversations with Elizabeth about Julia and it's clear she feels terrible guilt, loaded on to her by you. I'm sure you did want a simpering idiot to sit on your knee and pose as your 'princess' (Jesus – inside you are pure marshmallow) and I'm sure you made your disappointment all too clear to the poor girl.

I can still see you by that pool in Corsica. I think it was Julia's birthday. She was eight or nine, perhaps. Maybe ten. What she really wanted was a book. She had made that pretty clear. She wanted a particular book, obviously, because she wanted to be like her mum, who always had her nose in one. *Alice in Wonderland.* She had set her heart on it. You didn't think she should have a book. You had made that perfectly clear. You had told her she was getting a pretty dress, and that was what you got her. I happened to know that, like many other stupid people, you never really understood *Alice in Wonderland.* As she unwrapped the parcel, Elizabeth did her very best to keep the glass smile at the edge of her lips, but little Julia, with her funny glasses and her lank hair and her permanent look of anxiety, couldn't manage to conceal her feelings. She was a kid, Gerry. Give her a fucking break. Her lip was on the edge of trembling when you said, in that horrible, jocular tone you use when you're insulting someone – because that makes it all right, doesn't it? – 'You'll be pretty enough for it one day, darling, won't you?'

Then she did cry. As she ran into the house you looked around at us as if, for some reason, you thought we were the kind of adoring audience to which you usually perform – brainless bimbos, elderly judges – and you said, spreading those pointlessly large hands of yours, 'Did I say something?' I don't think Elizabeth said anything. She just got up and followed her little girl into the house. If anyone destroyed Julia's ability to be herself, it was you, Gerry. It is entirely typical of you that you seek to shift the blame on to your long-suffering wife.

'*You are certainly not a warm-smells-of-baking-bread-jam-on-the-apron-let's-make-potato-paintings-and-do-animal-impressions kind of mummy. Only that is the kind of mummy I would like to have in charge of my children.*'

Actually, Elizabeth does rather good animal impressions. You just never thought to ask her. Her wounded rabbit is hilarious. Her giraffe whose neck is trapped in a power cable is even funnier. But, of course, the mummy – a revealing word for someone brought up in the fifties – to whom you are referring is nothing to do with Conrad or Julia. She is the kind of mummy you want to have all to yourself, Gerald. Isn't she? From what I hear, your mother and father had the kind of happy marriage from which someone with an inadequate sense of themselves might well feel excluded; and, of course,

251

you would be much happier with a less intelligent woman. Barbara would destroy you in two weeks.

You have spent more than half your life with a woman and you have never really seen her. Shame on you.

I can't really send this letter to you as this is your house (well, half your house anyway) and you are not here. I suppose you will skulk back at some point. I am taking Elizabeth away from here and, at some point, I expect I will have the conversation I need to have with Barbara.

I think both of us feel we would not mind if we never saw you again. Ever. I suppose there is little chance of that. If I know anything about you, it will not be as simple as 'selling the house and dividing the proceeds' – all I hope is that Elizabeth never has to see you or talk to you ever again. Maybe this will be a chance for a lawyer, as long as it isn't you, to actually do something useful.

I am leaving this letter on your hall table, next to your cycling helmet. I hope it makes you realize how badly you have treated Elizabeth. No, that is not what I hope. I hope it fucking chokes you, Gerry.

John Goldsmith

From:
Barbara Goldsmith
The Palehorse Hotel
Little Bransyng
Norfolk
1 December

To:
John Goldsmith
101 Fellen Road
Putney

Dear John,
I hope you are getting on well with the farting noises.
However low you get, I know it is something that never fails
to amuse you. Jas and Josh did not mention that the three of
you had all bonded together by sharing this simple pleasure.
In fact, in the brief call I had with them, both of them said
they had not seen you 'for yonks'. In so far as either of them
expressed emotion of any kind, I would have said they were
worried about you.

'Where's Dad?' Josh said. I said I didn't know.

'Oh,' said Jas – they were both on the speakerphone in
Josh's car, ' that's a bit rough!'

'Why am I supposed to know where he is?' I said.

'Because – *doh* – he's your husband. *Doh*!' said Josh.

'Not for much longer, I suspect!' I said brightly.

That shut them up for a few minutes. Any suggestion that
human relationships may be under discussion is usually a
pretty good way of silencing them. I moved the conversation,
effortlessly, to rugby. They were on their way to or from a
match. At least that meant I didn't have to try to pretend to
remember their wives' names or make baby talk to February or

Solstice, or whatever the little swine are called. We talked about rugby for a bit – or, rather, they did. Then the silence returned.

'You're not really . . . leaving Dad, are you?' said Jas.

Interesting that they couldn't conceive of you having the nerve to walk out yourself. I think – as you rightly suspected – that that was why I kept the tone of that letter so consistently unpleasant. It took that to get you moving.

'Because,' said Josh, 'he is a good husband and father!'

I couldn't believe I was hearing this. I think I may even have said so. Good husband and father???? Out of what manual did they get that one?

'I mean,' said Jas, 'he's a really good doctor!'

'The jury's out on that!' I said.

Another very long silence. I could hear them groping for your other good qualities as Jas's BMW took them closer and closer to the enticing prospect of running around with twenty-eight other large men who have been trained from birth to feel nothing.

'He is,' said Josh, 'a good provider!'

He was clearly still reading directly from the manual that had provided his earlier insights into your character. It is interesting to note, while on this subject, that money earned by women doesn't really count. The fact that I earned about eighty thousand pounds last year doesn't seem to matter, as far as they are concerned. I don't think either of them has ever read a word of one of my books. Neither, from your brief remarks in what may well have been your last letter to me, have you. You are the man, John, who, when I asked him if he liked Nabokov, replied, 'Only with cheese on it.'

'You go on at him sometimes!' said Jas.

I suddenly felt very tired.

'It's all right, boys,' I said. 'I wouldn't worry about it. He doesn't listen.'

'It's very important,' said Josh, 'not to listen to women.'

I think this was intended humorously but, like all jokes made at my expense, it had the definite intention of putting me in the place I have steadfastly refused to occupy for the last thirty-odd years of their lives.

I have no idea where you are, John. I am assuming you will return at some point so I am sending this letter to the big, clean, characterless house where we have lived together for so long. What I am going to say is difficult – I don't think Gerry has yet had the guts to say it to Elizabeth – but I am going to say it and have told him I am going to say it so here goes.

I have been in love with Gerry Price for the last forty-three years. I fell in love with him on the day I met him on a hot summer's day in Oxford in the summer of 1968. Remember 1968?

I had been to see a guy I knew in Magdalen. It must have been the summer term of my second year. I had played Hermione in the OUDS production of *The Winter's Tale*, directed by this man (I think he was called Rick) who, for reasons none of us ever quite fathomed, decided to set the whole thing in Poland in the 1930s. He kept trying to kiss me, which I didn't like at all. I got out of his room and walked along the cloisters, looking out on to the cool lawn and the sunlight, and thought I was very lucky to be such a clever girl who acted in plays and got a great deal of attention from young men like Rick.

One of the doors of the studies that faced directly on to the cloisters was open and I looked in as I walked past. Gerry was lying on a sofa, smoking a cigarette. He had long hair in those days, right down to his shoulders. He glanced up and saw me. He smiled. He had that same great, jagged mouth and that same predatory look about him. His eyes were bright with mockery and fun and intelligence. We both just couldn't stop staring at each other. I don't know how long I stood there.

'You're Barbara Sharpe, aren't you?' he said eventually. 'You were in that play!'

I smiled and said I was indeed Barbara Sharpe and had, indeed, played Hermione in *The Winter's Tale*. I stood there, waiting for the compliments. They did not come. Instead he just lay on the sofa, staring at me. It was strange. Although his hair suggested hippie inclinations, he was wearing a dark suit, even on that beautiful summer day, and he had on a newly pressed clean white shirt.

'And may I know who you are?' I said.

The way he was looking at me had started to unsettle me. I couldn't have said quite why. I think – and this is something I have only just understood – it was sadness in his eyes. As if he had seen bad things ahead for both of us.

'Oh,' he said, 'I'm a boring lawyer and I'm going to leave Oxford and make a lot of money and be very, very boring.'

'I meant,' I said, slowly, 'what is your name?'

He didn't answer this question. He just kept looking at me with those eyes of his, and now it was as if he was laughing at the two of us. He got up off the sofa.

'I saw you,' he said, 'walking across Oriel quad.'

'I'm allowed to do that!' I said. I was beginning to be slightly irritated by him, but still I did not move. I felt that I wanted to stand there for ever on that hot summer afternoon, with someone down the corridor playing 'A Whiter Shade Of Pale' by Procul Harum. When they got to the end of the track, whoever was playing it moved the needle right back to the beginning. The organ kept on with that Bach-ripped-off riff and the singer managed to sound like he had something we knew no white man ever really had, i.e. the blues.

Gerry, who wasn't, of course, Gerry then, just some guy

in a room in Magdalen, was walking towards me now and I felt that something very important was going to happen, but I couldn't have said quite what. If he had kissed me, right there and then, I would not have objected. If he had asked me out, I would have said yes, but neither of those things happened. Instead he got that sad look in his eyes again.

'I don't want to be a boring lawyer,' he said, 'but that's probably what I'm going to be. Wouldn't it be great if you could walk away from the life that everyone seems to have chosen for you? It's not the life I want, but it's the life I know I'm going to get. A house in the suburbs and two point four children. Jesus!'

His face darkened. Then, suddenly, for no reason that I could see, he broke into a smile and he seemed much younger. I felt I knew exactly how he must have looked as a child. I remember thinking that, in spite of what he had said about being boring, life with him could be very exciting; but, just as I started thinking this, he started to close the door against the sunlight and the beautiful June day outside.

'I have to work,' he said, very gently. 'Goodbye, Barbara Sharpe.' It was only when the door was firmly shut against me that I realized I had not even found out his name.

The next time I saw him was in Putney. He was married to Elizabeth and I was married to you, John.

As a novelist, I would like to tell you a different story. To show you, perhaps, how, over the years, as parents of children who went to the same schools, we became part of a network of middle-class families who gave dinner parties for each other, played tennis and even took joint holidays in hired villas in France, Spain and Italy. How, gradually, at these enlivening social occasions, maybe at the St Jude's Wine and Cheese in Aid of New Playground Equipment or, possibly, at the Putney Choral Society's groundbreaking version of 'Easy

Bits of *Elijah* with Piano, Five Violins and Mr Goldberg on Cello and Timpani', Gerry and I found ourselves exchanging glances, then phone numbers and, finally, a room in a hotel somewhere for a bit of off-piste shagging.

It wasn't like that. It was simply that we had been in love with each other since, oh, since before we even met. We both put up with being apart from each other for all those years and then, one day, neither of us could stand it any longer. I don't think either of us ever spoke properly about what each felt about the other. There wasn't any need to say anything at all. We both knew. Perhaps there were moments when our knowledge of the simple fact that the two of us were meant to be together floated uncomfortably close to the surface but, certainly, nothing was ever said. For years, we were very careful not to touch each other. Or, if possible, even to get too close. Everyone thought we disliked each other and that suited both of us just fine.

Life is a stupid business, isn't it? I am not saying either of us was aware that that was how it was at the time. We were not, either of us, so bound by the conventions of marriage that we were struggling with feelings we knew to be wrong or anything of that sort. It is simply that this was how it was but neither of us could see it. You never know until it is far too late, but we know it now and, even if we did not know it then, we can see that that was what made us both the people we were. It is almost too late for me and Gerry, but not quite too late.

I am sorry, John. I could have wished I had not fallen in love with a man you disliked so violently. I am very anxious to stop you coming after him with, or without, a tennis racquet. We are going to be here for at least another week, and if you want to write or call, please do so. I suspect you may not even get this letter until things have changed yet again. Perhaps by then Gerry will have been able to face Elizabeth. I have tried to call you and find out where you are but you clearly do not want to see or speak to me so perhaps this may find you. I am genuinely sorry about what has happened.

You can't do anything about what you feel, John – and sometimes you simply have to act on it. We are staying in Room 12 here and, if you do get this letter and feel the urge to drive up the motorway with a sledgehammer, I should take the precaution of calling first.


Barbara


From:
Elizabeth Price
101 Fellen Road
Putney
2 December

To:
Barbara Goldsmith
The Palehorse Hotel
Little Bransyng
Norfolk

Oh, Barbara,
You can do so much better than that, can't you? Most of my girls could have managed a better brush-off letter. At Dame Veronica's we try to teach them to express themselves gracefully. The Latin I have been drilling into them all these years does seem to help.

I thought you were supposed to be a novelist. I thought

you dealt in credible motive and realistic motivation and all those things that make invented characters come alive. Oh, sorry. You're not that kind of novelist, are you? You are the kind of novelist who goes on about signifiers and signified and who, fundamentally, thinks words do not really mean what they seem to mean.

'Meaning,' I seem to remember you saying in one interview I read, 'is undecidable and indecipherable.' Certainly your novels are both of those things, which is probably why I usually throw them across the room on about page twelve.

We have to be very careful, of course, about language. The sort of people the snobbish part of me despises often, for example, use inverted commas when they come to a word that is worrying or perhaps overly important to them. They feel the need, when engaged in this business of writing things down, to put a distance between themselves and what it is they are trying to convey. Actually I now think their awkwardness is a kind of honesty. You have no awkwardness whatsoever when it comes to language. You think you can make it mean anything you want it to mean.

Hence your extraordinary letter.

*'It was simply that we had been in love with each other since, oh, since before we even met.'*

Excuse me, Barbara – what does that actually mean? How the fuck can you be in love with someone you do not even know? And how can you make a single casual meeting in an Oxford college the basis of a smouldering passion that smouldered away for forty-odd years and was then, for no good reason that I can see, suddenly allowed to flower, burst into flames, erupt and whatever other form of cliché seems appropriate to describe suppressed passion finally learning to hold its high head high, walk tall, etc., etc.

For fuck's sake, Barbara. What was really going on?

Have the decency to tell us – please. I almost prefer Gerald's cowardice to your horribly trendy lies.

'*We both put up with being apart from each other for all those years and then, one day, neither of us could stand it any longer.*'

*Doh* – as your really rather nice children might have said. So if you were 'putting up with being apart', you must, surely, have been aware of it, and if you were aware of it, it must have manifested itself in more than the odd sigh or rolling of the eyes. Are you expecting me to believe that that was all that happened? Come off it, Barbara – who are you trying to fool? Love from afar? With Gerald?????? Courtly love went out a very long time ago; it was never, ever an option for someone like you and most certainly not for Gerald Price QC. You weren't, anyway, 'apart' from each other. You were constantly tripping over each other at judo practice and Speech Day and at my house and your house. I have gone back over every encounter and tried to remember exactly how you acted together. Nothing. From which, Barbara, I deduce that there was an active attempt at concealment. You have both been at it for years.

When did you two first start fucking? Tell us. Just own up to the whole horrible squalor of it. Don't lie or, if you must lie, have the grace to come up with something a little more credible than the plot of your last novel but two.

'*We were very careful not to touch each other. Or, if possible, even to get too close. Everyone thought we disliked each other and that suited both of us just fine.*'

I don't think that anybody much thought you disliked each other. If that was what you were trying to convey, you made a very bad job of it. And as for 'not getting too close', how about that night in the swimming pool of the Villa Isadora? Or the hokey-cokey in and around the gardens of the Maison de Maître Île de Maquereaux, Bénodet, Brittany, on the night of 1 September 1984? And just how did the spoken unspoken agreement between you two sensitive flowers operate? You just 'knew', did you? Bollocks, Barbara. I may not be a highly regarded female novelist who earns nearly six figures a year (I just do not believe that figure by the way) but I do know bullshit when I see it and your letter is almost as near a liquid stream of bullshit as you are likely to find outside a dysentery hotspot in downtown Calcutta.

'*Life is a stupid business, isn't it?*'

Er ... possibly it is. Not a particularly original thought for a leading lady novelist. It needn't be, of course, if one tries to behave intelligently. Something that seems to be very low indeed on your list of priorities

'*We were not, either of us, so bound by the conventions of marriage that we were struggling with feelings we knew to be wrong or anything of that sort. It is simply that this was how it was but neither of us could see it.*'

Oh, perish the thought that anyone, these days, is 'bound by the conventions of marriage'. The conventions being, I suppose, that you try to look after, tell the truth to and generally support the person you are supposed to love. Oh, no, Barbara, you're an artist, aren't you? You can do exactly as you like and we – the poor benighted creatures who have not published novels that were well received by the *New Statesman* – are supposed to lie down and accept it.

The second half of that first euphoniously dishonest sentence is very revealing. You weren't struggling with feelings you knew to be wrong. Hang on. What was it you said earlier in the letter?

'*I have been in love with Gerry Price for the last forty-three years. I fell in love with him on the day I met him on a hot summer's day in Oxford in the summer of 1968. Remember 1968?'*

Yes, I do, Barbara. It was not a particularly interesting year. Principally because the world was full of people like you walking around with flowers in their hair and talking mealy-mouthed rubbish about universal love and brotherhood.

But, getting back to your letter, you were in love with him and not struggling, in any sense, with that feeling. It was just... there. You hardly noticed it, really. You didn't sort of get around to doing anything about this grand passion until you were in your late fifties. Why was this, I wonder? More time on your hands? Career not going so well? Or could it possibly be that it wasn't really there at all? It seems, as far as I can tell, to be based on the fact that he ogled you, briefly, in the cloisters of an Oxford college.

*'You never know until it is far too late, but we know it now and, even if we did not know it then, we can see that that was what made us both the people we were. It is almost too late for me and Gerry, but not quite too late.'*

Don't want to sound like a stuffy old schoolmistress, Barbara darling, but, if you really do think we 'never know until it is far too late', how come you can authenticate this mysterious feeling that kept you rooted to the spot when dear old Gary Booker was singing his heart out over and over again on that afternoon in Magdalen? You seem to want us to believe that it was a dream that sustained you as you struggled with the wasteland that is SW15 for thirty-odd difficult years.

*'I am sorry, John. I could have wished I had not fallen in love with a man you disliked so violently.'*

Well – this is a little nearer to it. Not, of course, in any way honest, but a little nearer than most of the rest of your truly awful letter. It is the only moment when you own up to the fact that your actions do have some impact on those around you and, while I do not believe for a moment that you care about what John may or may not think of your new choice of man, some of the badly expressed, half-baked ideas jostling around in that sentence do give some hint as to your real motivation.

It must be very sweet to take something from me. You have always wanted to do that. You have always wanted my approval but, like the conscientious teacher I am, I was never able to say about any book of yours, 'Darling, it was marvellous!' I am boringly programmed towards honesty. Towards saying what I genuinely feel and think, even if other people are going to be offended by it. Conrad always tells the story of our taking him, when he was about seven, on the Channel ferry. He asked me what the ship was made of and I said, 'Iron. Steel.' He said, 'So is it heavier than water?' I said, 'In one sense it is!' And he said, 'How do we know, then, that it won't sink?' I said, 'Darling, we don't *know* – but we can reasonably assume it might not.' Which left the poor little chap with a lifelong fear of the sea.

You have taken quite a bit off me over the years. There was that rather nice Provençal bowl in about 1981. There were no fewer than three blenders between 1979 and 1986. There was that very nice first edition of Lynd Ward's *Madman's Drum* – worth, I am told, four hundred dollars, these days – that you 'borrowed' and somehow never got around to returning and, of course, I did not ask you for it because I am not like that and you know I am not like that and that was why you kept it. There was the scarf. Oh, yes – the scarf. You must remember that because, for some reason, I did ask for it – over and over again – and you, with that famous charm of yours, said you *must* remember and you were *so* stupid and you *would* do it, you really would, and I looked at you

264

from behind my famously lidded eyes and puffed on a fag, and said, 'You won't, Barbara. You know you won't. Stop pretending. You just won't!' And you laughed with what some people think of as charm, and said, 'I know! I know!'

Perhaps, though, Barbara, I have, at last, taken something from you – even if it is something you do not seem to want.

I am writing this at the desk in your study, surrounded by unsold copies of your works. Many of them, for some reason, in Japanese. What on earth the Japanese make of you I cannot imagine. The sheer volume of volumes still *chez toi* might suggest that they don't make very much of you at all, but I am sure you improve a great deal in translation. Perhaps there is a small core of tasteless idiots in just about every country in the world who all sign up to pretending to like the same kind of rubbish.

Really, your house is a shocker. Did you know you have earwigs (at least I think they are earwigs) in your kitchen cupboards? And that the fridge door will not close? Why have you put that coffee-table in the front room? Why did you buy it in the first place? What on earth is that Monet reproduction doing in the lavatory? For how long, by the way, have you had separate bedrooms and how did you manage to snaffle the most comfortable bed?

John and I are enjoying it greatly. In spite of the rain falling on your shabby little garden. Although I think I may have painted the whole place green by the time you return to London. Oatmeal is so *passé*, don't you think?

Oh, in case you were wondering what I'm doing in your house, John has left a letter there, which will explain it all from his point of view. I will try to give my account of what happened between John and myself without resorting to any rubbish about being in love with each other in a previous life, or swapping glances at the school gates for the last however many years without really understanding their significance until last week.

I was devastated after Gerald left me. He is not an easy person to love – or even to like for that matter – but he was the person I loved. He was the father to my children, and I was under the impression that he was in love with me. I can't understand why else he would have shared my life for so long. If I had had the kind of problem with him that he seems to have had with me, I would have told him.

Out of the blue I got a letter from John, who had run away to France after your horribly twisted version of a Goldsmith Annual Family Round Robin Newsletter arrived on everyone's doormat. It seems that he has, for quite a long time, been thinking that he felt something for me that was slightly more than friendship. When he said that, I realized that I had been feeling almost the same kind of thing. I hadn't ever done anything about it because I was married and, or so I thought, in love with someone else. I suggested he look me up when he was back in London. He did. We found we liked each other very well. We want to live together. At the moment we seem to be living in your house.

I would suggest that when and if you do return to Putney you go to Heathland Avenue. John is still really very angry with Gerald and I don't think either of us wants an undignified scene, do we? Somehow or other we will have to get this sorted. For the moment, letters seem an easier way of communicating. At one level I think all four of us are so angry with our partners that meeting in person is a very bad idea.

Your former friend
Elizabeth Price

PS You also have moths. Quite a lot of them.

PPS I have had a series of extraordinary conversations with a funny little man called Gibbons, who is a private detective. He seemed to be implying that either Gerald or you may have murdered poor Mike Larner's wife. I think he is rather sweet on me actually.

# Chapter Twelve

*Orlando Gibbons has an Agatha Christie Moment. People try to take it away from him*

From:
Orlando Gibbons
Detectives Are Us
12 The Alley
Putney
14 December

To:
Mike Larner and Sam Dimmock, c/o 24 Beeston Crescent
John Goldsmith and Elizabeth Price,
c/o 112 Heathland Avenue
Gerald Price and Barbara Goldsmith, c/o 101 Fellen Road
Mary Dimmock, c/o Orlando Gibbons, Flat 12,
Woodvale Mansions, Keswick Avenue

Dear All,
This letter and its contents, which, I suppose, come to think of it, are the same thing, is and are highly confidential. I hope I have got everyone's address right! There have been

some pretty major changes in the living arrangements of our 'little group' recently, and if I have got an address wrong, I apologize!

As many of you know, I have recently become engaged to be married to Mary Dimmock as soon as her divorce comes through. This is someone on whom I spied in my professional capacity as a 'private dick'. She knows. She has forgiven me.

My darling, I still love you and feel intensely the great joy you have brought to me by agreeing to share your life with me, which, of course, Sam knows about. You have your 'hands full' elsewhere, Sam, by which I do not mean a cheap joke at the expense of your newly discovered and – to me – deeply moving awareness of your sexuality. What you have with Micky is unique and very precious in my view.

The purpose of this letter is to report on my current 'work in progress', which is to provide an assessment of the causes of death of Mrs Pamela Larner on 3 November 2000. Normally I would supply Mr Larner, who is my client, with an exclusive report of my conclusions, but I have already given him an early look at my 'result' and we both felt it would be appropriate to share my report with the group I have herein termed the 'Puerto Banús Seven', being a reduced number of the original 'Puerto Banús Eight' by one person due to the death of Mrs Pamela Larner on 3 November 2000.

It is this death on which I am now reporting. It is a story of passion and sexuality, which, in many instances, combines the two at the same time. It is full of squalor and ugliness but also beauty and nobility. And, also, regrettably, hideous violence and suppressed urges, which surfaced with tragic consequences for the people in whom they surfaced and also those near to them at the time.

I will attempt to keep my narrative 'plain and unvarnished' and stick to the facts as I have uncovered them. I have indicated my sources, where necessary, and checked my recordings with the respondents.[1]

Pamela Larner, born Pamela Figgis in Hertford, England, on 12 January 1948, was a petite brunette (we think) who had had a varied career in reflexology, hairdressing, secretarial work and Gestalt therapy. There is no firm evidence that she qualified at any of the institutes claiming to implement the now discredited doctrines of Fritz Perls but she had, almost certainly, 'read a book about it'. She also maintained she was a qualified Jungian analyst but I have been able to find no justification for this at all. Michael Larner has said that her therapy work was 'all bullshit, really' and that she 'just got people to roll around the floor, with their clothes off, if possible, to make it all look more intense'.

Although most people seem to agree that she was a talented hairdresser, she clearly thought that she was somehow 'above such a humble job'. She was the mother of three children: Barnaby Larner, who was last heard of in a high-security jail in eastern Burma; Leo Larner, who is an off-licence manager in Budleigh Salterton; and Milly (also known as Molly) Larner, who, after a brief career in local radio, has joined a lesbian commune for unemployed gay women over thirty in Haworth, Yorkshire.

Her marriage to Michael Larner was not a happy one. In the mid-1990s, when she was out of touch with all of the 'Puerto Banús Eight', including, by his account, her husband, she seems to have become seriously delusional and lost the loyalty of her children, if she had ever really had it. She became convinced that she had four, not three, children and one respondent, not part of the 'Puerto Banús

---

[1] Interviews with Mike Larner, Elizabeth Price, Mary Dimmock and telephone interview with Barbara Sharpe/Goldsmith. Mr Price refused formal interviews.

Eight' – who has asked not to be named – has reported her talking, at length, about her 'wonderful daughter Lucy', who had been to Oxford, got a first-class degree, married a man called Hugh and now 'has bought a beautiful farm in Gloucestershire where I go for weekends to ride her horses Dapple and Misty'.

She also persistently maintained that she had a first-class degree from Brasenose College, Oxford. She was not consistent about which subject she had taken but the most common skill to which she laid claim was medieval Spanish, a subject of which, as far as I can gather, she was entirely ignorant. In fact, she attended the 'Ox and Cow' secretarial college in Oxford where she acquired typing and secretarial skills.[2]

She began taking various drugs during this period, including a variety of sleeping pills, some of which were prescribed for her 'under the counter' by Dr John Goldsmith. He told me in a lengthy interview that he had been very careful about the amount he prescribed and, after a while, had said that she should consult her own GP about her problem.[3]

During this period Larner met Gerald Price by the cheese section in Waitrose, a place he often uses to make 'sexual conquests',[4] and their passion, which seems to have developed while they were staying in the Villa Maurice Barres in Calvi,

---

[2] I have been unable to verify the actual name of this establishment, which seems to have specialized in giving education in secretarial skills to girls from well-off families who could then claim to 'have been at Oxford'. Which Mrs Larner did – almost constantly, according to some respondents.

[3] Dr Goldsmith told me that this was the first time he had revealed this fact and did not want it publicly known. I have consulted him before mentioning it here and he has given his permission. He told me, in the Duke's Head, Putney, on 3 December, that 'that cunt Gerry Price may try to make something of it but I do not care'.

[4] Interview with subject who asked not to be named and had a brief 'fling' with Mr Price in 2012 after he approached her as she was buying a pre-wrapped portion of Jarlsberg.

Corsica, was reignited. Mr Price maintained, in his interview with me, that she was 'just a shag' and certainly, from his point of view, that would seem to be the case.

Not so, however, from Mrs Larner's perspective. Her demands on Mr Price grew more intense. She several times suggested they should 'go away together to somewhere hot and live on the beach', and when Mr Price responded negatively, Mrs Larner threatened to tell her husband, her mother and, on one occasion, Putney Police – apparently on the grounds that 'what he did to her in his kitchen when Mrs Price was on the school trip was against the law'. Pamela Larner's mother, who refused to be interviewed by me, works as a receptionist in a nightclub in Marbella, although she is in her early eighties.

On the night of 3 November 2000 Mr Price visited her at the Larner family home at 24 Lawson Crescent, Putney, a four-bedroomed family home arranged on four floors, having the advantage of a secluded garden to rear, which, although largely still in its natural state, has the benefit of several mature fruit trees. It is situated in the popular 'Putney Wedge' between the Upper and the Lower Richmond Roads.

It was a warm night for the time of year.

When he arrived Mr Price found that Mrs Larner was upstairs in the room she often referred to, during this period, as 'Lucy's bedroom'. He could see this as Mrs Larner's shape was clearly visible behind the blinds. It was 20.30 and this time, suggested originally by Mr Price, has been confirmed by Mrs Katharine Bildeeze, who was living, as she is now, in the opposite house and, on the night in question, was, as usual, at what she calls 'her station' in the upstairs front bedroom.[5]

---

[5] She maintains a more or less constant vigil in her chair by the window, claiming, in the course of several interviews I conducted with her, to be 'looking out for burglars'.

Mr Price called up to her and asked her why she had telephoned him, twice, on his home number, something he had specifically asked her not to do. Mrs Larner replied – this account from Mr Price is confirmed by Mrs Bildeeze, 'Because I love you!' To which Mr Price replied, 'Fuck off why don't you?'

After quite a lengthy conversation Mrs Larner let Mr Price into the house.[6]

We only have Mr Price's account of what happened next. According to him, they had a long argument about their relationship in which Mrs Larner, several times, threatened suicide. At one point she held up a bottle of what she claimed were phenobarbitolozone[7] and 'waved them around her head shouting' for several minutes. She said, several times, that she 'wanted to die' and that her 'husband is a fish'. Eventually she swallowed two or three and Mr Price hit her in the face 'to try to get some sense into her'. She then opened the french windows and said she was going out into the garden to kill herself 'so that the neighbours would see'. Then, according to Mr Price, he produced an item of 'male jewellery' that Mrs Larner had given him during a villa holiday in Chania, Crete, in 1982, and told Mrs Larner that it was about the only thing he had had from her and that it summed her up as it was 'gaudy, tasteless and worth absolutely nothing to anyone' because, like her, it was completely fake. She seized it from him and threw it into the garden, then retreated to the sofa, waving the bottle of pills and shouting, 'I will take these and die and then you'll be sorry!'[8]

---

[6] Michael Larner was on a field trip for the BBC filming a group of stickleback, or possibly gudgeon, in Hampshire.

[7] There is no such drug registered with the MHRA.

[8] They were temazepam – as confirmed in the police report, which I have seen.

Mr Price said she was welcome to top herself any time she liked and that as far as he was concerned he would be glad if he never saw her again. He then left the premises at – according his estimate – 'roughly 22.15'.[9]

Mrs Bildeeze (see Notes 7 and 11 and attached Appendix 'BILDEEZE') has told me that at approximately 23.25 'an unknown woman' approached 24 Lawson Crescent and rang the bell several times. There was no response. The woman then went to the side door and started to climb over it. When I asked Mrs Bildeeze why she did not contact the police, then or subsequently, about this apparent intruder on Mr and Mrs Larner's property, she said it was 'Just sex, sex, sex all over again and I didn't want to get involved.'[10]

I have reason to believe that this woman was also the person who approached me on 12 June of this year, pretending to be Mrs Elizabeth Price. I received a letter from a Post Office Box address in Putney in which I was asked to keep Mr Price under surveillance as she suspected he was having sex with someone who was not her. This person proposed that she deal with me purely by letter and told me that, in order to preserve 'confidentiality', she was against our meeting or communicating in any other way than by letter.

I followed her instructions faithfully.

On 14 July 'Mrs Price', who, I am now convinced, was not Mrs Price at all, told me she was 'going away for a few weeks'. This fact is important. Store it in your minds. We will return to it. I continued to investigate the issue of Mr Price's

---

[9] Confirmed in an informal interview with me in the Putney Shopping Centre and, also, by an interview with Mrs Katharine Bildeeze (87) of Lawson Crescent.

[10] She added, 'Sex makes me sick. I am eighty-seven and have had enough sex. So have the people in this road. They think about nothing else. It is disgusting.'

adultery for her and, in good faith, supplied her with pictorial, photographic and aural recordings of his activities.[11] The last occasion on which I received a letter from her was on 10 September. I wrote to her again on 5 November, which was when I began to suspect that 'Mrs Price' was not actually Mrs Price.

Something must have happened after 10 September to make her (or at that stage I thought, possibly, him) lose interest in the 'game of deception' to which I had been subjected. Another significant factor, the importance of which I did not appreciate at the time, was that a person she suspected was female had subjected the person on whom I was spying for 'Mrs Price' to several violent attacks. On one occasion this unidentified assailant ran up behind her on the towpath and assaulted her after a rehearsal of *Hamlet* in which she played Ophelia.[12]

Could it be, I reasoned, that the person attacking Mrs Dimmock was Mrs Price?

Let us return to the evening of 3 November 2000. The night on which, as you will remember, Mrs Pamela Larner breathed her last. 'Died', in other words or, if we are going to be brutally honest, and that is what I intend to be in this letter, was murdered by the placing of a pillow over her face in order to stop her breathing. There is a word for it. Asphyxiation. It is not a pretty word, but it is the only word that will do in these circumstances because it is what happened. Asphyxiation. Suffocation. Murder. That is what we are talking about.

---

[11] The person on whom I was 'spying' in what I now realize was a totally despicable way was my present fiancée, Mary Dimmock. I do not mean to suggest, by using the word 'present' that I intend to get another fiancée in the near future.

[12] Not, obviously, the assailant but Mrs Mary Dimmock, soon to be, I hope, Mrs Mary Gibbons, who received high praise for her rendering of the part.

When Michael Larner returned to the marital home, where he lived with his wife, on that fateful evening of 3 November, which is when she died beyond all question of a doubt and is confirmed by the police report, he found her, of course, 'dead' in such a final and absolute way that he knew immediately, or at least fairly quickly, that she could not be resuscitated.

The empty bottle of pills. The half-bottle of red wine. The single glass. It all screamed one word at him: suicide. Death. Two words – but with one meaning. And yet, as he looked around the room, decorated in Mrs Larner's favourite colours, turquoise and pea green, he saw something that made him think that perhaps another word or phrase might be more applicable here: 'murder'; 'homicide'; 'deliberate killing'; 'assassination'. And so on. There are many words for murder. And I have given you a few here – which, although I did not originally intend this, may serve to remind you of the gravity and seriousness of the offence we are talking about.

There was, ladies and gentlemen, a cushion on the floor. Not only that. Someone – Michael Larner was emphatic on this point – had rearranged the wine glasses in a way that suggested, along with the fact that Mrs Larner would never have drunk red wine on her own, that another person had been with her after Mr Price had left the premises. In other words, after Mr Price had left, someone, the woman who had been following him, climbed over the fence and entered the premises from the rear: the doors had been opened by Mrs Larner when she threw the 'man bracelet' into the flowerbed.[13]

Who was this woman?

Someone who was obsessed with Gerald Price. Someone who had been nurturing passionate feelings about him for years. Someone who wanted to know what he was up to

---

[13] See earlier reference to Mrs Bildeeze's evidence.

*without anyone knowing that that was what she was doing.*[14]
Someone who hated the idea of anyone else having him so
much that she was prepared to spy on his possible lovers
while, at the same time, ingeniously attempting to incriminate
the woman with whom he was living, who was, of course,
his wife of many years, which is to say Mrs Elizabeth Price
– without 'inverted commas'. The letters to me were written
on a computer and signed with what I have since ascertained
is a fairly credible imitation of Mrs Price's handwriting.[15]

It is, in one sense, a 'practical joke' but a pretty sick one in
my view. It is the action of a woman who is deranged, although
she appears, as many such people do, to be perfectly normal;
but murder, as I do not need to remind you, is not a practical
joke. It is a very serious business; and I am convinced that the
woman who initiated the 'fake letters' was also the woman
who held a cushion over the face of Mrs Pamela Larner.[16]

Who is this woman?

As soon as I became aware – in the early part of December
– that Mr Price had left his wife for Barbara Goldsmith,[17] I

---

[14] My italics.

[15] It is exactly the sort of ingenious scheme one might expect from this clearly
highly intelligent lady, who is, as you all know, a lover of crossword puzzles.
She is a very public moralist and at one stage in her life was a committed
Christian. If it was her, I knew I was going to be seriously disappointed
because I had decided, after several encounters with her, that she was not
one of those who said hello with Puritan enthusiasm, then sank her teeth
into your flesh. You know what I mean, Acrostic Fan!

[16] We have no firm evidence that the cushion was held over Mrs Larner's
face. When Mr Larner found it, it was on the floor. The pathologist's report
states that Mrs Larner died of an overdose of sleeping tablets and she had
ingested enough temazepam 'to kill a horse' to use the term employed by Dr
Ron Schnitte, the police pathologist. The crucial points of evidence here are
all related to the time of death.

[17] I first became aware of this on 10 December. I presented myself,
unannounced, at 101 Fellen Road, the marital residence of Dr and Mrs
Goldsmith. The door was opened by Mrs Price. She said, before I even had
the opportunity to explain that I was there on behalf of Michael Larner,
'Gerry left me for Barbara. He is trying to say they have always been in love

realized that there was only one possible candidate. There is only one person who has nurtured a disturbingly violent passion for 'the Beastly Barrister'. Yes, Mr Price, that is the name by which you are generally known in Putney. There is only one person who knows Mrs Price well enough to include in her letters to me certain telling details, which led me to think, even when I was fairly sure she wasn't, that 'Mrs Price' was, or could be, Mrs Price.[18] There is only one person who is adept enough at 'literary style' to provide me with letters that 'caught' Mrs Price's well-known, sardonic tones – even down to an obviously genuine quotation from Mr Price on the subject of the Archbishop of Canterbury.

That person is Mrs Barbara Goldsmith – or 'Sharpe', as she prefers to be known on the dust jackets of her well-regarded 'literary' novels.[19] Even if they are full of misprints and contain what can only be deliberate misinformation about the bus depot opposite the Green Man.

I have shown a selection of photographs of women to Mrs Katharine Bildeeze of Lawson Crescent. She immediately identified Ms Sharpe as the person who climbed over the fence at 23.25.

The police report puts the time of death somewhere between eleven and twelve on the night of 3 November 2000. Mrs Bildeeze also identified Ms Sharpe as the person who

---

but it's obviously not as simple as that!'

[18] In her first letters to me 'Mrs Price' managed to 'pull off' a convincing impression of the real Mrs Price's style, criticizing my use of 'inverted commas' and generally 'coming on' like a disgruntled schoolteacher. I have since learned that Mrs Price, a serious and committed teacher, is not often malicious at the expense of those less well educated than herself. This is not true of 'Ms' Sharpe.

[19] Not all are well regarded. In the *Observer* edition of 23 November 1996 the lead fiction review, written by Alison Hennehaugh, began, 'Dishonesty in fiction is the cardinal sin. Imaginary characters have to have feeling and strength and moral purpose, and Ms Sharpe's latest convoluted novel is peopled entirely by a cast of stooges who have neither.'

left the house by the front door at approximately 23.43.39. Time, I think you will agree, to have drunk some of a glass of wine with Mrs Larner, watched her fall into a coma and then 'helped her along' by holding a pillow over her face. It is possible that Mrs Goldsmith – or 'Ms Sharpe' or whatever she wants to call herself – even posed as a friend to the distressed woman.[20]

I have learned, subsequently, that Mrs Goldsmith has given an account of her relationship with Mr Price that is, frankly, incredible. She has, it appears, claimed that she and Mr Price have always been in love with each other and that they, although aware of their feelings for each other, had never, in all the time they had known each other,[21] begun a physical relationship. It is obviously difficult to speculate as to what exactly happens between two people when no one else (*not even a private detective!*)[22] is present – but a more likely alternative seems to me to be this.

Mrs Goldsmith had long harboured a violent passion for Mr Price, which developed into an all-consuming hatred for anyone with whom he was, or ever had been, involved. Although professing to share his feelings that their relationship should be unconsummated in any permanent way, she dreamed of nothing but total possession of him, in a way that destroyed her own relationship with her husband and children. She watched, from a distance, as Mr Price 'cut a swathe' through the women of Putney and

---

[20] I am told that some volunteer workers in the 'Samaritans' often 'help' suicides through the process of dying rather than trying to save their lives. A piece of moral casuistry (yes, I know the big words too, Ms Sharpe and 'Mrs Price' with or without inverted commas) worthy of one of Mrs Goldsmith's characters.

[21] A period of at least forty years, since both agree that they met at Magdalen College, Oxford, in June 1968.

[22] The italics are Mary Dimmock's.

the intensity of her hatred for these women[23] grew ever stronger with the years.

Above all, of course, she resented the woman who had kept faith with the 'Beastly Barrister' for so many years. Nothing is more unpleasant to the totally faithless (and, as I will show, Mrs Goldsmith has been constantly unfaithful to her husband) than faith. Writing a series of letters that not only satirized and provided a crude caricature of a woman whom she had hated for years and also, possibly, might incriminate her in a murder and a series of attacks on innocent local women[24] was a perfect release for a woman consumed with what seemed an unrequited passion for a man who, although almost totally lacking in moral qualities, seems to have been an irresistible magnet for many different types of woman.

I am prepared to admit, after much thought, that Mr Price himself is unaware of his new partner's history and was certainly totally innocent of any knowledge of the true circumstances surrounding Mrs Larner's death. All I have to say to him is that he may well, at last, have met his match! Don't go to bed with the lights off, Gerald!

The evidence, I realize, for 'Ms Sharpe''s involvement in these crimes is purely circumstantial. Mrs Larner died over ten years ago. The official verdict on her death was that it

---

[23] Miss Annabelle Kwok (1982-5); Mrs Sue Jones-Parry (1983-6); Mrs Pamela Larner (1985-2000); Dominique von Finkelkraut-Smith(2001); Alison Hennehaugh (2003-2005); Julia and Margaret Smith-Lewens (2006-2009); Ulrika Schwarzkopf (January 2010); Emmeline Hughes (May 2010); Jean Priest (June 2010, probably); Mary Dimmock (September-October 2011)

24 Alison Hennehaugh was 'set upon' by a 'masked woman' as she cycled home from the *Observer* in 2004. I have still not been able to ascertain whether the attack was motivated by pique at her review of 'Ms Sharpe''s novel or fury at Ms Hennehaugh's affair with Gerald Price. Dominique von Finkelkraut-Smith was also sprayed with paint by a 'heavily disguised and aggressive woman' on Putney Heath in October 2001. There may have been other attacks or, indeed, unexplained deaths for which Barbara Goldsmith was almost certainly responsible.

was suicide. The only evidence we have for the presence of Mrs Goldsmith at 24 Lawson Crescent on the night of 3 November 2000 is that of an eighty-seven-year-old woman who has been the subject of several court orders for harassment of her neighbours; in fact Mrs Bildeeze, whom I found a charming and co-operative witness, has recently been admitted to Queen Mary's Hospital, Roehampton, suffering from 'acute dementia and paranoia'.[25]

It is impossible to prove. Murder is often impossible to prove. That does not make it any less like murder. I would very much appreciate a response to my letter from all of you who have helped me with my inquiry.[26]

Yours truly,
Orlando Gibbons (PIAA)

PS It is also significant that Mrs Goldsmith was 'away at a conference' from 14 July – exactly the date of departure claimed by 'Mrs Price' in her letter to me.

PPS Mrs Goldsmith has had well-documented affairs with fourteen different men. She has also, by her own admission to an informant who did not wish to be named, had 'a brief fling' with Alison Hennehaugh of the *Observer*.[27]

---

25 She accused me, among other things of 'tampering with her brain' and 'letting electricity out to kill her'.

26 Although Mr Price and Mrs Goldsmith have been, to put it mildly, obstructive, I would also welcome a response from them. On my last visit to Heathland Avenue, where Mr Price now resides with Mrs Goldsmith, he threw a chair at me and called me 'a sneaking little rat'. My interest, I repeat, is only in the truth.

27 Hennehaugh also did not wish to be named.

From:
Micky Larner
Dental Nurse at
Dimmock Dentistry
'We Care About Teeth'
24 Beeston Crescent
Putney
16 December

To:
Orlando Gibbons
24 Lawson Crescent
Putney

Dear Orlando,
It's funny to be writing to my old address – but I think it's
so great that you and Mary have taken up residence there
permanently! I am doing so much work with Sam in the
surgery that it does seem to make sense for us both to live
here. Hope you like my new slogan for the practice! I'm
finding dentistry a challenge but I'm really loving being a
nurse. I don't think the exams will be easy but I'm determined
to make a go of it. Just carrying the spittoon to and from the
chair is thrilling when Sam is moving so purposefully about
the surgery, implement in hand!

My gay-animals film has hit a few snags. The Dutch people
proved somewhat unreliable, to put it mildly, and Jens seemed
more interested in Sam than he was in long-term relationships
between male squirrels; Channel 4, who are always chasing
the latest new thing at the expense of real, solid value, in my
view, say they now think it is a little 'too niche' for them.

'Niche'? Excuse me! Isn't it important that nobody seems
to recognize or, at least, publicly admit to the fact that

homosexuality among British mammals is a huge issue? For them and for us. If we cannot acknowledge gay bats or gay sheep, how the hell can we face up to our own sexuality? I tried to deny mine for years – as did Sam, who still, as you know, has something of a problem in this area – and it did not have a good effect on Elaine. Some of the sequences we have already filmed, including a devastating and moving sequence of two male badgers trying and failing to have intercourse on a motorway near Leeds, are among the best things I have ever filmed in forty years as a documentary filmmaker.

I realize I am not getting round to discussing the murder of my wife. My discovery that I was gay is not the only thing in the world. People are dying of starvation, for God's sake! Although I would say that Channel 4's attitude is, in my view, fundamentally homophobic!

Pamela. Sorry. Pamela.

I am not talking about my issues with Channel 4 because I am trying to deny Pamela. Although I detest homophobia, in whatever form it takes, I should say that Pamela is, or was, the mother of my children and, although we had some difficult times (the last fifteen years were very difficult indeed), I still have moments of intense fondness and sympathy for her. And yet, in a way, I was relieved when she died. A part of me would not have been unduly bothered if she had been thrown under an electric train or dismembered by wild animals.

But that is not the point. She was a person. Not an easy person. But a person. In many ways a despicable person. Sometimes a person you would like to strangle. Or choke to death. Or asphyxiate. I realize this may sound tasteless, given that, as far as I can see from your excellent report, she was actually asphyxiated. By a woman with whom I have been on holiday! But she was someone who could, quite easily, provoke you into holding a cushion or a pillow over her face and holding it down, hard, until her screams died away to whimpers and her limbs, after threshing uncontrollably for what seemed like an eternity, twitched their way into lifelessness.

I hated her, Orlando.

I have never hated anyone the way I hated Pamela. She was so boring! And the way she went on and on and on about her mother. My God! Her mother was boring but Pamela going on about her was even more boring. She went on and on, actually, about just about everything. 'Why do you leave your underpants on the floor?' 'Oh, you're not going to do a funny French accent again, are you?' 'Another film about fish? Who needs it?' Living with her made me feel physically sick. We had a memorial service for her after she died and I can tell you people were really scratching around for something nice to say. I will be honest with you, Orlando. Life is a lot simpler without her.

That being said, obviously murder is wrong and we have to think what to do about the revelations with which you have provided us. I want to thank you, by the way, for being so careful and patient with your enquiries.

What we do about it is anybody's guess. There seems to be, as far as I can make out, no way of definitely proving that *la* Goldsmith did it; although I must say your theory, which I suppose it is, rather than definitive proof, at this stage, sounds horribly plausible to me. Barbara is the Wicked Witch of the West and, in my view, if she had actually been operating in Oz during the period when Judy and the Munchkins were following the yellow brick thingy they would all have been strewn over it as roadkill before you could say Liza Minnelli. Murder is obviously wrong. Maybe Pam had already swallowed however many of whatever it was she swallowed and was going to croak anyway – but you've got to admire her, haven't you? I mean, what a bitch!

Actually, knowing Babs, I think it entirely probable she forced them down Pam's throat!

I love her style, actually. I mean, the old bag must be sixty if she's a day but she still wears those pencil skirts because she has the hips for them, and those blouses that reveal a positively embarrassing amount of tit. When she tosses her hair around, which is, I have to say, even if she did asphyxiate my wife, her best feature, everyone but everyone sits up and takes notice because she has style in a big, big way. She has passion. She has the kind of intensity you used to see in Maggie Thatcher when someone tried an awkward question. When she looks straight at you – which she always does – you are rooted to the spot. I remember her in Spain, sitting at the breakfast table and smouldering over a freshly squeezed orange juice. Dressed to kill at 08.45. Dear Johnny G. was never, ever able to handle her, was he? And the Beastly Barrister – who is, let's face it, a dish even if we hate him – has probably finally met his match.

I think probably the best thing is to leave it there. Nothing will bring Pamela back. Thank God. That sounds awful but in a way I think she is probably much better off where she is. She did not enjoy life. I do feel, at last, that my curiosity has been satisfied as to how she met her end and that I can get on with my life with Sam, which is the most important thing for me at the moment. I am glad to say that there is a strong possibility that Barnaby may be released from jail very soon; he is hoping to return to Putney and perhaps get some work experience in the media. Leo and I are getting on like a house on fire and I have had some very nice notes from Milly, so things are looking good.

Thanks again for all your hard work, Orlando. We will all meet very soon, I am sure, and I enclose a cheque for £2,056 in recompense for your labours.

Love from
Mike Larner


From the desk of
Gerald Price QC
112 Heathland Avenue
Putney
18 December

To:
Orlando Gibbons
Detectives Are Us
12 The Alley
Putney

Dear Mr Gibbons,
Do not be confused by the address at the head of this letter. This is Barbara Goldsmith speaking to you from what used to be the Price marital home. I am sitting in dear Elizabeth's study surrounded by unreadable Latin and Greek poets and even more unreadable books written about them by very dull scholars.

I have received some amusing letters in my time but I thought yours was a classic of its type. I am assuming it is intended humorously. Gerald and I were highly entertained. I read it to him in the bed he and Elizabeth shared for so long, and we laughed and laughed and laughed.

My personal favourite was Mrs Bildeeze. There is someone

like that, I am sure, in every road in Putney and, as a piece of comic invention, she is mouth-watering, even if perhaps a little too sharply drawn to ever be anything but caricature. I was particularly struck by the image of me clambering over the side entrance of 24 Lawson Crescent, a place I last visited in 1984 in order to retrieve one of my sons. I cannot recall which one but as they are virtually identical that doesn't really matter. I think they were restaging some sequences from *Return of the Jedi* with the aid of a few plastic light sabres.

What I do know is that I made a resolve, at the time, never to go anywhere near the place again. Pamela Larner, as I am sure your research, if we can dignify it by that name, has taught you, was a very difficult woman indeed. I have only recently become aware that Gerald had an affair with her – a lapse of taste that he ascribes to the particular difficulties he experienced in his marriage. I certainly did not roam the streets of Putney, with or without a blunt instrument, in order to peer at what the husband of a woman with whom I was, at the time, friendly was doing.

I had heard some rumour that Mary Dimmock was sure that she was assaulted on the towpath by an unknown woman. It may be true – although Mary Dimmock, as I am sure you are aware, since you seem to have made the mistake of becoming sexually involved with her – is a notoriously hysterical female. Her hold on reality is tenuous to say the least.

I was intrigued by the notion that I would impersonate Elizabeth Price's prose style in order to incriminate her, or at least suggest that she was somehow involved with Mrs Larner's death. It may be, for all I know, that she was. We are all capable of murder, especially someone with as heavy an investment in being a nice person as poor Elizabeth. What is certain is that I do not have the time or the inclination to go through such a ludicrously complicated routine of deception.

You also make some completely ill-founded and laughably inaccurate remarks about my sex life, which is, Mr Gibbons, nobody's business but mine. If you insist on making any of the allegations in your letter public, I will sue you for criminal libel; and, from the look of you, Mr Gibbons, I can afford a rather better lawyer than you can.

I trust you have not actually contacted poor Alison Hennehaugh. I am pretty sure you have not and that that part of your letter is pure invention. As far as I know, Alison is now working in an Australian university. It is true to say that she did not like one of my novels; but then, if you write novels, how can you stop some idiot saying publicly that they dislike them – and being paid to do so! It goes with the territory, Mr Gibbons. It is only their opinion. They have a right to their opinion. Many people, I am glad to say, find my novels amusing, which is why I continue to write them.

The names of Gerald's conquests are all, clearly, inventions. Gerald and I particularly enjoyed Dominique von Finkelkraut-Smith. I hope I am spelling that right. Gerald says to pass on his compliments and he thinks it is the name of a Senegalese hurdler who was third in an Olympic race some years ago.

That was the principal purpose of my letter and I am assuming that neither Gerald nor I nor anyone else will ever hear anything more of you or your ridiculously half-baked theories. If they are half baked and not intended as a deliberate piece of satire on all of us suburban monsters. I suspect there is a deeper purpose to your letter – for on the few occasions when I have met you, you have struck me as not at all stupid. I am baffled as to what it may be. Perhaps Mr Larner did not pay you properly. He is, or was, notoriously mean.

I suspect, however, that your letter does not really propose a theory at all. It tells a story, although I have not yet quite grasped why you wanted to tell it that way. Or, indeed, what it is all about.

It may be as well, however, to try to give you an idea of how and why I behaved as I did. Life is full of inventions and absurdities. As a novelist I try to invent stories that are palpably untrue in order to make a truthful, and I hope helpful, point about the real world. When individuals start to use their narrative skills to make lies seem truthful and real, for whatever reason, I think it is time for novelists to stand up for the truth.

I married a man I did not love. Many people do that, Mr Gibbons. I tried to live with the damage that decision caused for many years and, yes, if you must know, I was unfaithful to my husband on several occasions. There was, however, no doubt in my mind, at any stage during all of my miserable years in Putney, that I was actually in love with someone else; and that he was in love with me. No one else knows Gerald Price in the way I know him. No one else loves Gerald Price in the way I love him. No one else understands Gerald Price in the way I understand him.

I don't know why we waited so long. Love only becomes real when you start to act on it and we were, for so many years, frightened to do that. It seemed such a big step. We had children, we had a pleasant life; we had a shared interest in order and peace and harmony in order to be able to do the work we wanted to do. If England is famous for anything, it is for the fact that it has an ordered society in which people obey the rules. Our prosperity depends on preserving that and, as I am sure you know only too well, the suburbs of this right little, tight little island are full of people who have learned to compromise.

I was in love with the husband of a woman who was, at one time, my best friend, Mr Gibbons. It might be hard to believe that, but when Elizabeth and I first met at one of those ghastly primary-school functions, we were the only women who seemed to have anything in common. We had read the same books, been to the same plays, seemed to care about the same things. The core of those villa holidays was me and Elizabeth and Gerry and John, who, in those days, actually seemed to think they liked each other.

I recall one of those rare mothers' coffee mornings when I actually bothered to turn up. I was always much less good at being a mother than she. We sat in the sun in someone's garden and talked as if we would never tire of telling each other things. We neither of us could ever work out why we hadn't met at Oxford. I always remember Elizabeth saying, in that self-dismissive tone she does so well, as she turned down her mouth and reached for another cigarette and/or *The Times* crossword, 'Oh, I was an academic mouse who never left the library. And you were a glamorous girl who was in plays and knew famous people. Things haven't changed.'

It was never going to be easy for me and Gerald to act on what we felt.

We were afraid of hurting people too. Gerald is as good at playing the oaf as I am at playing the bitch, but that is not who we really are. We may not have managed to be decent or kind but that is what we want to be, and, of course, we did not manage it. In trying to do the decent thing, I became a shrew, utterly alienated from my own children and full of vicious but unspoken thoughts about my friends, which found their way, regrettably, into my fiction. And Gerald played the part of the suburban lout so well that he grew into the role until it possessed and poisoned him as surely as the shirt of Nessus poisoned Hercules. Be very careful about what you pretend to be – because it is what you will become if you play the part long enough.

You remain something of a mystery, Mr Gibbons. I have my suspicions as to who you are pretending to be but I could not say with any certainty quite what you are. We have never talked long enough for me to decide exactly what kind of phoney this makes you; it seems you go around telling people you were born on a council estate but you are, clearly, not that kind of boy. Or you have managed to get very good at hiding what must have been a very tough childhood indeed. 'Orlando' is not a familiar name among the tower blocks. Or is it? Really, one knows nothing about anything any more. One thing is, however, clear, from those pale blue watchful eyes of yours, the still way you examine the faces of people with whom you are talking and your facility with cultural reference. You are by no means an ordinary detective.

Gerald and I will be leaving England for good as soon as the legal difficulties with our marriages are resolved. John and I no longer even risk the intimacy of a letter, these days. Lawyers have to write them on our behalf. This, of course, makes communication almost as bad as it was in the years we spent shouting at each other.

Goodbye, Mr Gibbons.

Barbara Sharpe

From:
Elizabeth Price
101 Fellen Road
Putney
25 December

To:
PO Box 132
Putney

Dear Mr Gibbons,
I am sending this to our post office address. I think of it as 'our' post office address. I know you enjoy an inverted comma and I felt these were entirely appropriate for a letter in which I am going to be, for the first time in our relationship, completely and utterly honest. The disputed punctuation is a delicate way of marking the fact that it isn't really our post office box but one that I have started to think of as being precisely that. As – judging from your last letter – have you.

And so – to Post Office Box 132 for what must be the last time.

It is Christmas Day and the snow is deep in John's back garden. '*Vides ut alta stet nive candidum ...*' as Horace says. I suspect you have read the Odes, Mr Gibbons. I just cannot get used to thinking of it as 'our' back garden. You see, Mr Gibbons? Once you start using inverted commas you can't stop. The habit of honesty, too, is as hard to break as the habit of lying; lying, as I think you spotted when we met for the first time at that memorably unmemorable production of *Hamlet*, is not something at which I excel.

Jas and Josh's children have been outside playing snowballs and we have all had a great deal of fun. Jas's little girl is particularly sweet. Her arms stick out as stiffly as

292

a gingerbread man's and she wobbles like one of her own toys as she walks. Julia is very charming with her, which pleases me a great deal. The fruit trees are, like the ones on the Mount Soracte, in Horace's beautiful poem, loaded so heavily with snow it seems surprising they bear the weight so easily.

Christmas Day – and the house full of children. It is quite like old times, but now these all seem to be the right children in the right place. Conrad, who, if he was bullied by Jas or Josh, or both of them, at school, seems to have forgotten it. He and Elaine are planning to move into a flat together, and later on this afternoon, the Dimmocks – Mike Larner, as I am sure you know, these days consistently refers to himself as 'Mrs Dimmock' – will be coming round as, probably, will you and Mary. I know how devoted she is to her very nice daughter and I hope you, too, are getting to be as fond of her as everyone else seems to be.

You and I will exchange polite smiles and polite remarks and no one will know what we know because we will never discuss it. Things between us are as private as the confessional. I can't ever remember feeling so free as when I first wrote to you back in June. I have always tried to be a truthful person, and even when I started pretending to be someone else, I took the precaution of using my own name.

I didn't want to own up to what I was doing. That was really what it was about. I felt ashamed of spying on my husband and I could not admit to myself that things had got so bad that I had been reduced to acting like . . . like what? I was going to say 'a jealous housewife' (inverted commas again) because, in one sense, that was what I was, and yet I was not. I did not want to own up to those feelings. The woman I invented to write to you was not unlike me but she wasn't really me at all. I have my schoolmistressy side but

293

I am not – though Barbara would like to think I am – *all* schoolmistress.

Once I knew that my suspicions were correct and that he was up to his old tricks again, I did not want to face up to that either. The monstrous mask I had invented for my own face was fixed to it and I could not remove it. I could not really bear to write to you any more. I was trying to be someone different. I think we have all managed to do something like that in a few short months.

The jealousy wasn't really about what happened between him and Mary. It had gone very deep in me over the years and, like whatever it was, or is, that Barbara and Gerry feel for each other, it made me mad, unlike the person I am or, at least, the person I would wish to be. That being said – although I know you are not going to discuss any of this with Mary – I should tell you that I did not 'hit her on the head' that night on the towpath. I think I rushed out of the darkness, pushed her, like a bad-tempered schoolgirl, then fled back into the night. I certainly didn't attack anyone else!

It is, I fear, as it so often is, a very ordinary story. Life, unfortunately, is so rarely anything like your highly entertaining letter, all of which pleased me greatly. Gerald, as I am sure you know, only really had two affairs during our marriage. One with Pamela Larner and one with the lady with whom you now seem to be involved. I no longer feel any anger at Mary – though I am afraid we will never be anything like friends. I think she thinks I really am the woman I was pretending to be when I wrote to you. So maybe you and she will be a good combination.

The footnotes were great fun – and particularly footnote eighteen: '*It is exactly the sort of ingenious scheme one might expect from this clearly highly intelligent lady, who is, as you all know, a lover of crossword puzzles. She is a very*

*public moralist and at one stage in her life was a committed*
*Christian. If it was her I knew I was going to be seriously*
*disappointed because I had decided, after several encounters*
*with her, that she was not one of those who said hello with*
*Puritan enthusiasm, then sank her teeth into your flesh. You*
*know what I mean, Acrostic Fan!'*

I do indeed, Mr Gibbons. 'Puritan enthusiasm' is clearly
'zeal' and we say hello by saying 'hi' and I try to be kind and
gentle but sometimes I do sink my teeth into people's flesh
and 'bite'; add 'hi' to 'bite' and 'zeal' and you get Elizabeth.
We understand each other very well, do we not? Hi! I had
you figured for a minor public schoolboy the moment I saw
you weaving your way towards your shabby little office in
The Alley.

I am not, however, writing to go back over all the games
we have played with each other since the summer. Things
have changed.

What you really want to know about is Pamela Larner.
Which is why I am writing this letter. I am sure neither of
us wants to bother Mike with what I have to say. He has
always been so absorbed in himself that he is only dimly
aware that there is anyone else on the planet apart from him
and a few fish. Sam seems to be the first person ever to make
any impact on him at all. Though I fear 'impact' is a wildly
understated way of describing what seems to be going on
between those two! We may have to persuade them to go
into the garden to cool down later on today...

Nobody liked Pamela. I plead guilty to following the
general trend. It wasn't anything she actually did. It was,
quite simply, her and the way she was. She was desperate
for attention and quite selfishly unaware of other people's
feelings. I knew about her affairs before I discovered she
had got her claws into Gerry, but I disliked her about as

much before I found out what she was really like, as I did afterwards.

She was a victim, I suppose. There was something wrong with her; and because people know what other people are thinking, just as you knew exactly what was going on in my mind when we met that first time in the church hall, she knew that we knew just how damaged she was.

I made an effort at first, which I think she took as patronage. I don't give a damn whether people have or have not been to Oxford or Cambridge. I am not a particularly clever person. I was good at classical languages and I have loved living with them for most of my life, but I have never done anything distinguished, even in the one scholarly field where I have some qualifications. I can also remember when I started, foolishly, to advertise my doctorate, how Gerry said, 'Make sure you don't put it in the phone book and have some poor bastard with appendicitis ring you at four in the morning only to get a lecture about fucking Lucretius.'

He could be funny in those days, Gerry. He could be funny and he could be kind, though all that went away the longer we lived with the lie we had so carefully built.

I suspected she was up to something with Gerry when we were in Corsica but I never thought he would allow himself to be taken in by someone so absolutely ghastly. It wasn't until the mid-nineties that I started to suspect something was going on. He would be back late from work, sometimes bringing flowers. There were never any suspicious phone calls to the house – I think they were very careful. I think, too, that it probably started and stopped a few times, in a way that had something to do with my libido, or lack of it, during this period.

Just before the end of the last millennium I became certain he was having an affair, although I still had no idea who it might be. I shut my eyes to it. I didn't want to think about it.

Conrad was drinking, Julia was looking more mournful with every day that passed, and I suppose I was in the grip of a fairly major depression. I didn't tell Gerry about it. I have never been someone who finds it easy to tell anyone else their troubles.

I did take to following him. I made a habit of going through his jacket pockets and looking for letters. I monitored phones calls and sniffed the car, like a drug dog, to see if there was unfamiliar perfume hanging in the air. Because I was not loved, I became, rapidly, unlovable.

That night in November – I remember the eerie warmth of that evening as if it were yesterday – I was coming home from Barbara Goldsmith's house when, quite by chance, I saw Gerald on the other side of Putney High Street. He didn't see me. He was walking, with his head down, those long, loping strides of his eating up the pavement. I could tell from his face that he was heading towards some kind of confrontation and, of course, at first I assumed it was going to be with me. I realized it wasn't when I saw him turn right into the Upper Richmond Road. I ran, then.

I caught up with him as he turned into Lawson Road and headed down in the direction of Lawson Crescent. That was when I knew he was going to see Pam Larner.

At first I was going to go home. The last thing in my mind was any sort of scene. I waited on the corner of Lawson Road and the Upper Richmond Road for about five minutes; then I walked, slowly, down to that shabby house at the end of Lawson Crescent. As far as I remember, that lady opposite was not in her usual station by the upper window. She did take time off sometimes, Orlando – and whatever her name is or was, it is not Bildeeze.

The rooms at the front of the house were dark, but there was a light on in the upper front bedroom. I stood there, looking up at the window, expecting, at any moment, the familiar shape of Gerald to walk, in silhouette, against the linen blinds. Perhaps, I thought, I would see them kissing. Perhaps the light would simply be switched off suddenly, and I would know he was up there, with her, making love. None of those things happened. A dog barked in an empty house next door. A car roared up the street, screeched to a stop and two young people got out. They started kissing, and I imagined what it must be like to be young and kissing in the street without a care in the world.

I waited for what I now realize was about an hour but, at the time, seemed longer. I was walking away, in the direction of the river, when I heard the door of Mike and Pamela's house shut with a bang. I turned and saw him at once. I am surprised he didn't see me. I can't have been more than thirty yards away from him.

I don't think he was in the mood for seeing anything, though. He stood there for a moment, at the front gate. He was twisting his hands together, trying to control his fury. He turned away from me and, as he walked back towards the Upper Richmond Road, I could tell, from the angle of his shoulders, that he was in the grip of a rage that was not going to go away easily. Whatever he had been doing in that house, it wasn't kissing.

For a moment I really thought he might have killed her. He is quite capable of that.

It was that, rather than a desire to tell her what I thought of her, that prompted me to ring the bell. I leaned on it, hard, like a policeman. She didn't answer the first time. The next time I rang there was another long pause and then the sound of footsteps in the hall.

'Who's there?' I heard her voice say. She sounded drunk. I didn't see any point in lying.

'It's Elizabeth!' I said. 'Elizabeth Price!'

Another long silence. Then, 'Go away!'

I was about to do just that. In fact I was already making my way down the path when I heard her voice again. She sounded different. She sounded desperate now, like someone who has just been told that a person they have loved very much has died.

'Please don't go!' she said.

She didn't open the door, though, so I went to the side door and climbed over it. She was by the french windows when I came in from the garden. She was wearing jeans that were too tight, and one of her red chiffon blouses with ruffles. Her face was white and she looked as if she had been crying. Her hair, usually as immaculate as the cloth at one of her dinner parties, was ragged and out of place. She looked, I thought, pretty drunk. She stood there, swaying slightly, and for a moment I thought she was going to say something unpleasant. She was good at that. In the end all she said was 'Your husband was here!' Then she turned and swayed off back inside. I followed her.

She staggered to the sofa and sat heavily. Red wine spilled on the pale carpet as she slumped back among the cushions. She stared at me as if she had never seen me before.

'He's a bastard!' she said thickly. 'An absolute fucking bastard!'

'I am sure he is!' I said, trying to keep my voice as level as possible. I moved to the armchair, next to the coffee-table. There was a half-filled glass on it. For Gerald presumably. I sat and looked at her, hard. She didn't look right. It wasn't just the paleness of her skin or the visible twitch in her cheek. It was her eyes. I've seen that look in the faces of people in hospital waiting rooms. They have caught a glimpse of that thing none of us really wants to think about. That thing you see when they tell you there is no hope.

'I'm sorry,' she said. 'I'm sorry!'

'For what?' I said, although I knew perfectly well what she was sorry for.

'Oh, about Gerald,' she said.

I didn't know what to say to that – so there was another silence in the room. There was only one lamp, in the far corner, so it was uncomfortably dark. The french windows were open and, though it was warm, a slight breeze idled in from the garden and made me wonder if I should get up and close them; but I didn't. I knew something very serious was happening, but did not, yet, know what it was.

'I've taken forty temazepam,' she said, in casual, matter-of-fact sort of way.

'Oh!' I said. I sounded, I thought, curiously bright and cheerful. I knew I was supposed to do something about this. I could not for the life of me think what it might be. Make her sick. Pump her stomach. Call the police and the ambulance. 'I'd better call someone,' I said, after what seemed like hours and hours. I was getting up to do just that when she leaned across and grabbed my wrist, hard.

'I don't want you to do that!' she said. 'You mustn't do that!'

I sat back in my armchair. 'He's not worth killing yourself over!' I said – although that was not what I felt at all. In fact, one of the first things I had thought when she had told me she had taken pills was that I might ask her if there were any left in the bottle.

'I want to die!' she said, in a low voice.

I started to say something. She still had hold of my wrist. Her grip was surprisingly strong. I didn't say anything. I waited for her.

'It's nothing to do with Gerald,' she said eventually. 'It's nothing to do with anyone or anything. It's the way I feel. It's what I want to do. I've felt like this for so long. It seems like it's been going on all my life. I want to die.'

That was when I suppose I should have said something to make her feel that life was worth living. The sun would come up tomorrow. The birds would sing eventually. There were her children. I think I might have started to say something about her children. I don't think I mentioned her husband.

'Look,' I said, trying gently to disengage my arm from her grip, 'I think we should ring someone. It's not too late to do something.'

'I don't want you to call the ambulance or the police,' she said. 'I want you to sit there for a while.'

I didn't want to do that. I didn't want to sit there and watch her die. Calling in an emergency was, I saw, with horrible clarity, simply a way of avoiding this, but she still had hold of my arm. I tried to loosen her grip once more but she dug her fingers into my flesh even more tightly.

'I just want to talk to someone,' she said. 'Someone nice.'

I didn't know how to answer this. I have never thought of myself as a nice person. I have never liked the word much and, in the context of the terrible thing that was happening in front of my eyes, it seemed even more of a weak, hopeless way of trying to describe such an important quality.

'You're a decent person,' she said. 'You're about the only decent person among the whole lot of them. You're the only one I like. And I go and have an affair with your husband.'

'How long ago,' I said, trying to keep my voice calm, 'did you take the pills?'

She had been drinking. Had she taken them before Gerald came in to see her? Had she really taken forty of them? She seemed very lucid. Except for those eyes, which were already looking beyond me at something we must all one day face.

She did not answer this question. Neither did she loosen

her grip on my arm. 'I don't want you to call anyone,' she said again. 'I want to die.'

That was when I started to disengage her fingers. She fought me over this. I did not give way. In the end, she loosened her grip. All this time, her eyes never left my face. I still had it in mind to get over to the phone and call 999, but I couldn't get up. Not when she was looking at me like that. Not when she had said the things she had said. I had no idea how much time I had but I didn't think I had long.

'I want you to hold a cushion over my face,' she said. 'I want you to do that. I want you to do it now.'

'I can't do that,' I said. 'That's murder. I can't do that.'

'Sometimes,' she said, 'it isn't murder. People get killed every day. People drop bombs and blow up buildings and get drunk and stab people.'

She had grabbed my arm again. I couldn't bear the idea of prising her fingers off my flesh for a second time. More than anything else, I did not want to be sitting so close to her, smelling the alcohol on her breath, looking into those empty eyes and listening to her voice, repeating the same simple urge over and over again. I want to die. I want to die.

'Look,' I said, 'I'll get up and get a cushion. OK? Is that OK?'

'That is what I want,' she said. 'That is what I want you to do.'

She seemed easier in herself now. Her words, I noticed, were definitely slurred. I thought she was having trouble keeping her eyes open. Very soon she would be unconscious. Then I could get to the phone, call in the emergency and leave. I would have done the thing you are supposed to do if you are a nice person. That word again. Only a voice in my head kept saying, 'Whatever gave you the idea that you are nice person, Elizabeth? You are not a nice person.'

'Look,' I said, 'I'm doing it. Look.'

There didn't seem much point in trying to talk about all the things that made life worth living. I didn't think she had the right to do this. Not when I was in the room. I didn't want it to be anything to do with me. If she wanted to kill herself, let her do it in some hotel where no one would see. I simply did not want to look at her misery any longer. That was why I got up from the chair.

There was a cushion on the other sofa. She let me get up and watched me as I walked over to it. I picked it up. She really wasn't focusing very well any more. I did not have much time. I could walk over to the phone now and put in the call. That was what I was going to do. Her eyes, in that horrible, snake-like way she'd always had, found mine and stared deep into me.

'Thank you, Elizabeth,' she said, her voice definitely slurring now. 'Thank you.'

For a moment she looked so like Barnaby. He was the saddest of all her children; and they were a pretty sad bunch. She was always shouting at him, from the window as he tottered towards the school gates, as he trudged up the path to the front door or fell behind the others on one of those long, grim walks she was always insisting they take. She was not a good mother. She was not a nice person, and now she was looking at me like a dog about to be put down, grateful for any kind of attention, even if it was a bullet in the head.

I don't know how it happened. I found myself on top of her, forcing the cushion into her face. It wasn't for long. At the time I thought it was no more than a gesture. I would have said I had held it over those pathetic, dishevelled features for less than a minute, but maybe it was longer than that. I don't know. I really don't know.

I would swear, too, that when I lifted it from her, although her eyes were closed and she was breathing heavily, she was still breathing. I would swear to that but I am not certain of it. I believe it, for the reason we believe most things. Because I want to believe it. I flung the cushion away across the floor. I picked up the glass. I drained the last of the wine. For some reason I found myself thinking, There was wine in that when I came into the room. I am drinking some of what Gerald was drinking.

It became very important to get rid of any traces of him from the room. I had lost all interest in her now. She was just sleeping, I decided. That thing they write on gravestones, 'At peace at last.' I wasn't aware of myself either. It was as if I had never walked in on her, as if I had never listened to those things she had said.

I took the glass, washed it carefully in the kitchen sink and put it back in the cabinet. Then I walked out into the street, closing the front door behind me as carefully and quietly as if there was a baby asleep upstairs. I didn't ever think about Pamela Larner again. She simply disappeared from the face of the earth. We had lost touch with Mike, of course, years before that night. I tried not to think about what had happened.

But, of course, I did. That was really why I wrote to you. After finding out about Pamela, in that particularly horrible way, I could never stop thinking about what Gerry might or might not be doing. I was ashamed of how I felt – but I could not stop myself. Hence you, the private detective I did not really want to acknowledge I was hiring. Maybe that was why I wrote to you in what was not really my voice, almost a parody of the schoolmistress; and yet, of course, by pretending to be that crusty, slightly prurient character, I was brought face to face with what may be my true self. It is certainly how Gerry sees me.

I think about it over and over again. I know I did not do the right thing, but it is what I did. I have told no one any of this and I will never tell anyone else. I am telling you now because I know you, too, will never tell anyone. No, I don't *know* – but I am reasonably sure. I feel easier that I have told you, anyway, and am prepared to accept the risk.

I am not a risk-taker usually. I try to plan things carefully, and if I have had a dream, it was probably always for a quiet life. In which case, I hear you ask, why on earth did you marry Gerald Price? The answer to that is – I simply do not know. We do things for love and we do not know why we do them and so often they are the wrong things but it is what we do.

I know we will see each other later today. We will meet, too, I am sure, in the suburb again and again, and smile and exchange news, but we will never speak of any of this. It's all too sad. And we have not much time left ourselves, so it is, perhaps, better not to think about it all.

Ever your friend
Elizabeth Price